P9-CLB-415

Poutre du
Poutre de

VILLA OF DELIRIUM

ADRIEN GOETZ

Translated from the French by Natasha Lehrer

NEW VESSEL PRESS
NEW YORK

www.newvesselpress.com

First published in French in 2017 as Villa Kérylos

Library of Congress Cataloging-in-Publication Data
Goetz, Adrien
[Villa Kérylos, English]
Villa of Delirium/Adrien Goetz; translation by Natasha Lehrer.
p. cm.
ISBN 978-1-939931-80-1
Library of Congress Control Number 2019940461
I. France—Fiction

TABLE OF CONTENTS

PART ONE
THE BLUE ROCKS

"The Greeks discovered glory, they discovered beauty, and they brought to this discovery such jubilation, such an overabundance of life, that a sense of youthful contagion can still be felt even after the passage of two or three thousand years."

THEODORE REINACH

1

THE HALCYON TERRACE

I still have a set of keys to the house. During the summer months, every now and then, like today, I slip inside, my shadow merging with the shade of the portico behind the library, on the far side where there's no risk of being seen by anyone from the village. I listen to the birdsong. This time, I have decided, will be the last. I won't come back to Kerylos again. Over the years I haven't been able to resist stealing in occasionally, not telling a soul, to touch the bronze statuettes, look at the furniture and paintings, listen to the fountain in the courtyard, gaze out at the sea through the open windows. This time I have not come to contemplate. I want to reclaim what is rightly mine. It is time.

Kerylos, the Greek villa, has become legendary. Postcards of it are for sale at the tobacconist in Beaulieu-sur-Mer. I bought five or six, which I slipped into my camera bag along with some magazines. I haven't been back for over a decade. Among the postcards there was one of the mosaic floor depicting the Minotaur at the center of the labyrinth, being decapitated by Theseus. Theseus is holding him by one horn, blood flowing in tesserae of reddish ocher stones. Last week I received the same postcard in the mail, my address typed and instead of a message a stylized, slightly clumsy drawing of an ancient laurel wreath. There was no signature. This was no ornament representing Caesar's triumph, it had a flurry of leaves and fruits hanging between the branches, it was a majestic Greek diadem—the golden crown of Alexander the Great that every archaeologist in the world dreams of discovering. This is what has brought me back. At least now I know where the postcard was bought. Did someone from here send it, someone I used to know? Had certain people held on to the habit of sending anonymous letters after the war ended? My address in Nice isn't hard to find. Underneath the photograph is a simple caption: "Summer sun over the Greek villa Kerylos—mosaic in the reception room (Andron)."

Kerylos is still a secret place, not open to visitors, and its owners haven't thrown a party here for many years. When I was twenty it represented a kind of perfection. Today I find myself wondering how I could have ever found it beautiful. This morning all I can see is plaster cracking like old face paint, threadbare curtains, dead trees. The fountain isn't working; the pipe that feeds it must be broken. If this were the first time I was seeing its architecture, I would find it absurd, a page of poetry read at school and soon forgotten.

Since I left here and moved far away, I've liked houses that look like the pictures I paint: geometric volumes, bare walls. Inside I want only useful, everyday objects. All this ornamentation that I once looked upon with dazed fascination has lost its charm. How did people ever live in this place, which would have been my prison if I hadn't managed to escape? No one lives here anymore, except, I believe, the Reinach grandchildren and great-grandchildren for a few weeks every summer; it's the fashion now. They keep to themselves. They've left bottles of sunscreen and sun loungers on the top terrace. Everything has been reversed, and maybe it's better that way: when I was young, "the season" was winter.

As I walk into the house, I feel my adolescent reflexes twitch, as though somehow I have to be young in the house where I spent my youth. I climb the two floors—stopping to catch my breath, my body even more exhausted than these walls—to the uppermost terrace, my terrace, the big square at the top of the central tower from where one could film the entire panorama of the Côte d'Azur: the Bay of Beaulieu, the Villa Ephrussi with its pink facade and exotic trees, and on the other side, La Réserve, now a famous hotel, the cliffs of Èze, as stunning as those that soar over the sanctuary of Apollo at Delphi, Saint-Jean-Cap-Ferrat and its millionaires. I haven't brought my little tripod with me, so I must keep my hand steady. I want to leave these images for my children. The happiest people in the world might envy me. Once upon a time, I was happier even than they—and I left in time. Houses have been built, but at the very end of the promontory, where it disappears into the sea, if I turn my back on the villa I can still imagine I am on a Greek island. Today I have a clear view of the Tête de Chien and the Cap d'Ail, and I can even just make out the festivities in Monaco. If I were to stay here until this evening, I'd be able to watch the prince's fireworks—but I know I mustn't; by dusk I will be far away. I will have found it.

I put on my sunglasses and lay down on the mosaic floor. I once watched it being laid with the tracing paper the craftsmen used as a guide: the tesserae compose a series of lines, with the cardinal points like on old maps, the names of the winds written in Greek letters. I look at the sky, closing my eyes and opening them again, blinking regularly. The railings need a coat of paint. A couple of the bronze balustrades are coming off. Another few heavy gales and they will fall down onto the rocks below. Nobody knows how to make them anymore, I imagine. I can't bear to think that one day this house will be a ruin. That would be the best that could happen to it. Once, in a fit of anger, I had a mad urge to set it on fire. I stopped myself. If I had spent my life here I'd have been trapped, I would never have become an artist, I would have remained the good little boy who admires everything anyone shows him. One of the treads on the stairs is cracked and needs fixing. Forty years ago I would have shored it up and then gone to search for the right can of paint in the boiler room. How proud my mother would have been of her Achilles, the good boy she had so enthusiastically recommended to this charming family, and how I would have blushed with shy delight. Today, I am going to leave the step to cave in, despite myself. Nothing must give any clue that I have been here.

I open the door to one of the two bedrooms at the top of the house called "Daedalus" and "Icarus"—all the rooms here have names. I had forgotten how each latch was finely crafted in the shape of a palm, inspired by motifs from the ancient Orient, molded into shape and then burnished green to harmonize with the warm tones of the wood. The twin beds have been replaced with one large bed; the sun beats down on an ocher coverlet embroidered with sphinxes. A few more years and the faded, sun-scorched fabric will tear and there will be nothing left but tattered shreds. I recognize the odor of exotic woods, pass my fingers over the marquetry and inlay, then plunge my head into an empty chest, its perfume as intense as the day the first pieces of furniture were delivered. I was there when everyone was squealing with delight. When I think about the end of my childhood, here, it almost horrifies me.

Walking through the rooms on the ground floor, I notice the way the light is reflected between the chairs: the floor has been waxed. Who could have done that? Who uses a floor polisher on marble? Stone needs to breathe, it will die if it is regularly treated like that, everything will flake and crack and turn yellow. In twenty years, Kerylos will be dead. Another house will be built on this spot. All that will be left are yellowing postcards in old albums.

The mosaicists, who spent entire months on the floors, worked for the Oceanographic Museum in Monte Carlo. They fascinated me. I copied their designs for my own pleasure. On the floor of the dining room they created a great goggle-eyed octopus, my favorite animal. I copied it into my notebook, and later had it tattooed on my arm. People are always surprised when they see it and they ask if I used to be a sailor. No one ever dares ask me if I've served time. I had it done in Thessaloniki by an old tattoo artist in the port, in 1914, just before war broke out. It throbbed for a couple of days. I was glad to have a permanent trace of the extraordinary journey I had taken, away from Kerylos—without realizing that I had actually chosen, while on Greek soil, an emblem of Kerylos to accompany me throughout my life. When they finished, the craftsmen left instructions for cleaning the tesserae that must be written down somewhere among all the paperwork that the Germans pillaged. Theodore Reinach left detailed instructions for taking care of his house. What happened to this notebook, with its black leather cover?

If I don't write it down, no one will remember the December evenings in this house where Christmas was never celebrated, though everyone brought gifts; where heat rose up from the ground and the huge windows retained it like an orangery; no one will remember how when we were late, Adolphe Reinach and I, the "rascals," would clamber over the rocks to get home, sneaking back through the subterranean corridors; no one will remember all our plans for expeditions, or the hundreds of books we read, or anything about the tangled lives we invented as though we had already lived them in the time of Pericles at the Acropolis or Alcibiades around the mountains and the temples of Sicily. No one will know anything about my life or my loves.

I watched this white and ocher house being built, I lived here, worked here, fell in love here, knew every room as well as those of my apartment in Nice. The moment I walked in, these old familiar walls felt like home, in spite of everything, more so than for most of those who used to have their own rooms here, almost all of whom are dead now.

The first time I found myself alone here, I took a bath in the master bathroom, like the shepherd Paris taunting King Menelaus. I had no interest in seducing his wife—I wasn't fantasizing about Fanny Reinach as I lay back in the bubbles and hummed my favorite aria from *La Belle Hélène*—but I occupied his palace as if it belonged to my father and my ancestors, as if my chariot were waiting at the door with my armor, my shin guards and my shield adorned with legendary scenes, as if I had returned to my legitimate home.

I might have turned my back on this machine that soaks up the sun, this refuge for reflection, this ship on the ocean of time, this fragment of rational madness—but it still stirs something in me. It was the setting for all the stories I made up when I was still a boy, and the place where a few years later I first caught sight of the woman I was to love more than any other. It is the mosaic of my life. Joy marked out in tiny fragments of stone. She is the reason I come back, though not too often, to avoid too much pain.

We should never really have met. She was a little older, married, and I was poor—it took the wealthy Monsieur Reinach summoning an architect and asking him to build him a vacation palace, and a series of events that no one could have foreseen, for our paths to cross, for me to learn her name, Ariadne, and for her to notice me at all. Her name was surprising, especially when you think what pretty girls in 1956 are called, Nicole or Martine. Ariadne in the Labyrinth, Ariadne abandoned, Ariadne sister of Phaedra, Ariadne at Naxos. I cared nothing about all that; she was alive, she wore moccasins to the beach, she had a white cotton hat and a bicycle. She didn't come out of a book. I was called Achilles, in a family where no one before me had even heard of the Trojan War.

Our names, those of the men of that time—I was born in 1887—ended up chiseled on monuments to the dead: Jules, Antonin, Honoré, Paul, Simeon, Damien, Marius—all my friends from Beaulieu, I see you still, I know how you fell, each one of you. I owe to Ariadne that part of my intelligence that the illustrious Theodore Reinach, master of Kerylos, forgot to transmit to me. He only ever talked to me about antiquity, music, the poets he loved. As a young man I used to stand on the rocks below Beaulieu and recite poems from *Les Fleurs du Mal*:

"But the buried jewels of ancient Palmyra. The undiscovered metals, the pearls of the sea . . ." A red leather-bound edition that Adolphe, Theodore Reinach's nephew and my closest friend, picked up for me when we were fifteen, with the six censored poems, copied out by hand on pages pasted in at the end, that gave us butterflies. Adolphe was smaller and punier than I was, but he had something about him, an equestrian's elegant bearing, and a grave air that became instantly charming the moment he stopped being serious and began to laugh. I wanted to go and search for Baudelaire's jewels for Ariadne, in the sand, beneath the sea, in citadels deep in the desert or the most secret vaults of Atlantis. I wanted to see strings of pearls and gold draped over her shoulders and breasts as I embraced her. I was tired of loving statues. Told like this, the romance that transformed my life sounds like a fairy tale. Our love affair never ended; I hid it from my children, and of course from their mother—but when I come to tell them of Kerylos I want to bequeath them that as well, in addition to what I have come to claim this morning. Why should my children know nothing of the great love of my life? This house, that doesn't belong to me, that I stopped loving long ago, this absurd labyrinth that now seems quite grotesque to me, this house that will end up in ruins—I want to give it to them, room by room. This is where my life is.

The prince is marrying Grace Kelly in Monaco today. When I got up this morning the gilded waves were already covered with boats—like in that famous passage from the *Iliad* that I once had to translate—from cruise ships to fishing skiffs, all heading there to sound their foghorns. My little town of Beaulieu is quite empty. I thought I could come here without attracting attention. No one knows I am here. I suppose the caretaker and his wife will return from Monaco this evening around seven. I don't know if they are the same people I used to know—I think not though, they would be so old—but perhaps they are, after all the climate is splendid. They most likely won't venture beyond La Guitounette, their little house at the beginning of the promontory, but I don't want to take the risk.

I'll have just enough time to find what I'm looking for. If only I knew which room to search. Surely Theodore Reinach, in the years before his death, had left some kind of sign or pointer that nobody had been able to interpret. The house was full of chests and cupboards that used to overflow with letters, plans, photo albums, drafts of scholarly texts, school books; the Nazis upended everything, emptied it all out, and took most of it away. I've always wondered if they did it for the pleasure of plundering a "Jewish" home, or if they were trying to find something specific—if they were looking for the same conqueror's crown that I have come to find.

Perhaps the Reinach papers, if they weren't burned in Berlin in 1944, are still in sealed boxes in some Moscow archive. I can't imagine anyone ever being interested in them. I shall have to proceed by deduction. I knew the whole clan so well, the three brothers, their wives and children. I know how they thought—especially Theodore, the most brilliant of all the family, the creator of Kerylos. I refuse to call him "my benefactor," for he was far from doing me nothing but good. I don't blame him anymore. I miss him. He would be so old now, a wise old man who could tell us all the stories in the world, all our odysseys and journeys, like Homer or Herodotus.

I always go down the alleyway along the side of the house and enter through the vast kitchen, which is so cool. That is where I came in the first time, in 1902, when I was fifteen. Then it was the entrance to the site, though construction had barely begun. Among the deep holes everywhere it was impossible to make out where the foundations were. I'm not sure that the foundation stone had been laid yet. Rocks were smashed to pieces, some of the old trees left and new ones planted. I spent six years living in the midst of the construction work, alongside artisans, builders and painters, and then six more, the happiest of my life, in a Greek villa where I was often alone, like today. Then came the war. Everything changed. I became an adult. After 1918 life resumed, but it bequeathed us all more memories than plans for the future. I needed something new. I moved away. I couldn't stand this absurd passion for Greek antiquity anymore. I became a painter, I wanted to be of my time, I exhibited many paintings, destroyed others. I loved purity of shape. I was a Cubist. It was not the simplest life I could have chosen.

2

MURMURINGS IN BEAULIEU

As they watched the walls beginning to go up, the residents of Beaulieu began talking about "Chateau Reinach," what the Reinachs called "the villa," "the house," or simply "Kerylos." In the small seaside town, the project of building a home in the style of the ancient Greeks was discussed by the dairywoman in erudite tones and by the postman with a vague air that suggested that he had seen it all before. Monsieur Theodore Reinach, "a highly distinguished Parisian" according to the notary, had chosen the finest architect, who had actually worked on ruins in Greece. Another mystery—an architect who had learned his trade "on ruins."

A few people in town knew that Emmanuel Pontremoli was the grandson of the rabbi of Nice. The locals eyed him in his panama hat as he took his seat in the café and unfolded his plans. He had slender fingers, a drooping mustache, and always wore a light-colored jacket. When he spoke it was clear that he was an architect: he constructed his sentences so carefully that his interlocutors were tempted to repeat them verbatim, even as they realized they had completely forgotten what he had said. His tired eyes twinkled whenever he saw a pretty or well-dressed woman walk by. The notary, a dreary old fellow with round spectacles, who strung together clichés with the same attention he bestowed on certifying property deeds, had no idea about that. The Reinach family had "an enormous fortune," was "highly influential," and everything was being done with the most "opulent extravagance." The "chateau" would outclass all the little palaces in the area that vied to be the most "playfully inventive," the Moorish villas, the Palaces of Versailles in pink marble that made them look like powder rooms, and the Gothic castles concealing beach bungalows in their turrets. Everyone bet that it was going to be built in the Art Nouveau style, a "folly" that was just a little more outlandish than the others, like the Villa Gentil with its minaret—Monsieur Gentil was an art dealer—La Vigie, with its circular design—a friend of Gambetta and Waldeck-Rousseau commissioned it—Chateau Saint-Jean, the whim of an Italian-German banker—or the Villa du Parc, as big as the Prince's Palace in Monaco, whose owner, Monsieur Peretmere, used to be a Freemason. On the promenade it was all anyone was talking about; they had seen this Reinach fellow, rather unfortunate looking, but it was his wife they really wanted to meet, dripping in emeralds, apparently, and his two brothers; everyone said the three were inseparable.

The arrival of the first slabs of marble provoked much excited commentary in this pond of babbling frogs. Gleaming white, the marble reflected the sun onto the faces of the curious onlookers. Several months later, during the second phase, the colored slabs arrived, for the dining room, and some tiger-striped marble for the thermal baths—thermal baths! The arrival at the railway station of the enormous polished columns was met with applause. They arrived by boat, then took the little train, like everybody else, and were taken down to the site in drays that nearly collapsed under their great weight. Pontremoli had chosen a quarry in Carrara that hadn't changed since Michelangelo, from which was dug the purest stone. Those who had been imagining a brightly colored house were a little disappointed. The dairywoman knew: Greek temples were painted red, blue, and yellow, the statues in garish hues. She would take out her illustrated almanac, which she had had for years, stored in the lean-to behind the dairy, and show its engravings of Greek temples to anyone who betrayed the slightest interest. She had her own little library, its books covered with butter papers. That was how she was so knowledgeable about everything. She even looked a little like a librarian, orderly, methodical, with that hint of melancholy mixed with resentment born of a fate that had her cataloguing milk churns when she ought to have been dealing in first editions.

Since no one was allowed onto the Reinach site, and the workers were so well paid that they didn't sit about gossiping in cafés, nobody knew exactly what was being built. People imagined silver bathtubs and salons overflowing with indecent statues, and more naked bottoms than in a museum. Ancient Greek bottoms, according to the postman, are always "ambiguous." He preferred Fragonard and Boucher, or Watteau's *The Embarkation for Cythera*, which was a great deal more suitable. A Greek villa, that would be an extraordinary spectacle, an orgy of pediments and staircases, and the priest, forgetting Christian charity, said at once: "What marvelous ruins it will make after those people are ruined." Ruins: the word was on everyone's lips. Hearing the words "Greek villa" it was impossible to imagine anything else. You could already see the signs: "Warning—rockfall." It was an excellent opportunity for the naysayers, who mocked that it was going to be a pasteboard pastiche of the Temple in Nîmes, a hastily daubed theater set, or a picturesque curiosity with broken columns and collapsing arches, like a cemetery or a meringue, or it was going to look like a gigantic clock without a dome, facing out to sea. Without shutters the salt would destroy everything. As the house went up it was supported on a wave of rumors that ebbed, growing duller and fainter as the walls and terraces began to rise, then surged again with the arrival of the first crates of furniture. Even the pastry cook, the dairywoman's rival, albeit not as cultured—the most vituperative Fury in this choir of ancients that included the shoemaker and the laundry supervisor from the Hotel Bristol—was stuck for anything new to say. She stood, silent and morose, attacking neat rows of eclairs with great swipes of her piping bag.

Monsieur Theodore Reinach sported a goatee, always wore a three-piece suit, and whenever he went for a walk among the tall, sloping olive trees that lined the beach at Beaulieu, he put on a wide-brimmed gray hat and tucked a white handkerchief with blue polka dots into his breast pocket. When he first appeared in town he was only forty-two years old, though everyone thought he must be at least sixty. He was graying at the temples and almost completely bald on the crown of his head. The local children made fun of him: a man who lived in the ancient world surely bathed in the sea every day, ran races naked, wore laurel wreaths, and threw the discus and the javelin—and then this portly man turned up, his face creased, dark circles under his eyes as if he'd been up several nights in a row reading and studying, looking nothing like a statue. In his shiny patent-leather ankle boots he was anything but Greek, though none of the grownups mocked him. He impressed them, because of his immense fortune and also because he was the very picture of a scholar. His dog followed him everywhere. He had two, one after the other: the gentle Cerberus, who never barked, and the ferocious Basileus, whose name was the Greek word for "king," rather as Victor Hugo, when he lived in Guernsey, called his dog Senate; whenever he called the dog's name, his voice carried the authority of the Republic. Theodore cared for his dog himself: the whole point of a dog in polite society was to accompany his master on his constitutionals.

The fishmonger claimed the servants "over there" had to wear white skirts and shoes decorated with pompoms, and be able to speak archaic Greek, which wasn't easy, according to the priest. During the Third Republic, as during the time of Louis XIV, archaic Greek was terribly important. There were those who had studied it, and the others—well, everyone had learned more or less a little bit of Latin . . . and everyone could quote Molière mocking learned ladies. Greek was ridiculous, especially when spoken with the accent of the South:

> Greek, O Heavens! Greek! He knows Greek, sister!
> Ah, niece, he knows Greek! How sweet!
> What, you know Greek? Oh, I beseech you sir, for the love of Greek, allow me to embrace you.

The dairywoman wrapped her arms around the pastry cook. Occasionally their malice reconciled them.

Sometimes Theodore's brother Salomon came to visit, his brother Joseph a little less frequently, they all wore a pince-nez and a hat. The first time, the rumor went all around town in less than an hour. Everyone came out to see, even the postman interrupted his round. They looked exactly like each other. They were almost the same height, had the same beard, the same pince-nez. Salomon was the least bald, Joseph the most corpulent, Theodore the only one who smiled. The spectacle of this triumvirate at the Réserve de Beaulieu, sitting at a table facing the sea, took place about once a year. The waiter claimed he always heard them arguing, and conversation swiftly grew heated between the three brothers, though he could never tell what about, while Marinette, the maid from Monaco, said the three Reinach gentlemen always agreed on everything, and if anyone would know, she would, since she was the one who starched their shirts, which she was most careful not to confuse, identifying them by their embroidered initials. "There they are, the three of them, Minos, Aeacus, and Rhadamanthys," the priest said, and everyone made him say it again. They were the three judges of the Underworld. And then he added, his voice dripping with honey and gall: "Or perhaps they are actually Shem, Ham, and Japheth," the three unfortunate sons of Noah in the book of Genesis. The pastry cook shrieked with laughter.

No one disputed that the Bay around La Réserve was the most beautiful breeding ground for crustacean species along the entire coast. The French Riviera saw the arrival of lobsters, scallops, spider crabs, and langoustines of all kinds: exiled kings, courtesans turned marquises, cardinals in plain clothes and

French field marshals in grand uniforms, American writers trying to shake their alcoholism, half-veiled Russian ladies—but not many scientists, apart from those from the Nice observatory, financed with the largesse of Monsieur Bischoffsheim, and the Prince of Monaco's oceanographers, who were always between two polar expeditions. Astronomy and the creatures of the seabed were very specific areas of knowledge, everyone knew exactly what they were about, even if one couldn't understand a word. But this Theodore Reinach was a scholar in every field. No one dared open their mouth when he was around. At first everyone thought he was an expert only on ancient Greece. They soon realized that he read books in every language on every subject, he would leave a pile by his deckchair, and Marinette would carry them back up to his bedroom as though they were the Gospels. In his leisure time away from archaeology he devoted himself to chemistry, geometry, music, and the legend of Catherine Ségurane, who had beaten back the Turks during the siege of Nice at the end of the Middle Ages by showing them her bottom. It was intimidating.

Everyone agreed that this man, in spite of his woolen suits lined with red silk and his silver-knobbed cane, seemed happy. A greenhouse plant who was thriving out in the sun and the wind. He was no longer studying, he was composing. For the first time in his life, he was doing something other than reading and writing. He was like a musician, taking a theme, constructing variations, throwing himself into one movement then another, bringing in more and more instruments as he built up to the finale. Sitting on the pebbly beach and skipping stones, I listened. I watched. I amused myself with my harmonica. I bade my time. This building—with its dozens of laborers, diggers, draftsmen and surveyors, all working on the Anthill, the Pointe des Fourmis, as it had always been known, and which now suited it more than ever—was to be the culmination of his life's work.

3

THE ARCHAEOLOGIST AND THE ENGINEER

I decided to breach the rocky perimeter and speak with this Monsieur Reinach, I was not entirely sure how, nor indeed about what. I had done my research, I had spoken to everyone, I was the boy who helped the postman and ran errands for the priest, I received kisses on the left cheek from the dairywoman and on the right from the pastry cook, I was pleasant and helpful to everyone, I didn't hang around the shoemaker that much, I was good-humored—that had always been my principal talent.

I had never met Monsieur Theodore Reinach. I had only seen him once, from a distance, entering a hotel. I wasn't afraid of him. I waited calmly, watching for the right moment. I said nothing to my mother: I was too worried she would leap up like a devil and exclaim what an excellent idea it was and absolutely essential that her little genius be noticed by this brilliant and eminent scholar. I loathed the way she had of pushing me forward, in front of the other servants, as if she were trying to sell me at market: she made me recite the *Fables of La Fontaine* to the laundrywoman, the maid and the boys who came to help in the garden, for want of being able to make me perform in front of a public more worthy of me—or rather, of her. On the beach,

I was always afraid that she would undress me to show everyone how well I'd turned out.

Everyone was talking about the house, at the end of Mass, standing outside the school gates. Greek antiquity posed problems for the elementary teacher: would it be like the Parthenon? Or to be more precise the Erechtheion, the dairywoman stipulated, with a lubricious air. Would there be caryatids, processions, animal sacrifices? "And cothurni," added the shoemaker, referring to ancient Greek footwear; he saw a market opening up and carefully tore out the illustrations from the children's encyclopedia so that the priest couldn't show it to everybody. The baker, a dried out, stale old woman, was relieved to learn that the Greeks did not practice child sacrifice; the postmaster, who had read Flaubert, explained to her that that she was confusing them with the Carthaginians, whose land the baker struggled to find on the map. The postman wore a knowing look on his face. He liked to show off his erudition. He knew the people of Beaulieu were called Berlugans, the real name of the sea monsters on the margins of sixteenth-century nautical maps. The priest had the town's coat of arms painted on his tabernacle: there was a sun and an olive tree, with the motto *Pax in pulchritudine*, which he may have come up with himself. This "peace in splendor" suggested tranquil contemplation by the sea, when in fact everyone spent their time in endless argument and discussion. The dairywoman went off to get her giant atlas, the one that *Folklore* magazine—or perhaps it was the Family Museum—had given to all its subscribers. How beautiful was this France, which was just discovering compulsory and free public education. An entire generation had already learned a whole host of facts and was hungry for more; people kept dictionaries and books of grammar in their homes, which they handed down to their children. Nowadays, people in coastal towns read *Cinémonde*, and when anyone mentions the Minotaur, everyone knows they mean the jazz club in Juan-les-Pins, the favored haunt of starlets.

The priest, whose skull shone like an alabaster lamp in a chapel, said, "Greek is our language, the one in which the Gospels are written." He added that not everyone could, and indeed not everyone should, read the Greek text—as opposed to what the Protestants recommended—but he was not very clear in his explanations. I understood nothing, and to tell the truth, I didn't care. As far as the priest was concerned, Saint Jerome had translated everything into Latin, to be safe. I told myself, I who knew nothing, that the original was better. The Greek Orthodox hated Latin, and I still had within me something of my origins, a sort of irrational objection to what came from Rome and the Romans: I had always been told that my family had migrated from Greece to Corsica. I thought of myself as having noble origins, reaching far back into the past. "I'm Greek," I would tell my friends in the harbor, which in all honesty did not particularly impress them. At thirteen, I rebelled against my mother. I couldn't stand the interminable Masses at Nice Cathedral she dragged me to. The day I said, "I refuse," was the day I got my first slap. I was bitterly resentful of the priests, with their dirty beards, their incense, and their soporific chanting. Yet in front of other people, I remained proud of this distinction. My father spoke French and Corsican, my mother Greek. I was trilingual, a thoroughly useless talent. The notary confidently proclaimed that modern Greek was nothing at all, barely a dialect; compared to the Greek of the Gospels, the Greek of the fishermen from Lake Tiberius, it was decidedly inglorious. The Greek spoken by the orators of Athens, now that was something else.

Whenever I tell my grandchildren about these discussions that took place in the evening, on the small green benches along the promenade, beneath the olive trees, they think I'm crazy, that I'm telling them about the time of Catherine de Medici and her court of great humanists and pious astrologers. But no, this was how things were in my youth!

Among the people I saw every day, there was one man I venerated who was even more exceptional than the celebrated Monsieur Reinach. This was the brilliant man for whom my parents worked. He was, I later learned, among the few real friends of the Reinach clan. He was well known and highly respected in the town. An elderly, well-turned-out gentleman, puckish and rueful, with a short, pointed beard and white mustache, he was extremely attentive to his elaborate coiffure, which gave off the odor of brilliantine. He was the very embodiment of opulence and success and yet he spent his time lamenting his situation and telling me about all of his misfortunes.

As far back as I can remember, "grownups" always confided in me. I was no less fond of the domestic servants, with whom my mother played lotto into the night, than I was of the austere friends of the notary and the postman: I talked to everybody. I loved to laugh, and would mock them as soon as their backs were turned. They were like my family, all the people of Beaulieu. But this man was different.

This genius of the Republic lived in the most beautiful house in the entire area, a house built like a strongbox. He had taken a liking to me and always used to tell me his life had been a failure: he had made the whole world dream, was the embodiment of the twentieth century even before the nineteenth was over; but for himself and his family he wanted one of those big old-fashioned houses, in beautiful brick and stone, with classical arcades. He had come upon this sliver of nature well before the Reinach family, and perhaps it was he who suggested that the Pointe des Fourmis would make a delightful site for a house. That I never knew. Later on Theodore Reinach used to mimic the great man's monologues, beating time with his cane like a conductor desperately trying to hold back the waves. The dairywoman would bow slightly when she pronounced his name: "Monsieur Gustave Eiffel."

He used to tell me, fiddling with his heavy watch chain that gleamed in the sun, how every night he dreamed his masterpiece was going to be demolished on account of its lack of utility: "I asked Monsieur Reinach, of whom I am so fond, if, in antiquity, about which he is one of the most learned specialists in the world, great monuments had to have a purpose. The lighthouse of Alexandria, yes, I agree, it did have a purpose, but what about the Pyramids? The temple of Zeus at Olympia? What was it really for? Their villa, you shall see, it will be a marvel in the Greek style, and they will use it every day. But my tower. Did you go and see it, in Paris, my tower, my poor tower? No? You must go to Paris, you who are as handsome as the day. I suggested it to mark the anniversary of the Revolution, I wanted there to be 1,789 steps. All the big names established a petition opposing it, from Maupassant to Gounod, not forgetting Charles Garnier, chocolatier-in-chief, with whom I worked very happily all the same on the Nice observatory." I answered, bravely, but the conversation marked me. "If I had built my tower in 1870, during the Prussian siege, you know we would have been able to observe the movements of the troops, we might have pushed back, we probably would not have suffered such humiliation and defeat, the loss of our beloved provinces. By the 1900 Great Exhibition, nobody even mentioned it anymore, even though it was still standing; all anyone cared about was the tunnels built by that mole, Fulgence Bienvenüe, their cursed, stinking subway trains and moving walkways. Surely a tower is more impressive than a walkway! It is a terrible thing to survive one's masterpiece, to live long enough to see oneself go out of fashion. Who will remember the Eiffel Tower? It shall end up being scrapped. The future, you'll see, I wonder if Greek art won't be . . ."

My ignorance, contrary to what the sour dairywoman told me, didn't prevent me being taken on by the Reinachs. Eiffel the engineer led me to the archaeologist. I had read no Plato or Aristotle, nor any of the ancient historians whose names I didn't know, and didn't miss. When I arrived at the Reinach house, I knew nothing about anything. I had only one weapon: many young people used to come to see Eiffel, to take notes and draw; for my tenth birthday Monsieur Eiffel gave me some thick sketchbooks and pencils. He taught me how to draw perspective with a central vanishing point, make diagrams, create a sectional view, and as he saw that I was becoming rather good, he continued to furnish me with paper and sketchbooks to practice.

The first time I met Monsieur Reinach I had a sketchbook in my hand, in the Italian landscape format, in which I had amused myself by drawing the new villas that were going up. He looked through it attentively. In the Eiffels' garden, the conversation fell silent. For a long time I thought, not a little conceitedly, that it was because everyone was looking at my drawings. Years later, I realized they must have been talking of unmentionable things—secrets. It's all come back to me today, on my final visit to Kerylos. I will set down my memories in this notebook, the name of the woman I still love, the names of friends who have died, and also clues that I shall leave behind for how to locate the extraordinary object I have come to find, I hope, in this empty house. I've put it off for too long, I should have done this a long time ago. Yesterday I felt as though my heart was going to fail me at any moment—I could hardly breathe—and I resolved to visit Kerylos one last time today.

4

SKETCHES OF VILLAS BY THE SEA

The shape of the house follows the headland and the sweep of the rocks where algae cling. Its long, whitewashed walls lounge in the sun, the mortar between the foundation stones painted red, the large balconies adorned with bronzes, terraces meeting at an angle. There is nothing regular about it and yet there is a harmony to it that no other villa possesses. The wind caresses it as if it were a beautiful, streamlined yacht.

From a distance it looks like three sugar cubes on a saucer at the beach café. Olive trees grow by the water's edge, the cove protecting them from the mistral. Through the branches, the sun blazes over Kerylos; lattices of sunlight on the sea isolate this mysterious principality perched on the rocks.

Guests entered by the wooden gate—if it were in Ithaca, it could be the gate to Ulysses's palace, but here it used to swing open for the first automobiles—and immediately fell under the spell of the place. Up a flight of steps, at the top of which the door is painted a beautiful antique red, the color of Minos's labyrinth at Knossos. The first striking thing was the sound of the fountain, the coolness, the square courtyard with columns, an oleander bush sloping over the ornamental basin, the soft colors. They would wander over to the library that looks out onto the Mediterranean, discover stairs, corridors, bedrooms.

An umbrella pine made an edifice for the birds, stirring gently in the breeze. Theodore Reinach never wanted a proper garden around the house. He left the most beautiful trees that were already there and planted others here and there—cypresses for shade, roses, succulents, and palm trees from the Riviera. A few wooden benches placed at random for reading and meditation, looking like they came from Japan. Inside the porch there is a fragment of a painting from Pompeii, protected by a pane of glass, its colors changing according to the time of day. It could almost have been discovered here. It's not a picture of anything, just some beautifully executed garlands. It lends just the right note, like a quotation cut out and pasted onto the first page of a novel.

It glows. Other villas built in that era were eye-watering, suffocating, cluttered with furniture, sideboards with balusters and gilded chairs in the Louis XVI style, padded like elderly society ladies. Colors were aggressive—fuchsia, Empire green, bordeaux, standing out against a stained walnut background like the walls in prefectures and town halls. Some were cavernous, dark and bronze, with lampshades rustling in every corner, flounces, glass globes filled with birds from the tropics, lacquered tea caddies from Japan and Coromandel screens. Others resembled wedding dresses, in the Louis XV style, white on white, chandeliers tinkling with crystals. Local society went from one to the next, evincing a vague disgust. The heady smell of kerosene lamps. Even burglars were tired of it all, only bothering with the jewelry, and still suspicious it might be gold plate and paste.

But at Kerylos the visitor, gaze drawn far out to sea, could breathe. Guests awoke in rooms flooded with sunshine, pure white light dancing on ocher stone, the sea sliced into large rectangles. There was the smell of salt, freshly starched sheets, olive oil, and resin. There was no reason to be discontented.

The omniscient dairywoman was sure she knew all the crimes of the Reinach family, though she got tangled up in her explanations. She claimed that Monsieur Eiffel too was a convicted thief—it was no accident that the two fat, wealthy bastards got along so well. She was talking about the scandal in Panama, "like the hat," a terrible case that tarnished the name of Ferdinand de Lesseps, who had brilliantly pulled off the Suez Canal during the reign of Empress Eugenie, only to find himself mired in a sticky financial situation. Eiffel, she claimed, received millions. She talked about the suicide of the banker Jacques de Reinach, though she couldn't say if it was the same family as "our" Reinach from Beaulieu, but she believed it was. Her best customer, a shrewish woman of the parish, responded that the planet was horrible, dishonest, and that humanity only cared for money. With the fishwife and the butcher's wife, they formed a circle that was worthy of the empress's ladies in waiting. They were duchesses.

When the house, blindingly white, began to rise up, the dairywoman repeated to anyone who would listen that it was proof that this Monsieur Reinach was an imposter, for he clearly was less of an expert on the monuments of Greece than she. The postman, helping himself to another glass of rosé, confirmed that on envelopes Monsieur Reinach was never "Monsieur de Reinach," though it could be a different branch of the same family: "Some took the noble 'de,' a mistake they clearly thought was neither here nor there."

The postman did his rounds of gossip, telling everyone about Chateau Amicitia, with its columns and grand staircases, which made a great impression and into which an American diplomat had just moved. There were dramas and goings-on all over the place, and the priest, sweating gobbets on his bicycle, started on about the Dreyfus trial again, making the point that no one really knew if the captain, now exonerated, was really as innocent as all that. This holy priest was received at the Eiffel residence, where he prattled endlessly, saying whatever came into his head. Monsieur Eiffel could renovate his church! Some solid metal girders, but plastered over on the inside! My mother had to listen to them for hours. Madame Eiffel, whose name was Marguerite, died young, at thirty-two. In a way Monsieur Gustave never stopped mourning, though they had five children, three girls and two boys, which could have made for a lively household. But they didn't laugh much. There were always pretty women. Eiffel instilled in them all a certain rigor and reserve, and a grand Louis XIV style in their house in Paris, Rue Rabelais, a veritable palace, with a salon like the Hall of Mirrors in Versailles. It bore no resemblance to his famous tower. The priest, who visited once—to ask for a Christmas payment—remembered it as a fairy tale; at the home of the king of riveted steel he saw lace-canopied four-poster beds, finely woven Persian rugs, and chimneys carved like the high altar of the Cathedral of Notre-Dame.

What really dazzled the priest was that Monsieur Eiffel had achieved it all so young: at the age of twenty-six, he had been in charge of the construction of Bordeaux's metal footbridge. For those who are intelligent and "capable," there's no reason to wait fifty years to prove oneself. And, as he explained to the postman, that is called progress.

5

THE BARBARIANS AT THE GATE

I ought to have left Kerylos and tried for a place at the École des Beaux-Arts. Pontremoli encouraged me to do it, they still taught "good architecture" there—the kind he practiced himself—I might have become an artist sooner, in any case I would have been free. I should have left with the love of my life, instead of leaving with someone else; I should have left with what I had found in Greece, with my own hands, which was taken from me—I would be a famous archaeologist today—without feeling the slightest gratitude to the Reinachs, without regret; I should have left when I failed to bring my best friend's corpse home with me, I should have left without saying thank you, rather than being chased away like Candide from the Chateau of Thunder-ten-tronckh, with hefty kicks up the backside. But I stayed, like Ulysses spellbound in Calypso's cave, Ulysses among the Phaeacians, Ulysses drugged by Circe, Ulysses dazed and unable to escape from the belly of the Trojan horse. And today, I have tiptoed back inside.

It took the last war for this sanctuary to be desecrated. After 1914, I thought I had seen the worst. During that war, I saw monsters who wanted to destroy civilization, who sought the opposite of all that the Reinachs had taught me. When the

Germans burned down the cathedral in Reims, I was sure that we had reached the apogee of horror. My friend André Pézard told me about the months he spent living like a mole in the subterranean passageways of the Vauquois hill, crawling among the rats in the dirt and filth, to lay mines beneath the tunnels dug by the Germans. Whole months without seeing the sky, breathing death. He survived; he was lucky. He has lived in Italy ever since, he never wants to see anything beautiful again, he translates poets of the Middle Ages as a way of healing himself, and as much as he can, avoids talking about the things he saw.

I never imagined that just a few years later I would witness the absolute triumph of the barbarians; that I would see people I loved, people I knew, die in a way that is impossible to say, impossible to describe, in the wake of which would be an echoing silence. A silence that is just beginning to be broken, just a little, not quite yet.

A moment ago, going up the stairs, I noticed something I'd never paid attention to before: the sun falling on the altar at the far end of the Andron, the most beautiful of all the rooms in the house, in such a way that only the inscription on it could be seen: "To the unknown god." I wondered if it was the villa's epigraph. I understood it in my own way: God remains unknown to me. I prayed to Him occasionally, that He might help me find my Ariadne, lost forever—I am a simple man, impoverished in my spirit—He never heard me, and He left me desolate.

The first thing I learned about the Reinach brothers was that they were all three very close, and that there was a simple way to remember their first names. Joseph, Salomon, Theodore: their initials formed a kind of motto in French, *Je Sais Tout*, meaning "I know everything." They were the embodiment of science, art, literature, politics—everything that made the France of that era.

Joseph was a politician who also wrote for the newspapers. If he had wanted to, he might have become a great teacher, an inventor, a curator at the Louvre—even the presidency of the Republic was not beyond his reach. Salomon and Theodore were members of the illustrious Institute of France, they wore the elaborate embroidered green suit, the uniform of the category of men known as "Immortals," who were addressed with the words "Cher Maître" twice in every sentence. They were members of the Academy of Inscriptions and Belles-Lettres.

I was the son of a cook, who began as a maid, and a gardener, not even head gardener. I quickly discovered that in France there had been, since the era of Colbert—I knew about him, my schoolmaster had spoken of him—a kind of parliament of learned men who elected each other. On the list of famous names that the notary had given me, the only one who had been mentioned at school was Champollion, but that was enough for me. Theodore was also a politician.

The priest, with a smile, used to talk about "the brothers 'I-know-everything-and-even-more-than-that,'" and then wander off, chuckling like a Boy Scout. Over the years I heard all kinds of jokes: "The Reinach brothers know all there is to know about everything, but they don't know anything about anything else!" "Those three know-it-alls, grimacing like monkeys." "This is Orang, this is Utan, and this is Orang-Utan, the youngest," "Monkeys, yes, but terribly learned, they marry goats who are terribly learned too," "At night, we put them away in jars on a shelf"... These were the kinds of things people said in Paris, they made fun of them in the cabarets in Montmartre, just because they were famous. I saw caricatures, horrid little figurines that turned my dear Monsieur Reinach into a monkey, with a sign around his neck on which was written *Theo dort*, "Theo's sleeping," another one I didn't immediately understand, because it was related to one of the great mysteries of the house, where he was applying something to a sort of sleeping cap with a paintbrush: *Theo dore*, "Theo's gilding." They were the focal point of jealousy, not because they were erudite, powerful, brilliant at everything, but simply because they had inherited a fortune, something people would have willingly forgiven if they had been a little dimwitted. At the time, I confess that these jokes amused me, I saw nothing terribly wrong in them. It was I who was a little stupid.

"*Je sais tout*"—I know everything—was an insult I didn't understand at the time. Like all true geniuses, the three Reinach brothers wrote many pages in which they made clear what they did not know, in which they acknowledged their mistakes—I found this note by Theodore, for example, in the margin of a Greek book by the historian who cited the name of Christ, Flavius Josephus: "I take back my criticism, in favor of my original assessment." There are many such passages in their works, and this was indeed one of the lessons Theodore taught me: anyone who says "I know everything" cannot be a truly great scholar. How many times did I hear him end an explanation with: "I know only one thing, and that is that I know nothing." In their youth there was still the possibility that one could know everything, unlike today, when we will soon be sending men to the moon. It was not until much later I understood what "*Je sais tout*" signified: malice, ignominy, contempt.

Before I came to know the Reinach family, I understood nothing about the Dreyfus affair. Adolphe Reinach, Joseph's son—he was, almost to the day, the same age as me, and passionate about politics—became my best friend. He had undertaken to write down the details of the affair in a large scrapbook, with illustrations of the protagonists. At fifteen, I had vaguely heard about it, like everyone else, nothing more, all the uproar was so far away. I didn't even really know what it meant "to be Jewish." I am not sure if I understand much more what it means today, but what I do know is that none of the jokes from that era make me laugh anymore.

All these taunts and caricatures were nothing but hatred. The hatred that was used against Captain Dreyfus, the same hatred that later spread everywhere. People lowered their voices as much to praise them as to slander them: they were geniuses, benefactors, men of taste and talent; they were thieves, imposters, counterfeiters, "foreigners." They were implicated in a scandal in Paris. I sensed that I was not being told the whole story. I asked my mother, who reassured me: "The fine upstanding people here know nothing at all. I have made my enquiries. There are no people better than this family. If you go to work for them it will be with my blessing, my child."

I couldn't possibly have imagined what Villa Kerylos would become for me—and for them—at the threshold of hell. I entered the house because I was determined to. The rock was so close, right beneath my eyes, it took me barely any time to get past the gate. I was still barely more than a child, yet already a small, rather self-assured young man. In the early months of the construction project Monsieur Reinach used to visit frequently, usually staying at the hotel opposite the railway station, signposted, in capital letters, *Le Palais des Anglais*, or occasionally at the Métropole or the Bristol. An entire floor would be reserved for him, he would turn up with his wife and children, English and German governesses, chambermaids and butlers, dogs and cats in baskets. Impossible to imagine such a thing today. He was more famous than a movie star. His arrival would be written up in the newspapers, along with that of all the other bigwigs who set up residence for several weeks in winter—the Côte d'Azur in the summertime was only for the poor, or for workers doing repairs on the villas. It was said that each of his six children had their own valet and tutor, as Joseph, Salomon, and Theodore used to have, until they entered the lycée. I used their schoolbooks when Monsieur Reinach was helping me catch up: they were given written lessons, which they studied on their own, then their tutors would spend hours taking them through everything to ensure that they had understood. It was their father who had invented this convoluted way of learning. It meant he gave them a great deal of freedom, but in such a way that he was able to control them, his three geniuses. You have to imagine my education, in 1902, in this sort of peasant village, invaded by royalty, rich ladies and stars, next door to Villefranche—the fishing village, that my mother despised—where not everyone went to Nice every week. The people who lived there worked in the big houses and the hotels, which produced a small consortium of poor, snobbish gossips. In ten years, said my mother, the fishmonger had more than tripled the price of mullet and sole.

I was witness to it all, right up until 1908, the date of the inauguration of the villa. There was no ribbon cut with a small pair of gold scissors by the elegant Fanny Reinach, no photographer was summoned, the rabbi of Nice did not recite prayers in front of the house, no one burst into song in honor of Poseidon. There were no closets in the bedrooms, there were boxes of books still to be unpacked, the curtains had yet to be hung, but the Reinachs began to come down regularly: Kerylos was ready.

I was arrogant and ignorant, but I had the advantage of being aware of it. I knew that I had changed for the better. Year after year, I had made hundreds of drawings, which I sent to the Reinachs in Paris or kept for myself. I drew the foundations, the construction, surrounded by loose stones, the trees wrapped in wicker to protect them from damage, the arrival of blocks and beams, the painters and plasterers at work, deliveries of fabric. This was what I had been asked to do, and my original function, before I made myself indispensable. "Monsieur Theodore Reinach, of the Institute of France," "parliamentary deputy of the Savoie region," did not intimidate me. Seen from Beaulieu, this little man in a topcoat, with a goatee and a slightly stooped gait, who always had a book sticking out of his pocket, was a character, not a human being. I only began to think of him as a man when I saw him living in the house he had built. I liked him a great deal when I first met him.

Kerylos became the town's main attraction. I adored it as a family home, though the Reinach family was not mine. Later I lived through two wars, and saw my friends die. I saw wounded men and heroes. It was in this setting, which represented the peak of civilization, that I saw the triumph of the barbarians.

During the last war, the Germans behaved as though they were at home in Monaco. It was said they had ransacked the Villa Gal, in Villefranche, one of the richest houses around, and two or three others that they settled into. I was there when the Nazis came to arrest Julien Reinach, one of Theodore's sons, whom I had known since childhood. He was five years younger than me. He always came to see exhibitions of my paintings and had encouraged me when I decided to become an artist. I can still hear him: "So Achilles, you've gone from bodybuilding to Cubism? I suppose one might call that progress."

He had an austere demeanor, and at twenty-five seemed older than me. During the difficult period before Theodore died, when he no longer wanted to see me, Julien carried on regarding me as if we were cousins. He was Councilor of State. He had dedicated his life to the law, and to the study of what he called "comparative legislation." When he took the time to talk about it, it was very interesting. He was appointed Councilor of State in 1940, the same year he was de facto excluded from the civil service because of the anti-Jewish laws decreed in October. Not so long ago he told me, in his terribly distinguished voice and carefully chosen words: "Twenty years ago I took the competitive examinations for the civil service, and I became a young auditor, full of passion for the Republic. They had no choice but to appoint me councilor; normally, you know, it is a question of seniority, but they appointed me a Councilor of State straightaway; so you see, truth really can be stranger than fiction!"

He was in the library translating Gaius, the classical author of works about the laws of ancient Rome, when he was arrested.

The Croix de Guerre he had been awarded after the 1914 war offered him no protection from the French police.

He was interned at Drancy, the concentration camp outside Paris. His wife, Rita, presented herself to the authorities and requested to join him. Was she aware that this might lead to their deaths, as was the case for Léon, her husband's brother, who was at the beginning of his career as a composer, and his wife, Béatrice?

Julien told me that he saw the architect Pontremoli's two sons at Drancy—they were killed in 1944. What must they have talked about? They surely spoke of Kerylos, and happy memories. The Council of State is the highest institution in the country, and those who sit there guarantee the rights of all citizens—and when he uttered the word "citizen" I immediately thought of Athens, and he, too, no doubt. In Drancy they wore the yellow star, they were French citizens and the guards were Frenchmen too. Julien was kept there out of sight of other prisoners, before being sent to Bergen-Belsen in a cattle car. He escaped death by a miracle. Freed by Allied troops, he resumed his work with rigor and zeal. Outwardly, it was as though nothing had happened.

6

FIRST ENCOUNTER

"Achilles, hurry, I need some help!" I went over, reluctantly. I never liked assisting my mother at work when she wore her white apron, but that day, I shall never forget it, was the most important day of my life, the end of my childhood. She knew exactly what she was doing when she called, a little too loudly, "Achilles! Achilles!" I was afraid she was going to show me off like a monkey in a circus, I knew her look at moments like that: even in front of the Eiffel family, she always wanted them to say, "How good looking he is," or "Is it true that you make him recite the *Fables of La Fontaine*, Madame Leccia?"

It was because of my name, and the fact that I was "Greek"—though really I felt Corsican, I loved it when I heard someone call me "a proper little Corsican bandit"—that Monsieur Reinach, as I referred to him, never suspecting that one day I would call him by his first name, chose me. If it hadn't been for my mother, who used to say, brandishing her iron, "you have to strike while the iron is hot," I would never have been able to seize my chance. I'd have become a hotel manager in Nice or Ajaccio, or an orange seller, or a gymnastics teacher at the Lycée Masséna in Nice. I was determined to meet Monsieur Reinach, but had so far failed to do so. Without mentioning it to me, she'd had the same idea, which infuriated me; I was still at the age when one obeys one's mother—except when it came to standing through three hours of Easter Mass chanted in Slavonic.

My mother's bedroom was on the first floor of the servants' quarters, a small house on the grounds of the Eiffels' villa that overlooked the Pointe des Fourmis. I slept in a small adjoining room; our two windows were side by side, and I left mine open whenever I could. Today I still have trouble falling asleep if I can't hear the sound of the waves. I took to sneaking out at night, wandering through construction sites—the village, which fifteen years ago didn't have even five hundred inhabitants, was filled with half-built houses. I would borrow the priest's bicycle, which he habitually failed to secure properly, and dash off to Nice, getting there around midnight. I'd wander around the port, Place Garibaldi, observing everything, but I never became a thief or a libertine. I just loved to feel free, not dependent on anyone. I was suffocating in the domestics' citadel: I wanted to meet people, to talk, to experience different things. I imagined myself at the head of a fleet, I was an admiral; I imagined becoming an architect; I wanted to become a general and save France, open a fishmonger's, drive a locomotive, marry a Spanish dancer. I spent all my time spinning yarns to myself. Nowadays, the domestics' little house, where the gardeners also lived, would be the most coveted, because you can go straight over the blue rocks to swim, but back when the Eiffel family moved in, the main house was surrounded by a large garden—it would not have been elegant to build it right by the water.

In the huge grounds of the villa, Eiffel installed rain gauges, barometers, thermometers, a seismograph, a Campbell heliograph and a Robinson anemometer, which he concealed behind fake Roman arches and Medici vases. To me they were toys with needles and numbers. These machines in the garden were "scientific." Monsieur Eiffel himself set up his contraptions, and compared the results with the other meteorological stations he had built, which were, I believe, located in Bordeaux and Meudon. Waving sheets of graph paper, he demonstrated to all his staff what everyone here knew already: Beaulieu has a most agreeable microclimate. A person who kept to a healthy diet might reach the age of a hundred without much difficulty—my mother caught my eye, expecting gratitude. When I knew Eiffel he no longer rode horses, as he had done for years, though he continued to flaunt his love of sport by organizing fencing tournaments like the ones they wrote about in *Le Petit Niçois*, which his friends followed with enthusiasm, lying on their blue and white striped deckchairs. I loved his boat, too, called the *Aida*, in which he took us all—members of the family and the household staff—without trumpets and drums, for picnics in the surrounding coves. All the crew would hum, mouths closed, the great triumphal march of Verdi's opera.

My mother had gradually managed to inveigle herself into the kitchen, where she rapidly took the helm: she inspired respect, knew how to give orders, liked variety, invented dishes that were quite different from Parisian recipes. Her diet of fresh products pleased Monsieur Eiffel, who had been advised by his doctor to eschew sauces, fat, and heavy dishes. It was thanks to my mother that he discovered the Corsican cedar, which he loved. He planted arbutus, myrtle, and heather. When I was a child I loved picking citrons, hard and bitter, heavy in my hand.

They were soaked for a week in one of the big stone sinks, then boiled in eight successive sugar baths to turn them into candied fruits. My mother slipped pieces of them into fresh fish, caught the same day: nobody had ever tasted such a thing! Except perhaps, as Monsieur Reinach said one day, Alexander the Great, when he arrived with his army in sight of the foothills of the Himalayas: "Madame Leccia's candied citron is rarer than caviar from the Caspian Sea!" My mother didn't even blush, for she knew it was true.

The walls of our bedrooms were whitewashed with lime, like in the monasteries of northern Greece that I was to visit a few years later. The interior of the Eiffels' villa, in comparison, seemed to me a real palace: Venetian chandeliers, tapestries from Flanders, Gothic chests, carpets from Smyrna, Henri II tables collapsing under the weight of Sèvres porcelain, porphyry bowls overflowing with flowers, paneled ceilings and woodwork in the style of an English manor house. I was fascinated by a panel of tortoiseshell inlay that ran the length of an imposing chest of drawers. There were embroidered and starched tablecloths, cunningly folded towels: nothing to suggest this was a seaside house, or that one was in the home of the genius who had designed the Eiffel Tower. While my mother was making herself indispensable, I was receiving an education; I attended a small lycée in Nice, to which I traveled each morning in a horse-drawn cariole paid for by Monsieur Eiffel to transport the children from the village. I didn't yet have a bicycle; it was all I dreamed of, that and a fishing rod that I saw in a shop window in Villefranche. I went in one day, clutching my coin purse—how the seller laughed when he realized that

I had mistaken the length, displayed alongside the most beautiful rod, for the price. Otherwise my passion, since the age of ten, had been for lead soldiers. Monsieur Eiffel had some very beautiful ones—he let me take them out of their boxes and set them up on the dining room table when they didn't have guests—and he bought me some as well. I made Joan of Arc's companions and Napoleon's grenadiers fight each other; I had twenty warriors from the Macedonian phalanx, my elite troops. I spent entire evenings having Joan of Arc captured by Alexander the Great's soldiers, who demanded a ransom; I launched my Marshal Ney against the Cantonese vases in the grand salon depicting sites of the battle of Waterloo; I played the *Marseillaise* on my harmonica. I should never have been permitted to play in the master's apartments, but no one bothered me: "Unhappy man, thou wert reserved for French bullets," Monsieur Eiffel said, quoting Victor Hugo, whenever he walked past the bravest of the brave, "But please be careful of my pots." My mother was proud they let me play in the salon, and she would come in for no reason, carrying a silver tray, and I would pretend not to see her.

Our surname was Leccia, like many Corsicans, but my mother's maiden name was Stephanopoli, and she never forgot it. That famous day, toward the end of lunch in the Eiffels' garden, my mother had the idea of calling my name over the hedge. She had a pretty voice. Monsieur Reinach lifted his head: "Is there someone here called Achilles? He is not very swift to obey. Tell me, is this Achilles a tortoise?"

I peeped out from my shell. He uttered something that I didn't—yet—understand.

Sing, Goddess, of Achilles' fury,
Black and murd'rous, that cost the Greeks
Immeasurable pain, cast the countless souls
Of brave heroes into Hades' dark . . .

He drew on his cigar and added: "You recall, my dear Gustave, that very dusty translation, it sounds so much better in Greek! Μῆνιν ἄειδε θεὰ Πηληϊάδεω Ἀχιλῆος." Later I learned that these were the first lines of Homer's *Iliad*, telling of Achilles's anger. I stood silent as I listened to him; he watched me, as if waiting for a smile or a frown. "This Achilles does not understand Greek, Gustave, he wants to learn his real language, no? It shows! First lesson this afternoon, in the shade of the olive trees on my new land. We shall have coffee with the ants."

Piqued, I replied, Κατάλαβα, *catalava*, "I understand." My mother's face glowed. She didn't drop her pie dish; an excellent actress, she continued serving. A young boy who spoke modern Greek was just what Theodore needed, and living right next door to his future home. That's how I remember it today at seventy years old. Like every man of my age, I have lived through the worst horrors, cowardices, bombardments, deaths. I had friends who were tortured, others whom I loved at school who ended up as collaborators in the *Milice*; I saw my mother die when the ration cards ran out. I have as many memories now as old Homer behind his hollow eyes. But that day has remained intact.

During my first encounter with Theodore Reinach, I wasn't overly timid. My ignorance was my armor. I vaguely knew that a different world had existed, populated by dead writers, by gods whom no one believed in anymore, and by epic heroes. I just needed to get close to them, and I think I vaguely wanted this even before I met this strange tribe. I had only read Jules Verne and several *Lives* of Napoleon, written for young people and given to the children in the local schools back home in Corsica, with illustrations of the Battle of Arcole, the coronation, and Waterloo. My father had received all this in books he had been awarded as academic prizes, and he gave them to me, along with my harmonica, my lucky charm. I left Corsica at the age of eight. I saw in the Pointe des Fourmis a sort of blend of that mysterious island and the island of St. Helena. The building that was going up would be my dream palace.

I was resourceful, clever, and amusing, so people said. The construction site was my playground. I was one of the few who had the right to follow the work, to look at everything, to wander around as if I were part of the family. I had been asked to make drawings, my mission was to observe everything, and I called the villa that was under construction, loudly, in front of the dairywoman, the postman, the priest, and the whole choir of ancients, by its real name, "Kerylos," the Greek word for halcyon. The halcyon swoops over the waves; it is the bird of sadness, the bird that weeps in poetry. Halcyon is also the ornithological name for the kingfisher, that odd creature with its sarcastic and smug little cry that ends in a trill. The three Reinach brothers, Joseph, Salomon, and Theodore, born with beautiful regularity each two years apart, rather resembled kingfishers, birds that build their homes on the water, twig after twig, to raise their families poised upon the sea. Everyone said that the Reinach men were very ugly, and had married pretty women who were all even richer than they. I always thought that

Theodore Reinach had a noble head, his turned-up nose making him look like Socrates. He had fire in his eyes—my mother's expression, I think of her as I write it down. When he spoke to me he was straightforward, and I immediately understood whatever it was he was explaining to me. He proposed a deal to me. I was to send him my drawings twice a week, so that he could, from Paris, follow the construction.

My first lesson in archaic Greek took place that day among the bees and surrounded by rosemary bushes. My mother followed us with cups and a coffee pot, while the Eiffels remained behind chatting and Monsieur Eiffel, in a straw hat, made giant strides to measure what would be the width of the building. The vegetation had already been significantly cut back, and everything smelled of grass. Cerberus sat placidly sunning his muzzle at his master's feet. I perched on a rock in silence. Monsieur Reinach, seated on his folding leather chair, looked like a soothsayer: he had dust on his gaiters, his cuffs, and his hat; his white shirt was black and his black jacket was white. He didn't bother me with grammar; he chose two words, democracy and demagoguery, and explained the differences between them, telling me about the Chamber of Deputies, elections, and speeches. I loved listening. I was a grownup. I saw the sun, the sky, and the birds. I gazed at the horizon.

Fifteen years later, in 1917, in an ambulance, I spoke Greek with a wounded German soldier—he had studied the comedies of Aristophanes at Heidelberg—and together we recited in Greek a comic dialogue between two frogs, full of onomatopoeia, and we swore to do everything in order that one day there would be peace. He gave me his pocketknife. I still have it.

Perhaps it seems naive. But two people had had their legs amputated next to us, the air was foul with the sweet smell of putrefaction, we had seen our comrades die; and because he quoted Aristophanes I did not consider him, lying there on his cot, as just a Boche to be left to die so that we would have more water. When I told my children this, they looked at me mockingly. My grandson, in a disrespectful tone, rolled his eyes and whispered, "No more war!"

That sunlit day, in my memory I see windows that don't exist. Monsieur Reinach picked up the sketchbook I'd placed alongside the coffee cups on the little bamboo table, and drew doors and bay windows where they were going to go. He explained how the largest ones would go here, there would be a simple aperture, that was the location of the staircase, in this room he wanted three, like a lantern.

I saw the windows being put in during the months that followed; my mission was to draw their progress every day. Even today, I still know how to open them, with the system of a handle fixed to a runner along the vertical bar. It moves both up and down to turn the latch into the window casement; it's very modern, but from a distance it looks ancient. Eiffel was astonished when he saw the small geared wheel turning in the center of the mechanism. Archimedes himself might have invented it. Monsieur Reinach and Monsieur Pontremoli would sit and discuss these technical issues for hours. That year I saw them spend entire days poring over the plans: since windows that wide did not exist in the fifth century before Christ, they had to invent an entirely original system for opening them that would appear old. There was no question of making latches with dolphins or sphinxes. You cannot put Greek decorations on a modern window, or copy a genuine ancient window that doesn't open and has a polished alabaster plate through which one cannot see a thing; they had to invent a window with a Greek *appearance*, that allowed the sun in and through which one could see the sea. This difference delighted me. And while they were at it, they had fun designing the tableware. Christofle had reissued in silver several pieces from the Villa Boscoreale, copied from the Louvre—a fabulous gift from the Baron de Rothschild. Monsieur Reinach bought some of these pieces, which were in vogue at the time. But a family in ancient Greece would not have used such bowls, heavy with decorative reliefs, every day, and they were going to need forks that looked like they could have been used centuries before the fork was invented. I found that very amusing. That was my environment, the one that I loved. Theodore Reinach was, as much as Pontremoli, the architect of his house, and between them they thought of everything. They were like me with my boxes of little soldiers. One thing only struck me after two years of construction, though it's quite obvious: houses in the Mediterranean, in Algeria, Morocco, and Greece, the ones we saw in *L'Illustration*, don't have so many windows, and they open only onto patios and courtyards. Theodore wanted windows everywhere; that would be the main difference between his "Greek villa" and the houses of antiquity; he was not going to imitate, he was going to create, to compose an entirely new text in archaic Greek. Not an ersatz palace of antiquity, but a home for him, for Fanny and the children.

Each of these windows served as a frame for a fragment of landscape. I became aware that this coast I thought I had known forever was beautiful, that nature becomes a painting if an architect creates an opening through which to see it. During the Kerylos years, whenever I sat studying with my friend Adolphe, Theodore's nephew who was the same age as me, I would open all the windows wide; I could sit for an hour on one of the top floor balconies, "Daedalus" or "Icarus," staring at the clouds. I drew all these windows with their red shutters. I still have the watercolors I painted in a series, like Claude Monet, at different hours of the day, different seasons, always the same rectangles of light, year after year. Before leaving here, I am going to open the window in the bedroom that bears the name Philemon, the central window in the Andron, one of the windows in the library. I would never have written the word "window" ten times in my notebook if I hadn't come back here. Today I'm going to use my movie camera, the latest Kodak, to frame, film, fix what used to be my sky, one last time. I like filming static shots: when I get home later, it will be like having one large photograph with moving clouds.

My mother, to my great surprise, objected to what was in effect the kidnapping of her son—Monsieur Reinach had declared the very first day that, before the building work was finished, as soon as a part of the house was habitable, I would move into Kerylos. I thought it would make her very happy. She ranted and raved. Was she not capable of raising her son properly? A Corsican woman doesn't let her children go. And when she was old, she would need her eldest son. By what right did these gentlemen of Paris think they could take her cherub from her? I didn't dare protest too much, for fear of her fury. It was she, after all, who had pushed me toward Theodore Reinach, she who told me so often how much she liked the family; she liked to look at my sketches, she too was interested in the new house. I perceived it all as the most terrible injustice. She thought that "Monsieur Theodore" did not pay me enough for my drawings, given all the time I spent there. It seemed to me she was, deep down, accusing him of being miserly. My mother knew no Jewish families in Corsica. She and the sour dairywoman said things that made me feel ashamed; with knowing looks they said that everyone knew these Reinachs had "crooked fingers," at which point I exploded and I took the side of my new benefactor. She realized that nothing was going to make me change my mind. One day she knocked over the pile of books at the foot of my bed: "Did your Monsieur Reinach give you those? Your bedroom will end up looking like a hovel." I was old enough to shout back. Monsieur Eiffel had to intervene in person to pull us apart. He told me that I should not raise my voice in the presence of my mother. But afterward he took her to one side, and then she ignored me for two weeks.

It was not until a year and half later that she finally allowed me to leave with my notebooks and my boxes of soldiers—Monsieur Eiffel had given me some, Gauls from Vercingetorix, to complete my battalions, of which I was extremely proud. The house was not yet habitable, but I was the first to be given my own room, in what later became one end of the corridor on the ground floor of the servants' quarters. I had a cot, my drawing materials, a few clothes that I washed myself. It was an observatory, I did favors for the workers, helped the cook who made their meals, watched everything, followed the progression of each floor as it went up. I thought it was going to take ten years.

In fact, it all came together very quickly. Even before the upper floors were finished, the painters were already setting to work on the ground floor rooms. The plans were so well executed that there were no nasty surprises. Inside the house I felt like I was on a ship, an apprentice sailor atop the main mast. Some winters the waves were violent; the rocks protected the house, but I had to spend entire days cleaning windows that were cloudy with salt. I couldn't stand it after a while. Every day my mother had given me work at the Eiffel villa, silverware to shine, shoes to wax; she had a well-developed theory that children are slaves sent by God, and she looked at me coldly when I didn't obey fast enough. It was Madame Reinach, not my mother, who bought me my first pair of long pants, from the Lily of the Valley boutique in Nice. She chose a warm, light fabric. I didn't dare show them to the children of Beaulieu. I swaggered around the principality of Kerylos dressed like a prince, and happy to have found a family that wanted to make a man of me. Gustave Eiffel was undoubtedly the first to grasp that the time I spent living with the Reinach family, for whom I did a minimal amount of work, would be enormously valuable to me, and would help me gain a basic education, because I was quite clever. He brought over the brass to be polished and the shoe cream. My mother, who never lost face, told me, "Monsieur Eiffel says this Monsieur Reinach is a fount of knowledge." She lingered with relish over the word *fount:* "A *fount* of knowledge, my little one. And you will be someone too, one day, I know it"—but when she couldn't tell me who I laughed at her, and she ended up laughing with me.

What intrigued me at the age of fifteen was why Theodore Reinach, so witty and warm, was called a thief. Whom had he robbed? Why was he, in the eyes of the notary and the priest, some kind of crook? An agent in the pay of the enemy? There was a story that no one wanted to tell me. I was an idiot: I thought that by getting close to the family, I would find out when, why, and how they became so rich; I was planning an investigation—and all I discovered was a man filled with passion, who told me about distant countries, the rivers of the Russian Empire, the mountains of Ceylon, the royal dynasties of Java, the French Republic, the caravans that cross Arabia Felix, the love affairs of the gods; he was authoritarian too, he wanted to teach me a whole host of things, I was discovering a whole other world. I loved it. Every Saturday I went home to help my mother, and then on Sundays, to please her, I sometimes agreed to go to Mass at the Russian cathedral in Nice. At Easter I finally dared to put on my new pants, like a young dandy, and a slightly too-short jacket that Adolphe no longer wanted. I added a folded pocket handkerchief and borrowed a tie pin. She looked me up and down with an expression that made me tremble—I had decided to face her down—and hugged me.

Learning archaic Greek meant a lot of grammar. It was torture for me. I worked five or six hours in a row, copying out pages of texts, which I then learned by heart and recited when I was alone in my room. At night, I dreamed of little Greek words with paws, clambering in line along my pillow. I could recall snatches, which impressed the Reinachs, but I never experienced that moment when learning a language you feel as if you have crossed a border, the barrier lifts and everything is natural, easy, with its own logic and beauty. Plato's Greek was still a rock-face for me, on which I tore my nails. I was never tempted to give up. I wanted to be taken seriously. I began sneaking out at night again—I couldn't stop myself. After whole days spent with my head inside my books, I wanted to be in town, I craved the long tree-lined streets and rows of apartment buildings. I had my bicycle now, a De Dion-Bouton, bought with the money I had earned. No one was keeping watch on me, but it felt like I was fleeing as I headed into the night for Nice. With each push against the pedal, I'd hear the declensions, intone a verse, try to sense the stress. I couldn't read Demosthenes' speeches in Greek, I used to cheat, I used the translation, I knew no one would help me and I was desperate to earn my place in the Reinach orchestra. My mistakes made them laugh, which incensed me. Theodore remained patient and kind. Whenever he sensed that I couldn't keep going, he would give me a history lesson, and I liked listening to him talk about Spartan warriors, Philip of Macedonia's wars, the defeat of the great king Darius. I asked him questions about ships, the lines of rowers, triremes, I wanted to understand how there was room for so many soldiers in such small vessels. Had any been found? I stroked Cerberus. How did we know what the ships in the Battle of Salamis looked like, in the "night with the dark face"? I even managed, I think, to say it in Greek. It's all gone, wave after wave, like an exhausted swell in the cavern of my brain: I can't remember any of the things I knew when I was eighteen. The builders had completed the foundations. I was drawing the rooms and corridors in the basement: that's how I know there is no hidden underground room, no secret chamber. At least it will save me some time today. Monsieur Pontremoli didn't end up walled up like the pharaohs' builders in the Hollywood blockbusters that I loved so much in later years. Once, I had all the plans in my hands; this morning, I have them all in my head.

Playing this game whose purpose was to turn me into a historian, Theodore often used to tell me stories of the great adventure of the Jewish people. If he had chosen to make films, he could have been one of the great directors of the early days of cinema, making French epics in the Victorine studios. He showed me photographs of ancient coins in books, told me about Solomon's Temple, the seven-branched candelabra and the Ark of the Covenant that contained the Tablets of the Law and was carried on a golden bier surmounted by two carved cherubim. He described the molten sea, the large basin the Hebrew priests used for their ablutions. Always standing, he would mimic the Queen of Sheba all-aquiver, linger on the Jews' captivity in Babylon or the Golden Calf. He explained the Athenian constitution at the time of Cleisthenes—what a strange name—or the construction of the Greek temples of Paestum—I learned that the most beautiful Greek temples are found in Italy, that people photograph old coins and make books about them, that it was not only in the Bible that the Hebrews are mentioned, and that people only burn incense in front of Orthodox icons. My astonishment lasted all of two minutes, after which I knew it all, and later I would astonish my mother and the dairywoman.

At the lycée I was soon one of the top students in the class, though my mother of course was the kind who was entirely unsurprised and never rewarded me. She'd adopt the tight-lipped air of the head housekeeper and say: "Well done, keep it up." It was so unfair: when everyone complimented her on her cooking, she would cock her head like a little dog at the sight of a sugar cube. I think I hated her then, when I was winning prizes and she never said a word. One day she tried to go and see Fanny Reinach, to explain that she had lent the family her son, and they ought perhaps to pay her a little something. Madame Reinach looked at her and didn't answer. My mother shouted when she told me. I was ashamed. She was right though, if I put myself in her place; what had happened to us was very strange. She denounced Theodore and Fanny's greed, and went to talk to the priest. I was afraid that they would send me packing if all this came out at Kerylos. She talked about sending me to live with one of my father's brothers, a gardener at the prefecture, who would be able to get me a paid job as a day laborer. I wept. I knew I would never be good enough at Greek and history to be kept on at the Reinachs'. I began to have nightmares.

7

CONVERSING IN THE ENEMY TONGUE

The people of Beaulieu had no idea how to pronounce this "German" name: the butcher and the blacksmith said *Reinasheu*, with a strong accent. The people who said Rynack didn't like Jews. They didn't much like Germans either, and they never tired of repeating that the Germans had defeated us in 1870 and stolen not only Alsace but also the most beautiful part of Lorraine. One might have thought that for Corsicans, all those operations in the east were a long way away, but no: it was as if someone had torn off yet another piece of Napoleon's greatcoat, the final stages of the dismantling of the great French Empire. My mother forgave the Germans nothing.

One winter morning, I was horrified to overhear—without understanding a word—Theodore Reinach, who was holding Cerberus on a leash, and Gustave Eiffel speaking German together as they stood on the seawall.

I was alarmed. I wondered if I had arrived at a very bad time, if I had been right to leave my mother, if I should return to Corsica to look for work in Ajaccio. There were some Germans in the village, right next door in fact: in 1905 the Villa Livesey—built by a very elegant British railway engineer who had once hosted James Gordon Bennett, the man who established the world's first hot air balloon race—had been sold to Prince Alexander of Hohenlohe-Schillingsfürst, governor of Haute Alsace. No one ever spoke to him, nor to any of his servants, but everyone knew his complicated name by heart. In Beaulieu, Eiffel was admired, but no one spoke of the "Villa Eiffel," instead it was called the "Maison Salles." That was how letters there were addressed. As far as the postman knew, the real owner was Monsieur Eiffel's son-in-law, his eldest daughter Claire's husband, Adolphe Salles; the brilliant engineer wanted neither to draw attention to nor advertise his name, which rang so oddly to southern ears. Was he afraid of an attack? I only understood much later. Why were Reinach and Eiffel speaking German? Were my mother and I living among spies? I couldn't bear for her to start spreading another scandal, so I told no one, kept it to myself, one more anxiety to nurse as I memorized the pages of my books of Greek. Fanny Reinach's smile when she brought me cakes while I was immersed in my studies barely soothed my anxiety.

The next day Monsieur Reinach, as though he knew I had overheard his conversation, said to me in his reedy voice: "You know, learning German, because it's the language of our enemies and we are going to have to fight them again, is like already having committed to fighting another war; learning English, to fight alongside other men in red uniform, that's also wanting war; even going into some kind of passing trade, if that kind of thing grabs you, learning any living language, means thinking about defending borders, conquering, invading. But the man who studies Greek is going to learn how to think, how to love, and anywhere he goes in the entire world he will find other people who chose to learn the language so that they could share the understanding, the sense of nuance, and the progress that we all make, to some degree, in self-knowledge."

He didn't really say all that to me that day, of course, in one go; I'm embellishing. But it was what he led me to understand, during my first six years there, the period when the villa was being built. A man who knows a little Greek, or who learned some in his youth, will be drawn to other cultivated people, people who love theater, architecture, history, the beauty of statues, the feeling you have when you weigh a coin in your hand, thinking about all the people who held it before you, over the centuries—so many things that are beautiful and serve no purpose, serious and joyful, tragic and poignant, comical and sad—and you don't even think about whether they were German, Italian, or British. Learning Greek is like loving music, or speaking a universal language.

I didn't really understand. No one spoke the Greek of Homer anymore. I had enough wit to see, at least, that Theodore did not intend to turn me into a scholar. He saw that I had difficulty learning and I was much slower than his nephew Adolphe. So what was the point? If I eventually became, through great effort, reasonably good at Greek grammar—at one point I even understood oddments like the "oblique optative" and the "second aorist"—it was because I couldn't bear looking stupid. And also to impress Monsieur Theodore. I wanted to turn cartwheels before these people who were in the process of adopting me. Today, I can only remember a few snippets of all the things I learned back then. I remember Theodore once giving me a book by Saint-Marc Girardin, and quoting him: "I do not ask that an honest man should know Latin. It is enough for me that he has forgotten it." Of course now no one remembers Monsieur Saint-Marc Girardin either. I am a relic.

I forgot everything. How delicious it is. The cool breeze on the tip of my nose this morning. I escaped from Kerylos. Theodore fashioned me. And then I ran away. Greek, the language of peace: what a beautiful notion that was, except it wasn't true. All the Greek texts I liked, once I began to understand them, were about warfare, sieges, battles, heroes who killed, massacred, broke the bodies of their enemies by tying them to the back of their chariots. The Reinachs, peaceful scholars, weaponized their articles to fight German specialists. Universities were at war with each other. There was an archaeologist from Munich called Furtwängler about whom they spoke with deep respect, they owned all his books, and yet at the same time, it was very curious, deep down they seemed to hate him, a strange blend of resentment and admiration. All French people felt like this about the Germans.

On the terrace of the restaurant of La Réserve hotel, the Reinachs always sat together as a family. Nobody dared approach them. Everyone watched them and there were always the same comments: "Those girls are not pretty in the least, they inherited their looks from their father, look at their bulging eyes, and look at those boys, as serious as little Orthodox priests!" They didn't have extravagant things, gold-topped canes or fancy dresses, which bellboys and snooty old crones alike were swift to note. They were quite content with their English parasols, gray jackets and ankle boots made in London, imperceptible luxuries. It was impossible to know anything about them. They were never seen at the Great Synagogue in Nice, which did not go unremarked.

It would have been preferable, in terms of gossip, for them to take their places in the first row. They fell into no obvious category: the nabob with his courtesans, the marquis trailed by his pageboys, the gentleman from Paris ruined by gambling, the English dandy, smoking slim cigarettes and wafting around like Oscar Wilde, all so easy to describe, you could talk about them endlessly, while not actually saying anything at all. When it came to the Reinachs, everything anyone said in town was wide of the mark. It never crossed anyone's mind to pick up one of the books they'd written. The only clue to them that anyone could find, which was endlessly repeated, was the rather limited observation, in any case rather to their credit: "They are great friends with Monsieur Eiffel, a man of judgment, and not at all pompous. Do you really believe he made money from the Panama affair? Personally I don't think so, though that said, there is no smoke without fire . . ."

There was one story, however, that no one told me, and even the dairywoman knew only snippets of it. The notary, polishing his loupe, said: "They were a little crooked, I think. They paid out a small fortune on behalf of the Louvre for some pieces that didn't belong there." He said it in a pontificating tone of voice, but went no further. It wasn't until much later that I found out the affair had been in every newspaper and had provided inspiration for multiple caricaturists. But you have to imagine what passed for news at the time in a village like ours: the notary barely lifted his nose from his deeds and was so careful with money he didn't even subscribe to *Le Figaro*, and the dairywoman whipped up everything she heard, while distrusting the few actual facts that passed within her reach. I soon found myself locked up in the heart of the Reinach citadel, studying all day every day, where no one ever alluded to anything that might upset the master of the house, at least in my presence. It took me several years to untangle the skein, when I could have just gone to the public library in Nice to request the bound volumes of *Le Figaro*, or *Le Temps*, which had reported daily on all the various affairs in which the Reinach name was mentioned. But I was so busy with all the new books that I'd been given. At the age of fifteen or sixteen I developed a passion for classical authors and their tales of tormented and sometimes tragic love affairs, I would read the same page three times to understand what was going on, or skip ten to get straight to what happened with Daphnis and Chloe. My mother was a little taken aback to see me like this, but she gradually softened—after having started off saying to me, "Don't you see, if everyone acted like them, no one would ever get anything done."

The main topic of conversation was still the "Affair," and at Kerylos we used to talk about it late into the night. I was obsessed. I knew all the details, down to the most minuscule twist. Dreyfus was innocent. Adolphe knew his entire story; his father, Joseph, Theodore's highly respected elder brother and head of the family, had written hundreds of pages about it. They were all in awe of the family of the wretched prisoner on Devil's Island. Joseph became the self-appointed official historian of the case. At that point I hadn't met him yet, I had only seen him from a distance. I found his books interminably long, but I read them all the same; they were less demanding than Greek grammar. But I preferred to listen to Adolphe telling me about

Commander Esterhazy and the French maid at the German embassy going through the wastepaper baskets.

These mysteries, which I didn't fully understand, concealed another one, of which I wasn't aware at the time. There was one question I never asked myself: what did they want from me? I enjoyed an unusual status. I was the only person who could eat whenever I wanted with the domestic staff in the big kitchen below, where everyone knew my mother, and who was also allowed to eat with the Reinach children and their cousins upstairs when they came down for the holidays. Nobody was shocked by this. I was aware that I had been taken in by a broadminded family, where progressive and philanthropic ideas reigned. In England or Germany, in a grand Italian family, such a thing would never have been allowed.

A few years later I happened to be walking past the room that separated Monsieur and Madame's bedrooms, where they would meet to read and talk together, and I heard Madame Reinach ask, "And what about young Achilles, my handsome, clever friend, who's so agreeable to everyone? When are you finally going to let him play the role you've been secretly preparing him for? He wants to get out, you know, you can't keep him locked up at Kerylos at his age. You're holding him captive; when Adolphe isn't here, he's bored, and he's bound to escape from your gilded cage eventually. Now is the moment, believe me." I kept what I heard to myself. It had never occurred to me that I was not in this house by chance, or by a simple act of kindness. Theodore was, apparently, planning something in which I was to have a starring role, I knew nothing about it and no one had ever mentioned it to me.

Alas, nobody could have guessed what was going to happen. The tragedy that eventually played out had no single perpetrator. Adolphe, my one true friend, was killed in 1914, in the Ardennes, right before my eyes. He didn't live to see the birth of his son, Jean-Pierre. I met the child when I came back from the front. He too died in combat. In 1942 he joined the Free French, went underground with the Resistance, and was captured. He managed to escape and get to England, where he married Naomi Rothschild at the Great Synagogue in London. Their daughter Jocelyne was born the same year he was parachuted into Occupied France with Jean Moulin. She never knew her father either, because he too, like his father, died for France. The same story played out again. I knew them all so well, loved them so much, their story is part of my own. Today the peeling walls of Kerylos stand empty, telling me how utopian were their dreams, how much better they might have done spending their money more practically, how unaware, how *blind* they were, how they understood nothing of their times. They toyed with me; I amused them and I was too much under their influence to rebel. Joseph was too selfish to help me get into politics when he could have made me an attaché in some ministerial cabinet; Salomon could have given me a job at the museum in Saint-Germain-en-Laye where he was the director; Theodore could have encouraged me to try for the École des Beaux-Arts in Paris—I blame all three of them, but I will always revere Adolphe and his family.

I was not going to become, as my mother had thought in the early days, Monsieur Reinach's secretary. According to Monsieur Eiffel, he dictated texts filled with quotations in Greek, Latin, Hebrew, and Coptic, languages that his secretary would need to know in order to be able to follow. Some months earlier, a filmmaker had wanted me to act in a film about the kings of Spain, but my mother put her foot down. The director had seen me at the beach. He told me I would wear a black doublet with slashes in the sleeves, he thought I looked like an *infante*. My mother responded with a single sentence: "No one in our family makes money because he has a nice smile." I'd been picturing myself on a big screen, wearing a uniform with a golden chain, my name on the posters . . . And in one week I was at the Reinachs', having done nothing but stammer, I had a job, a salary, a second family—with my mother and my father nearby, it was ideal. When my little brother Cyrille was born—there was a large age gap between us—Theodore said: "Cyrille? I hope he's going to work methodically." He went on to become one of the most brilliant engineers at the Eiffel shipyards. Gustave Eiffel gave him a reference for Sainte-Barbe College, in the shadow of the Pantheon in Paris—where he himself had once been a student—and then helped him prepare for the competitive examination to enter the prestigious Central School of Arts and Manufacturing, where he had also studied. At the time, the Republic functioned as smoothly as the elevators in Eiffel's eponymous tower: two intelligent boys were given a chance, and two highly distinguished men did not think it was beneath them to facilitate their chances. Things worked out better for my brother. His protector was more efficient than mine and less of a dreamer. Between the two wars the system fell apart; today, as the country rebuilds itself, such a trajectory is once again conceivable for grandsons of a mountain shepherd, like us. Long may it last.

A short time before her death, Fanny Reinach took me up in a hot air balloon. She was very frail by then, but she couldn't deny herself the pleasure. I think we children provided an alibi for her. Theodore didn't come. She organized everything; it was to be a surprise for Adolphe and me and the little ones, Julien, Léon, Paul, and Olivier. We were ecstatic. The balloon lifted up from the gardens of the neighboring property. We could see Kerylos from the air. I can still picture her slender, gloved hand as she waved farewell in the breeze.

8

FACING THE RED FRONT DOOR

The house wasn't ready yet, but the front door had been fitted, two imposing leaves with massive hinges that made me think of a historical monument. I must film it today, before I take my leave for the very last time. There's nothing Greek about it. It's lacquered like a Japanese box. The heavy bolts, which look a little Egyptian, were made to order by Bricard, the best locksmith in Paris. The huge studded hinges look like ones I've seen on cathedral doors in Chartres and Amiens, or the ones in Victor Hugo's *Notre Dame de Paris* that drove Biscornette to despair (he was, I believe, a medieval locksmith who has a street named after him near the Place de la Bastille). The gate through which you could see visitors as they arrived looks like ones I saw at the monasteries on Mount Athos. The massive handles are imposing enough for the coffers of a Roman emperor. I'm still impressed today. Kerylos is a fortress. At the very moment the doors were mounted a ray of sunlight broke through the cloud. We were standing around in a semicircle, watching in silence. The dog strolled across, as languid as a cat.

The red paint, stark against the white walls and the little gravel-lined esplanade, was the color of our wounds. I can picture the summer day in 1914, twelve years later, Adolphe and me showing off our new uniforms. Again we were all standing around in a semicircle, this time in the salon of the Reinach residence in Paris. I stood there in my blue tunic and red pants looking at the old, heavy furniture in the rococo style, a symbol of worldly success, a large painting by Gustave Moreau framed by purple curtains, the women in dresses by Worth, the glasses of champagne, and all of a sudden I realized it was all over. Yet for the family it was just the beginning. They were completely confident that they would be joining the great French legends like Carnot and Casimir-Perier. The sons craved glory. The three brothers were the second generation of a family that had made their fortune and finally gained entry to Olympus, and they wanted to go even further. Maybe one of their grandchildren would become head of state, as Joseph had once dreamed of being, but he had the intelligence to realize that it was too soon in the family history—their name needed another generation or two before it would be celebrated all over the world, before it became universally known, like those of Pasteur and Poincaré. But I, who knew nothing at all, standing there in my brick-red pants, in a split second I knew that it was all over, so much sooner than expected. The Reinach era had only just begun and it was already coming to an end. The era when the very wealthy could also be intellectuals. Nowadays the rich are never scholars, and scholars are never rich. The end took several more years, till the next war. I witnessed it all. I saw them suffer, die, wiped out. Somehow I avoided the bullet that could have killed me too. I owed them everything, not least that moment when, at the age of twenty-seven, I suddenly understood the concept of time. I could hear voices that I'd heard a dozen years before. In the empty house today, I picture again the years of construction and this image:

Theodore at the Pointe des Fourmis, telling me all the things I have to learn, teasing me. I must be fifteen or sixteen. He pushes me into the water. *Don't tell me you're going to spend your life chasing vipers among the rocks, or learning to swim, or studying music, or history and geography, or translating Homer when you're fifty—you have to do it all now.* I've grazed my knees on the rocks, he pushes me back into the water, miming the breaststroke from the shore, newspaper in hand. In the December sun, the house rises up behind him and as I grow taller it grows taller too.

9

THE MOSAIC IN THE ENTRANCE HALL THAT REVEALS NOTHING ABOUT THE FUTURE

I once heard Theodore telling someone that the mosaic in the vestibule dated from antiquity. He was making very free with the facts. Fanny listened, her eyes lowered. When he spoke it was impossible not to believe him. He had bought it in Rome, he was saying, but it was as exquisite as Alexandrian-era decoration. He went into great detail describing the antiquities store where this particular fragment came from, recalling how he had hesitated a little, for the pleasure of haggling, having been offered an asking price that was clearly too high: he couldn't help coming across as a very rich man, his manners betrayed him, even when he dressed like some middle class gentleman of leisure. The subject pleased him, it was ideal for the entrance to the house: a rooster, a hen, and some chicks. A modest family portrait. He embroidered his story in the certainty that none of his guests would contradict him. He had indeed found it in Italy, but it came from a mosaicist who worked at the Vatican museum. It was a fake. Of course he would never have let a genuine antique chef d'oeuvre under visitors' boots, ladies' heels, Cerberus's water bowl. It does look entirely authentic: the beautiful rooster with red, blue, and white feathers is the image of Theodore, it is him, it is the singing Gallic rooster, his back arched, like Edmond Rostand's *Chantecler,* it is France.

In Greek houses, the vestibule, or porter's lodge, was called the Thyroreion. Which is what I always called it. When I was seventeen, as far as I was concerned, this was perfectly normal. I wasn't aware of the monstrous anomaly that was my everyday life with the Reinachs. "I left my umbrella in the Thyroreion," I would say, straight-faced. I adopted the words they used and kept my accent. I loved their house so much, a love that grew slowly, was built up stone by stone, piece by piece, becoming more beautiful with the first floor and then the second. I can still see myself as the young man I once was. But when I came in this morning, I couldn't believe I had ever been taken by this architecture. As an artist, I've done the opposite. From my very first painting, I tried to kill everything in me that was Greek.

At the age of fifteen I wanted to look like an ancient Greek athlete. The only work of art that interested me was myself. I grew very fast, and all through the time the house was being built, I carried on exercising. I learned the butterfly and the "Australian" crawl, as we called it then, with the retired non-commissioned officer who gave swimming lessons at the Hotel Bristol, one of the last men who still cultivated a resemblance to Napoleon III. Every night I went down to the sea to swim; I wanted muscles like those of Hercules in the huge books of paintings I found in the library—nothing like the athletes of 1910, hybrids of cavalrymen and funfair wrestlers. It took time, but I had few other leisure activities aside from eating like a wolf. I was Greek, and I had to prove it. The essence of Greek was first and foremost the body. The fat Orthodox priests were horrible Greek decadence.

I understood this instinctively long before I was able, through endless recitation, to understand the fragments of Plato's dialogues given to me by Theodore, who pushed me toward the baccalaureate and the love of truth.

I was a pleasant, uneducated boy whom he set about civilizing. A good boy. I drew and sang—gradually the Corsican folksongs of my childhood were replaced by the operatic arias whose scores Madame Reinach used to lend me. She'd noticed that I sang quite well, I could hold a note for a long time without quavering. I began as a page-turner. Two years later she was accompanying me on the piano. We practiced Nadir's aria from *The Pearl Fishers*: "Yes, it is she, it is the goddess," which I sang as a duet with Adolphe, whose voice dropped soon after mine. We sang it as we walked toward a copy of a statue of Athena Lemnia, in the vestibule with the staircase leading up to the bedrooms, cackling with laughter. Back then we didn't have many distractions. I sang *La Belle Hélène*, my triumph: "I am the fiery Achilles, the ardent Achilles, and I would be perfectly tranquil, were it not for my heel . . ." I played it all to my advantage. I think I knew how handsome I was, with my wide, dark eyes and my hawker's smile, a lock of hair slicked over my forehead, I certainly intended to make the best possible use of it all to forge ahead in life. I bought myself a pair of spectacles, because I was also self-conscious about my intelligence. I was a nasty little brat really. I used to steal Adolphe's cravats, not that he cared. What could be worse than a young man who reads in his mother's eyes how handsome and special he is, and who has a clear conscience, for after all his mother is right (which is why she so rarely pays him a compliment)? When I said this to my beautiful blue-eyed

Ariadne, she answered, unsmiling, "I suppose a child whose mother tells him he's ugly."

At the age of sixteen I was barely presentable—which didn't matter, since I was never invited anywhere. It was my good fortune to know the Reinachs, who brought me down to earth, and whom I so revered. Sport was the only area in which I could easily best them. I worked even harder at it, to infuriate them, because they dared not tell me it wasn't worthwhile. Soon I was reciting my declensions as I swam, or conjugating the famously difficult "mi-verbs," one of the pitfalls of Greek grammar. I would go down to the kitchen where little Justine, who was sweet on me, would grill me a steak, and into the garden, still reciting, to lift sandbags and do pushups.

I dreamed of Athena and Aphrodite. I exulted at the thought of Poseidon splashing about with mermaids, I devised new ruses for Odysseus, I recounted Solon's laws to myself and invented new ones, even more just, for the people, the army, the slaves, for the dairymaids and the pastry cooks, I made cutout paper models of the monuments of the Acropolis, I read aloud tales from Alexander's youth, I broke in Bucephalus by turning him to face the sun, I killed Penelope's suitors with my bow, I made the prettiest girls from Sikyon pose for a painting of the most beautiful woman in the world, I crossed the Bosphorus on a bridge made of boats. I cried, *"Evohe, Evohe!"* in the waves and strode naked along the beach at night, I memorized prayers to Persephone and Hades, god of the underworld, smoked bay leaves in an incense burner in my bedroom, fought the Lernaean hydra and slayed the Stymphalian birds on the marshes. I was so happy.

I was not in love. That came a little later, and I couldn't tell a soul about it. I've had a long time to think about this: how this house also gave birth to love. I could only ever have met Ariadne, Homer's Ariadne with her beautiful braids of hair, at Kerylos. She looked just like the young Greek women of my imagination. She liked to wear sandals and dresses by the great couturier Fortuny (who drew inspiration from the Charioteer of Delphi), with draped silk falling from her shoulders to her ankles, like Artemis the huntress. She also liked to draw. My love for her was like my love for Kerylos: it grew slowly. The difference is that today my love for Ariadne remains intact.

It was to Ariadne that I first sketched out a glorified version of my family's history, dissimulating the fact that my mother was a cook and my father a gardener. I didn't lie, but I stressed the elements that I thought would please her most. My parents had moved to Beaulieu when I was eight. It wasn't easy to find to work in our village in Corsica. Cargèse is quite probably the only Greek village in France. My mother used to tell us the story of our odyssey for hours at a time, like the other mothers from Cargèse, each of whom must have embellished her story in her own way, but the basic facts were true, what happened to us was a historical fact, just as much as the Trojan War. It's a terrible thing to seduce a woman by telling the very same stories that you hated to hear coming from the mouth of your mother. I knew it was all probably only half true. Ariadne was enthralled by "our" history. In the sixteenth century a boat pursued by the Turks arrived on an unknown shore, parched but beautiful, somewhere between the banks of the Liamone river and the mountains. I don't know how many pilgrims were on this Mayflower filled with Orthodox priests, but by the end of the nineteenth century several hundred intrepid people were living there—not necessarily all related to each other, for a fair number of them married Corsicans—peasants who had altered their Greek names to make them sound Corsican or French. I used to wish I'd been named Stéphane, like my cousin, or Nicolas, or Paul, Alexander, or Alexis. Achilles was a little far-sighted. In the France of the Third Republic, such a name wasn't entirely unheard of, people my age might have an Uncle Hector or Nestor—I once met an old duke named Sosthenes at the Reinachs' house, who told me we ought to set up a club for people with Homeric names. He had a cousin named Antide, which was extremely rare. I laughed when I saw Proust had given one of his characters the name Palamède.

In our village, Cargèse, there were two churches opposite each other, one Catholic and the other Byzantine. We followed the "Greek" liturgy, which was a little complicated because when they arrived on the island the Greek Orthodox monks had been forced to pledge allegiance to the pope, after which they were considered to be Catholics practicing eastern rites. The Archimandrite had the good sense to also serve as the curate; he simply changed his regalia depending on the ceremony. He maintained links with his fellow Orthodox priests in Athens, Saloniki, and Corfu, with whom he corresponded rather more than he did with the bishop of Ajaccio who was supposed to be his superior. Whenever we were in Nice, my mother would go and light candles in the Russian Orthodox cathedral.

The Thyroreion glowed red in the early morning light when the front door opened onto a view of the sea and the rocks. The walls on each side are painted with frescoes whose symbolism is not hard to interpret. Reinach for beginners: on one side, a basin, with birds, on the other, a shield. As if Theodore had wanted to site his creation between war and peace. The book I might write, were I to continue filling this notebook, would be some version of *War and Peace*; there are so many characters, stories, fights, and love affairs. It's as though this adventure encompasses a whole world.

We have lived through more wars than any generation since Napoleon and the tsar. Theodore, for all his plumpness and fine manners, was a fighter. He and his brothers faced real enemies at the time of the Dreyfus affair. He lived through the 1870 Franco-Prussian war, the siege of Paris, the battles of a vanquished France, when the raging fires of the Commune added so dramatically to the humiliation of defeat. Theodore told me of the loss, in the Tuileries fire that almost destroyed the Louvre, of Napoleon III's entire library, illuminated manuscripts and incunabula, a huge part of the legacy of the kings of France. Prosper Mérimée's house in Paris was burned down, with its great library and all his paintings. He came to Cannes to die, so as not to have to witness the end of his era. According to Theodore, war and peace was the story of mankind. Sometimes he would bring up the case of Gilles de Rais, going over his trial to show how he had been wrongly accused and dragged through the mud, portrayed as a sadistic and bloodthirsty Bluebeard, simply because everyone was jealous of his prodigious wealth. He knew by heart whole pages of dialogue from the trial of Joan of Arc. He knew who did what in the battles between the Armagnacs and the Burgundians. He lived and breathed history as religious people live and breathe prayer. He told me, laughing, of monasteries where monks, ignoring the passage of time and keeping only eternity permanently in their sights, continued to pray for the conversion of Saint Paul or that Saint Augustine should renounce lust.

None of this prepared us for winning the war.

The 1914 war horrified the Reinachs, though it came as no surprise. Forget historical documents; now families received telegrams with the names of those who were missing or killed in action. One morning it was Adolphe Reinach's turn, my best friend and comrade. How I wish he could have seen how happy I became, that he had been at my first exhibition, that he could have read the first articles written about my paintings. Theodore did not live to see the next war, he died in 1928. He never knew about the yellow star. He didn't see his grandchildren perish in a death camp.

In the summer of 1945 I happened to be in Paris, where I saw a documentary about Nazi war crimes. It showed everything. I stayed till the end. After the Liberation I had imagined mere prisoner of war camps, and I supposed the conditions there had been a little harsher than in the others. I'd thought we would celebrate the return of the survivors. But when we saw them they said nothing, and we didn't want to ask questions. It wasn't until I sat through this long film, in which I first heard the names of the sites of death, that I understood how Léon, Theodore's son, Béatrice, his wife, and their two children had died. And that I understood that they had not been the only ones, there were millions.

The narrator barely mentioned that the majority of those whose bodies had been piled into mass graves were Jews. It's hard to admit what occurred to me then—I have to write this, I need to be scrupulously honest with myself—that all the Reinachs' culture, all their knowledge, all that they knew and taught me, had not protected them from hell. Their genius was of no use. They believed that ideas, beauty, enthusiasm, knowledge had been passed down from generation to generation, going all the way back to Athens. They had fought to recover the links in this chain in order to revive it. All this to end up in mass graves. As I left the movie theater, I thought about how wrong they had been. How their lives had only served to revive dead things, before they themselves died in a horror that cannot be compared to any other. Everything I believed in died with them. It even occurred to me that I had been right to flee Theodore, to reject Kerylos, to live only for myself, to create abstract art, for the path on which they had set me led only to mass murder. I don't want to think like that anymore, of course. I am not so bitter now, but it is difficult. I feel terrible that I almost felt angry with the victims, who suffered so much, as no one had ever suffered before. I have not erased these images from my memory. If I hadn't seen that film, I wouldn't have believed it.

I still tell myself that if my children know nothing about Kerylos, nothing about ancient history, after all . . . I never handed any of it down to them, I didn't want to inflict an entire useless culture on them. Let them sell my books to the first second-hand dealer who comes along. But I did tell them very early on about what had happened in the camps, about the Nazi genocide. I knew Theodore and Fanny's grandchildren well. I still dream about them sometimes. They were like my nephews. In my dreams I can hear them, telling me I have grown too old.

After the Normandy landings, I found an essay by Salomon Reinach that I was once given by his brother, who was always telling me to take home various books and pamphlets, perhaps hoping that I would eventually understand something or at least be entertained. The barefoot boy from the Corsican mountains ended up with a library in Nice worthy of that of the university, and I've kept it all. In Salomon's essay, published in 1892, I underlined a sentence in red that must have been noted by other people, and ought to have been read by many more: "To talk about an Aryan race that existed three thousand years ago is to make a gratuitous hypothesis: to speak of it as if it still existed today is quite simply absurd."

10

"REJOICE"

By the age of seventeen, armed with a little culture and burnished with classical literature, muscular as a god on a sarcophagus, I was certain of one thing: I was not going to stay at Kerylos. I dreamed of adventure and travel. The house would soon be finished. I had learned a lot, now I wanted to go to sea, to see the world. I didn't stop telling my mother I wanted to leave. She was apprehensive, but knew she could do nothing to stop me; I had grown tall and strong, as she said. I wanted a boat, a voyage, to live as they did in *The Mysterious Island*, *Two Years' Vacation*, and *Dick Sand, A Captain at Fifteen*—no one pointed out to me that while he was writing my favorite novels, Jules Verne barely left his house. I wanted to be a sailor. I would have liked to be an architect, but I don't think I would have had the necessary precision. I didn't inherit the organized spirit of my mother the cook; if she had been allowed to study she could have become a chemist. She became the Marie Curie of ratatouille, a rather less dangerous recipe than the one for radium. The Reinachs believed that radium would heal humanity and all its ills, long before we understood the consequences. She was the only person who knew how to cook each vegetable separately and for how long, and in which copper pan. My father, the gardener, died shortly after my brother Cyrille's birth, leaving us penniless. I owe my stamina and my strength to him. I often think about him. He knew almost nothing about my life. I used to wonder if he was watching over me from on high, what he would have thought of me, of my paintings, my exhibitions, if we would have looked alike if only he had been allotted time to become an old man.

XAIPE, pronounced *kirie*, is the word written on the threshold. It means "rejoice," and it can be read both upon entering and upon leaving the house. One can believe it, or not believe it now. When the Reinachs weren't here, I sometimes found myself alone in the house for a few weeks at a time, and then I did indeed rejoice. The servants would take advantage of their absence to take time off, and I was left looking after everything. Sometimes during the holidays Theodore would have me come to Paris, where I would see the whole family, before happily decamping with a suitcase full of books.

For Theodore Reinach and his children, especially after we first sailed around Greece, I was like Passepartout in *Around the World in Eighty Days*: their factotum, and occasionally their friend. Once I have found what I have come to look for this morning, I'll leave by the spiral staircase that goes directly down to the courtyard at the back, and then I will continue to write my chapters, piece by piece, like a puzzle, from memory, on the terrace of the café in Beaulieu, on one of the green benches, on the beach, looking from afar at this gilded palace at the tip of the headland.

Then the awful person that I am will deliver these pages to the notary. I will make sure that one of my descendants publishes them, after everyone involved has died. Because I also intend to reveal a secret, concerning Greece, historians, and archaeologists. A fortune could be made from it . . . A secret even more shocking than the Glozel site and the inscribed tablets discovered there, which the academic world still insists are fakes, and that I believe should be in the Louvre or at the Museum of National Antiquities—now they can only be seen in the little private "museum" that the owner of the field where they were dug up (among the skulls, a whole field of the dead) has opened at the side of the road, with an entry fee of four francs. I need to talk about this too, though I find the story extremely troubling. I used to dream that I would be the person who deciphered the Glozel tablets.

How amusing would it be if my great-grandson—especially if he is not particularly bright—ends up making his fortune with this notebook, in which I intend to reveal everything. Reinach will at last have been useful for something: making the cook's descendants rich.

And how stupid it would be at my age to die like that, swallowing the key, how inelegant, lacking all panache, as Rostand would say—still my favorite writer, even if no one reads him anymore. Like me, he was born on April 1; he even founded a club for people born on that date. I've always had a feeling of fraternity with the great master, who should by rights have supplanted Victor Hugo.

11

PHILEMON AND BAUCIS RESTORED TO YOUTH

It was in one of the two ground floor bedrooms called Philemon and Baucis—all the bedrooms had names—that opened onto the passage to the peristyle that I experienced my first night of love. Not my first night with a woman; I had already slept with several dozen, though rarely more than once—that was the difficulty. I had stayed in just about every big hotel in and around Beaulieu. I could grade the level of service, the quality of the breakfasts, the plushness of the carpets. I could compare English, Scottish, Spanish, even German girls. None of them set out to make a play for me—I was poor, I was vain, and I thought Greek grammar and gymnastics were acceptable topics of conversation.

Still, I had plenty of affairs. I'd seduce a girl then never see her again. I used to confide in Adolphe, who was envious of my easy conquests. This was all during the happy period when the house was finished and death had not yet made an appearance. We thought the world belonged to us. Love didn't interest me particularly. I supposed I would get married one day, it might be a little hard for my mother, but she would get used to it. I didn't really think about falling in love, and wasn't even sure I wanted to.

I'd seen the two rooms on the ground floor when they were just finished and still redolent of fresh plaster. Because they were intended for older guests, they bore the names of a couple of aged mythological characters, Philemon and Baucis, simple folk who had become close to Zeus. It was time to dust them off. I thought about it every time Fanny Reinach, with her sly humor, opened one up for some distant aunt. In Kerylos, the rooms were never allocated definitively. Philemon, Baucis, Daedalus, and Icarus were—depending on the time of year and whether the house was full or not—for friends and visiting cousins, following the rules of Greek hospitality. From time to time I slept in one of them, especially in the winter, when Theodore found it convenient to have me close by so he could dictate texts to me, which he had taken to doing more and more—my archaic Greek was now of a decent standard—or tell me his latest hypotheses, and also, or so I liked to think, to do me an honor. I loved sleeping in these beautiful bedrooms, rather than in my cell next to the kitchen scullery: falling asleep with the embroidered curtains half-open, drifting off looking at the painted garlands and the stylized stars, waking up to the morning sun filtered through the beige and pink silk. I loved the colors of the walls in the evening light, the gray tones as they grew warm and deep, with an orange glow against which the roses and palm trees stood out in red. Every time I pulled open a drawer I felt exhilarated, and from the window I could hear the sea and the wind. I no longer suffered the nocturnal anxieties I had when I was younger. I stopped going to Nice at two in the morning. I felt like I was on a boat, but sheltered from any storm, or all at peace inside a lighthouse that was also a library, a garden, and a diving platform. I don't think I have ever been happier than in Philemon, where I slept quite often, and used to spend hours watching the boats in the bay. I have just pushed open the door, trembling.

Ariadne was very young when she married one of Pontremoli's assistants, the one who helped him with his plans. She had been in love with Grégoire, an architect–designer. She was as gifted as he. Everywhere she went she took a block of paper and her box of watercolors. She filled in the colors for him. Pontremoli had several assistants: Mazet was the one with the most confident hand, who played around with axonometric cross-sections and elevations and was a virtuoso with Indian ink, but for color Pontremoli swore by Grégoire Verdeuil—he had no idea that everything in his palette had been done by his wife.

It took so many coincidences for Ariadne and me to meet! If I follow the chain of causes and consequences, it goes right back to the Great Exhibition of 1900, when Eiffel was driven to despair because his tower already looked like an antiquity, while Theodore Reinach thought himself rather modern for making the acquaintance of a brilliant architect named Pontremoli. They only met by chance. Theodore found in him an interlocutor who knew Greece in a different way. Pontremoli was not so knowledgeable when it came to classical texts, but he had been on excavations and come up with a design for the reconstruction of the Pergamon monuments, the city that reached the peak of its glory under Alexander's successors, where an exuberant, unbridled artistic style developed: monuments laden with draperies and garlands, statues that were restless and tormented. In a small gallery, Pontremoli was exhibiting drawings that showed the citadel as it might look after restoration. They talked about the more austere temple of Apollo at Didymaion, the site the architect-archaeologist would be working on next. The subject fascinated the archaeologist, who had always dreamed of becoming an architect. They had found each other.

Pontremoli had been very ill, he'd contracted malaria, and as he was from Nice and well acquainted with the invigorating climate of the region, he had spent some days convalescing with the fishermen in the fresh air and sunshine of Cap Ferrat. In the neighboring town of Beaulieu, Reinach had recently purchased a piece of land on the Pointe des Fourmis. Pontremoli knew the Eiffel family. Everything was coming together. The architect was dazzled by the aura of the Reinachs. Grégoire, Ariadne's husband, who had recently joined the practice, was sent to make the first surveys of the site to be conquered: the rocks, the crevasses to be filled in, the mature trees that Theodore insisted on keeping. I had already seen Grégoire in the village, though I didn't know who he was: tall and dark-haired with a slender mustache and a smiling face, a handsome man with a slight belly who always wore a light-colored suit. I never suspected that one day I would come to hate him.

It was Grégoire Verdeuil, Ariadne's husband, who suggested to Pontremoli that they build a terrace along the promontory overlooking the sea, to maximize the scope of the property and allow it to be extended. The physiognomy of the Pointe would be altered, but in keeping with the spirit of Grecian rocks, according to the plans, which Reinach and Pontremoli, using tracing paper, compared with peninsulas in Chalkidiki and the

Peloponnese. If Viollet-le-Duc had dreamed of remodeling and improving Mont Blanc, there was no reason not to touch the pebbles in Beaulieu.

Ariadne and Grégoire soon moved into their own house in the town. Pontremoli visited regularly, and the major structural work was progressing rapidly. Often, when I returned from my morning swim Ariadne would be reading up on the rocks on a chaise longue—she gave no impression she was expecting me—and the three of us would have lunch together. I thought her a pleasant and very pretty woman, but the idea that I might fall in love with her never crossed my mind. She would look up from her book and smile at me. She was reading Zola's novels, and she lent them to me one at a time; we laughed at Gervaise's misfortunes, Nana's innocence, and poor Claude Lantier, the cursed painter, our favorite character. She came from a world that I could barely imagine, the world of grand Parisian architects, and I never felt entirely at ease talking to them both. Usually I would ask Grégoire to explain something to me, or show him a sketch that Monsieur Reinach had asked me to send. I was impressed by Grégoire: he recognized when my drawings were weak, was brilliant and generous, it was obvious that his work satisfied him. He was very encouraging and he used to show me how to improve my drawings. Once or twice he even asked Ariadne if she might like to color them.

Once the building was finished I saw them less and less. Grégoire was responsible for the ongoing work there, but he didn't always come up to the house with his wife. I began to be aware of my disappointment when I didn't see her. I wasn't in love: I was still having fun with my Russian and English vacationers; I was having an ongoing affair with a cousin of the dairywoman—who knew nothing about it—and years would go by before the belle dame with her box of watercolors became something more to me than an unattainable fantasy, a woman with a parasol, a woman I would have loved to have had to myself in another life, if I had only been born in an elegant part of Paris and had a little money to my name.

Several years later, wounded, desolate, and broken, I returned from the front. It was she who had suggested to me one evening at the Reinachs' just before we left, when Adolphe and I turned up sporting the brick red pants of our soldier's uniform, that she become my "wartime godmother." She promised to send me letters and parcels. I accepted without thinking. Grégoire interrupted, "I give you my blessing, Achilles. I'm too old to take up my rifle, unless the war lasts a long time and my battalion is called up. But this is going to be a short war." He could have signed up as a volunteer, as many others did. How my grandchildren will mock me when they read this: a love affair with my wartime godmother, against a backdrop of antique columns. And yet that is exactly what happened.

The letters we exchanged were brief. I dared not write too much. I told her about life at the camp and gave her news of Adolphe, of whom she was very fond. He was an officer. I was not. She asked me if, centaur that he was, he was continuing Achilles's education: well versed as I was in mythology, I was flattered. She wrote to me in rhyme; I replied in prose. Playfully, I told her that I missed her eyes. I was courting her, in a lighthearted way. During the first months of the war, I realized as the weeks went by that I was thinking about her all the time.

Distance had brought her close to me. She was becoming part of my life in a way that she had never been before, more than any of the other women who until then had never given me the time to fall in love with them. My love for her was growing, bit by bit, and I barely realized it was happening.

Instead of postcards written so as to facilitate the job of the military censors, she sent me drawings on which she stuck a postal stamp, with a note telling me that she had drawn herself onto the picture like a little greeting. She was easy to identify, a discreet figure in one of the galleries of the Louvre or the gardens of Versailles. She painted Nike, the Winged Victory of Samothrace, standing on her grand stone steps. She told me she had plucked a feather from her to use as a brush. When I looked at those outstretched wings, the folds of fabric draped over her body, I forgot the horrors and my mood lifted, I felt a little hopeful again.

Nike soared upward, the wind that plastered her tunic against her body not as powerful as the goddess's momentum. A second after the moment was set in stone by the sculptor, away she flew, stark naked.

I stuck this watercolor inside my soldier's canteen. She sent me another one: the statue protected inside a wooden crate, nailed together by the curators at the Louvre in anticipation of aerial bombardments. You couldn't see her anymore, she had been packed away in anticipation of our eventual victory.

I read her letters in the camp, showing them to no one. She told me her husband had been conscripted to paint camouflage over the lawn of an old house in Fontainebleau. Cubists were making tarpaulins for tanks—at least this new style of painting served some purpose, she said—and it was through her that I first heard of Georges Braque, without ever imagining that he would one day become my friend.

I was allowed to sleep in Philemon while I was convalescing, after being wounded twice the day after the battle at Tyranes farm, before I left again for the front. The contrast between the straw mattresses in the trenches and the bed prepared at the Reinachs' house made me cry. I pulled myself together. My mother wanted to stay with me all day, but I managed to convince her to leave me in peace. I told her the doctor had prescribed solitude and complete silence. I began reading one of the most famous books of the nineteenth century, Sir Edward Bulwer-Lytton's *The Last Days of Pompeii*, in an edition stuffed with illustrations, scenes from antiquity that took place in porticoed houses, beneath latticed stone balconies, or in front of not unfamiliar-looking fountains. I was no longer the son of the Eiffels' cook, that was the past. I had been Adolphe's comrade-in-arms, and now everyone's mission was to take care of me, nourish me, leave me alone to read and to rest. Pontremoli continued to come and work in the library. His assistant was there too, with his wife. I knew that when I came back I would see them, that I would see Ariadne again.

Grégoire had to go to Monaco for a couple of days to conduct a survey of the old palace that the prince wanted to modernize. The plan was to repair the floor of the chapel that leads out into the interior courtyard of the Grimaldi fortress. Grégoire looked a little older, but he was still attractive, he wore rimmed spectacles and often went home to sleep after lunch at La Réserve. He joked, "Whoever it was who designed the floor of the Sistine Chapel is the artist I pity more than anyone else in the world!" One day Ariadne remained behind at the hotel. I invited her to come up to the house, that is, to Kerylos. She accepted immediately. We had written each other hundreds of letters without ever saying anything. We had exchanged enough drawings to cover not only the vaulted ceiling of the Sistine Chapel but the *Last Judgment* too.

Ariadne came into my room. Nobody was occupying Baucis, the bedroom next door. There was no one in the house that afternoon at all, no noise except that of the waves. A few years ago this would have been unseemly; since the war, it didn't matter at all. I was sick, I was healing slowly. There was a thrumming in my ears. I walked toward her. We shook hands, in the English way. She sat down on my bed, like a nurse; she inspected all the vials and ointments that the doctor had left on the nightstand. She played her role as a postwar godmother perfectly. She was beautiful. I was hopeless.

She talked about herself, which she had never done before. Or rather, for almost an entire hour she talked about her husband. She told me about everything that had brought them together, I had to listen to her talk about their future, about the drawings they did together. I stopped listening. She was erecting a line of fortifications between us. I brushed her hand as I handed her a glass of water; she pretended not to notice.

She loved Grégoire. She had never been unfaithful to him. She was piling up sandbags. I drew my head back into the trenches. At that moment, I stopped loving her. I chided myself—for at the front you become an adult, there is so much time to think. I told myself I had no right to seduce this woman.

She was being honest. She understood the situation and felt she had to explain. My duty was simple: I had to respect what she said. I had to be able to hear her and stop thinking about her. I had been absurd. The trenches can drive you mad, give you crazy ideas. And what was it anyway, this love affair that wasn't, that had gone on like this for years? It was grotesque. Who spends a whole year courting a woman? What woman would put up with that? It took me under an hour to renounce my love for her. I was happy to renounce it. I understood it meant that I was getting better.

We joked about the friends of Madame Reinach who usually slept in this room. She opened the window. I believed I was happy, pleased—almost—that in my mind I had stopped being in love with Ariadne, right there in front of her, with her, thanks to her, it was an excellent thing! I talked to her about *The Last Days of Pompeii*. She stood up. I quietly handed her her hat and her red silk scarf and draped her coat over her shoulders like a perfect gentleman.

We both stood facing the closed door. She was leaving. She didn't say anything. I reached for the bronze latch to open the door. We looked at each other. We threw ourselves at each other.

I wanted to see every bit of her, her breasts, her hips, her feet, I wanted her to promise to pose naked for me whenever I asked, to swear to come back to this room every day to make love. She kissed my wounds, and every part of me that wasn't injured. She bit my lips and my thighs. She lay down on my bed, she let me kiss her, caress her, love her as I had never loved anyone before. I didn't care about Pompeii, about Romans or Greeks, I wanted only her, and she wanted only me.

It lasted. She came back. The drawings where she poses naked in the large chair, and where afterward she made me pose in the attitude of an enraged Achilles, date from that period. Since I had cradled the dead face of my brother-in-arms in my lap, I had not been able to touch a living body or hold anyone in my arms. She gave me back my life.

I remember this scene as the absolute essence of happiness, ecstasy. In that moment I was Everyman, a man for all seasons, made up of all the fragmented, chaotic images in my head, from the waves of my childhood smashing against the blue rocks to the artillery shells that had exploded next to me. If God exists, I'd like to ask him to let me experience that moment one more time, at the moment when I sense my death is near. I content myself with tracing one word with my finger on the wall of this room that no longer serves any purpose, because no one is coming back to live in Kerylos: *Ariadne, Ariadne.* The jealous women of Thrace hacked Orpheus's body to pieces. His head lay on the beach, and when one of them picked it up his tongue was still moving, murmuring, "Eurydice, Eurydice . . ."

12

THE PERISTYLE, A SEPULCHER FOR ADOLPHE REINACH, KILLED IN ACTION

There is a photograph somewhere—which I can still picture, although I haven't seen it since the last war—in which the three brothers are posing under the peristyle, each leaning against a column. I don't know when the picture was taken, although I was there. Maybe I tore it up at some point, when I could no longer bear Theodore Reinach.

It was a nightmare when the three Reinach brothers were together under the same roof. By the afternoon you couldn't remember which of the three you'd talked to in the morning, you'd reply to one having forgotten that it was one of the others who had asked the question. They were like three goats pursuing me in my dreams, Jolomon, Sanodore, and Theoseph, I was going crazy, it was like having three bucket loads of science, philosophy, and grammar poured over my head, it was unbearable. This three-headed monster had undertaken to turn me into a fourth monster. I took refuge in the water, where they couldn't get to me to teach me yet another thing. The year the work on the house ended was the year I first came across the cartoon "The Nickeled Feet" in the magazine *L'Épatant*, the characters Filochard, Ribouldingue, and Croquignol. It was them! I had the scholarly version, the one and the same loathsome Mister

Know-It-All! It's as if I've got this lost photograph right in front of my eyes and I'm exasperated and amused by it. Joseph is serious and frowning; Salomon is affable and smiling; Theodore stands a little apart from them, no doubt worried about having the two visitors whose judgment he fears the most in his house.

Joseph, the eldest, was the politician. In the early days, I didn't like him very much. He was very dull. Within the family, everyone admired him. His brother Salomon, director of the museum in Saint-Germain-en-Laye, often consulted him about works of antiquity or Gallic remains; he said that Joseph was an expert, maybe the finest of the three, and that politics had kept him from a fine career as a classical scholar. The great man wrote articles like other people drink coffee—one or two a day, sometimes more—and produced several series of books in ten or twenty volumes on an infinite variety of subjects, which hardly anyone read. He wanted to recount every detail of the Dreyfus affair, to which he penned a monument in I don't know how many volumes. His brother Theodore wrote a concise, clear book, *A Brief History of the Dreyfus Affair*, which was very convincing and very successful. During the First World War, Joseph, under the pseudonym Polybius, wrote daily accounts of the fighting that fatigued even the indefatigable General Nivelle, he of the famous "Nivelle offensive," who once declared, "Either Polybius stops writing or I stop conquering." The texts of the original Polybius, who recounted in Greek the wars of the Roman Republic, are already a little hard to follow, but the continuator surpassed the master. (Collected together, Joseph's articles filled twenty volumes, becoming the masterwork of the brother who was known as "the Reinach who does not write," because his brothers wrote so many books.) I didn't understand at the time, and it wasn't until years later that I realized it was an in-joke for history buffs; anyone who had studied at a good school would have recognized it as a play on an epithet by Boileau, the great historiographer of Louis XIV, who couldn't keep up with the successes of his sovereign, and substituted satire for praise: "Great King, stop conquering, or I shall stop writing." No one had taught me that.

I would watch, captivated, the illustrious Joseph taking his breakfast in the gentle morning air, just outside the music room we called the Oikos. Everyone—Theodore and his sons first—laughed at his impeccable technique for buttering his toast, sometimes on both sides. In his articles he repeated things he had already said, explained what he meant, and detailed what he would not say while specifying what he had not said. He told me about his first encounter with Dreyfus, whom he had not met before. Neither expressed the slightest emotion. Dreyfus merely held out his hand and said, "Thank you," and I can still hear Joseph's pompous observation, "That was all. Just those two words. I had the audacity to deem the exchange a credit to us both." I learned to dread his war stories even more: "That day our men certainly merited a mother country that, though exceedingly forgetful, nonetheless managed . . . " They were never-ending. When he came to the villa, Joseph relaxed, was natural and open, he admired everything, he was always given the same large bedroom on the second floor and he had conversations with his brother that lasted entire afternoons. He used to say, "When I am here, I am in my safe harbor."

Joseph and Theodore sprawled, one facing the other, in the low chairs in the library, blowing smoke rings with their cigars toward the inscriptions on the wall extolling the glory of Demosthenes and Plato. Floating in the air, they looked like the *spiritus asper* and the *spiritus lenis,* those accents in archaic Greek like little broken circles placed over the initial vowels, or over the letter *rho*. One of the defects of modern Greek is that "it no longer has spirit"—one of Theodore's jokes I must have heard a hundred times.

I took most of my meals in the big kitchen, but afterward I would go up to the library to talk a little with my "master," and, when they were there, Salomon and Joseph. I wasn't their servant, it wasn't my job to remove the breakfast tray. One of them might say, "The right-wing newspapers won't stop mocking this ironic attempt to link the Socialists with a policy of law and order. The world of business gains confidence as soon as it senses a steady hand holding the reins, don't you see, Theodore?" I didn't know which of them I felt more sorry for. But they all got on terribly well. They were heroic in the way that they supported each other. Their wives never ventured to join their conversations. The one I never really got was Salomon. I suspected he was the most amusing, people said he was a seducer, a hedonist—a word I didn't know then—he had a knack for making conversation with the maids, whose names he remembered from one year to the next. He never asked me questions, as if he didn't see me. Years later I came to know him better when I worked for him, and even today I still wonder about him. The blend of jocularity and seriousness, the way he paid no attention to detail, made him seem the most aristocratic of the three, but perhaps also the least intellectually serious. He had a tendency to show off, was never bored, he made his brothers laugh and dared to laugh at them. In every family, there is always one whom the parents forgive everything. Salomon and his wife would leave after a couple of days, before I had a chance to get to know them. Salomon was the only one who understood that at the seaside you're allowed to wear a seersucker suit, swap gray for blue, take off your boots and wear comfortable English shoes instead. None of these details escaped me, but I couldn't imagine what Joseph and Theodore made of him.

In Joseph's house in Paris there was an engraving inspired by a painting by Fragonard (I don't know where the painting is) called *The Bolt*. It had a frame that would have been more fitting in Moïse de Camondo's mansion: eighteenth-century style was now taken seriously, an indication of both a large fortune and impeccable taste. For a long time the engraving seemed to me a vision of another world, a fragment from a different, happy, strange planet, an instant of joy that didn't mean much to a young Corsican shepherd. I always thought it would be wonderful to experience a scene like that, but it was so far from my life it was like a dream, like furtively reading a poem by Verlaine. Later, after I had fallen madly in love, I would walk down the corridor to look at *The Bolt* again and think about my Ariadne. The intensity of the young man, the woman who is resisting but looks very much as if a moment later she will stop pretending to resist. Exactly what I had experienced in the bedroom where I had spent my convalescence. I kept picturing her about to cross the threshold, then turning back to kiss me. I have never forgotten that closed door, except its bolt was made of bronze and looked as if it might have come from Alcibiades's house. Even at Joseph's house, I found myself thinking about her.

In the years that followed, Joseph grew very fond of me, because I had gone off to war with his son, because I was so valiant that even after being wounded twice I returned to the front, then was demobilized with a formal recognition and a military medal. The dullest of the three brothers became my protector, though I had no desire to be his child, to take the place of his fallen son. Adolphe and I left school in 1907. We did our military training in Mourmelon. Joseph used to take me aside for brief conversations, just the two of us; I was, he knew, his son's only real friend. He loved me, though he might just as well have hated me or at least wanted never to see me. Because I had seen Adolphe—my comrade, the boy I'd grown up with—die. And because I, son of nothing, knowing nothing, serving no purpose, inheritor of nothing—I was the son who was still alive. Yet in spite of that he loved me. I let him, in memory of the evenings in the camp when Adolphe used to tell me that he was never sure that his father, so intimidating and serious, really loved him.

When I told my grandchildren about this, they dared to make vulgar jokes about Achilles and Patroclus. Masculine friendship, the camaraderie of soldiers—in the years since 1918 we have dared to give it another name. Homer is very clear: Achilles and Patroclus were united by an unbreakable bond, they had been inseparable since childhood, they were cousins. Adolphe and I—how ridiculous to write this today—were united by our patriotism. My grandchildren don't understand. We only ever talked of victory. There was nothing going on between us. I was never able to confess to Adolphe my epistolary love affair with Ariadne; I barely even admitted it to myself. I would have loved to tell Adolphe how, without planning to, I had experienced my own version of *The Bolt* with her. I wanted to. But he was no longer here. I'm certain I would have gone to find him, to tell him, and that he would have asked me the most intimate details that I wouldn't have shared with him, not this time. The moment when I kissed Ariadne was the moment when I understood, after four years of war, "I'm alive. I'm going to live."

The evening of *The Bolt*, alone again, convalescing, I was afraid. I thought Ariadne would be angry, would refuse to talk to me. But she came back the next day, with a drawing of the two of us. We made love at every opportunity, until I was better. We sketched each other twenty times or more. I thought only of her, and less and less of the war.

Then she disappeared. Grégoire and she stopped coming to the villa. I never really understood why. Pontremoli told me that Grégoire, his right-hand man as he called him, had opened his own architectural practice. It was high time he became independent. She stopped writing to me. All I had left were a few drawings—Adolphe, the only person to whom I might have confided, was dead. A year after the armistice, I met the woman who became my wife; my children know the rest of the story by heart. We danced at the wedding of a friend from my regiment, went for a walk along the road to Villefranche, and the same evening decided to get married.

The bond that Adolphe and I had is sacred, nothing can change it. Time has passed: Adolphe's son, born after his father's death, is dead now too. When his son died I mourned my friend a second time. They were truly brave. I wasn't cowardly or spineless, I'm not ashamed of myself, but I wasn't a hero and I survived only by chance. In mythology, I recall, Theseus, in error, hoisted black sails on his ship; his father Aegeus, believing he had died, threw himself into the sea. It was I who hoisted the black sail, but not in error. Aegeus wept on my shoulder for his son.

My generation knows by heart the citations for friends who died for France. Whenever I repeat these brief, sober words, like an inscription on a marble stele, I weep: "Reinach (Adolphe), cavalry lieutenant, on assignment from the Forty-Sixth Infantry Regiment (liaison officer). In all circumstances, he distinguished himself by his sang-froid and his exceptional bravery. On August 30, at the Tyranes farm, at a time of great difficulty, he grouped about him some ten men, and, all the while remaining on horseback, led them in the assault, thus allowing a battalion to remain in position."

Adolphe's body was never found. I would have taken him with me, dragged him through the mud. There was shelling from every direction, explosions and screaming. I didn't hesitate. I began to run. In his office in Paris, a sumptuous apartment on Avenue Van Dyck filled with chandeliers, paintings, and eighteenth-century engravings, Joseph asked me how his son had died. He wanted to know where his child's body was, of course he did. I recounted everything, minute by minute. We had ended up abandoning our position to the enemy. If I'd been weighed down with Adolphe's body, the Germans would have shot me too. Joseph looked at me, and I knew that he understood, agreed that I had done the right thing. He didn't say, "I would have done what you did," but that is what I understood.

In Villefranche-sur-Mer the famous Villa Leopolda had been transformed into a hospital for the wounded. All anyone was talking about was the ravaged faces of the disfigured soldiers. Wooden huts had been erected in the gardens, and the young Belgians who slept there gave their accounts of life at the front. This colony of survivors, just a few minutes from Kerylos, intensified the terrible grief of the Reinach families. In his preface to my friend's posthumously published monograph about painting in ancient Greece, Salomon wrote that no one knew what had become of his nephew's remains. They had planned to go together to Tyranes farm to open the mass graves and look at the faces of the dead one by one. They were told that the bodies had been almost completely pulverized. I can't read Salomon's words without trembling. I had held Adolphe's "remains" to my breast. But I've never regretted having fled with the others in order to save my life. Three hours later I was fighting again. I killed three Germans in hand-to-hand combat, with my sidearm. I had never killed a man before that day. My hand didn't tremble. This morning though, it is trembling, I'm too hot, I'm not used to this movie camera, my fingers keep moving, my film will be blurry, jumpy, it will show Kerylos in disorder, a kaleidoscope of shaky images that follow on from each other haphazardly and make no sense. Joseph, after the death of his son, was also adrift, suddenly losing the thread in the middle of one of his endless, rambling, pompous speeches—but I think I began to love him then, this man who sat with his hands on his knees, saying less and less.

Poor Joseph never became a minister of state, the thousands of pages he wrote have been forgotten, his name means nothing to anyone anymore. He believed in the glory of literature and his duty as a parliamentarian; he would be heartbroken and extremely surprised to learn today that he survives in the collective memory, unhappy man, because Marcel Proust turned him into a character: Brichot, who bores all the guests at Madame Verdurin's dinner parties. I took my time to read *Á la recherche du temps perdu.* I found it amusing, so similar to the world I knew before the Great War. Proust was not fond of the Reinachs. He knew Pontremoli a little. He wrote to Joseph to ask him to send a letter requesting he not be called up to fight. One can only imagine Joseph's reaction. Not to mention Proust's embarrassment, in the years that followed, at what he'd done. To make things even more complicated, in 1914 Theodore had just lost the elections in the Savoie, to a certain Paul Proust, who bore the same surname as Marcel, though they were not, I believe, related—and this Paul Proust died gloriously at the hand of the enemy, on October 14 that year. His name is inscribed on the monument to the dead at the Assemblée Nationale. We were not permitted to utter the name of Marcel Proust at the villa, which is why it took me so long to discover this.

Proust must have envied the worldly status of the Reinachs and the connections they had, that his own parents didn't have, and the three brothers' talents for serious things. He came from a similar milieu, albeit a little less impressive: a family with Jewish origins, talent, a passion for libraries, museums, and art. He had managed to shorten his military service by putting off his call-up, and, in the famous questionnaire (which people who don't know better call the "Proust Questionnaire," as if he had invented it), in answer to the question "the military fact that I admire the most," he replied: "My volunteering." Many of his friends were killed in the war, some of whom I had glimpsed from afar, like Bertrand de Fénelon and Robert d'Humières, and he might perhaps in the end have shown courage if he had ever been under fire. No one knows how they will react when they hear shots being fired. When I left for the front I asked myself that very question. We all did, though we never talked about it. At the first shot, I got my answer: I wasn't afraid. I took no pride in this. That's how it was. I didn't need to drink brandy. I didn't think that I would be killed. Had Proust been killed by the enemy, he might have been entitled to a military citation: "Proust (Marcel), with tireless courage . . . " I figured all this out when I read him. I never met him. He certainly took his revenge. The Reinachs were always writing, but the only real writer in their world, the only one they would have rubbed shoulders with, would have been Proust, though I doubt that any of the three brothers would ever have guessed it.

My Adolphe was much funnier than his Brichot-like father, which wasn't difficult, and as talented a Hellenist as his uncle Theodore, which was quite a feat. Although he was the same age as me he was of a rather more "scholarly disposition," as people used to say, subjected from birth to having his "head stuffed," an expression that was all the rage in 1914. He didn't give a damn about any of it: "They've raised me like a well-trained animal," he said to me once, "But you'll see, I'll surprise them." He would have been the one who continued the three brothers' research, wrote even longer books, the child in front of whom Gaspard, Melchior, and Balthazar would have prostrated themselves. We journeyed to Greece together. I was thrilled by our voyage, which allowed me at last to leave Beaulieu. Without Adolphe I would have withered at home; it was thanks to him that I discovered my love of travel—in my family no one ever traveled, we moved from one place to another, but it never occurred to us to go on expeditions to far off places, or even to go on vacation. Greece may have been far back in history, but he showed me that we were just a few days away by boat.

I'd been enlisted to keep him company and help him learn his lessons. For young Adolphe, the family tradition was to continue: a mathematics teacher, an English tutor, and I, whose role was to help him learn some useful bits of knowledge. In reality, it was I who got an education. Adolphe, in the early days, distrusted me. I was his uncle's new recruit, the less scholarly monkey who pronounced Greek all wrong, who distinguished "eta" and "epsilon," instead of reading both as "e" like every schoolchild in Europe since Erasmus. Perhaps he thought I was some little social climber from the village who God knows how had somehow attracted the master's good graces and was trying to escape my destiny in domestic service. I was of negligible value, *epsilon*. But he very quickly realized I was the ideal companion for staving off his solitude—these interminable lessons had been inflicted on him for years. He told me that as a child he had hardly ever played. His sister Julie, two years older than us, was also very serious. Julien, their cousin, the future member of the Council of State, Theodore's son, was five years younger, and his brother Léon was only six, which at that age is a vast gap. They were hardly going to play together in the garden. Fanny and Theodore's two younger sons, Paul and Olivier, had always been "the little ones," whom I pretty much ignored. Their siblings didn't waste their time playing with them either. Theodore's only living descendants are the children of Julien and little Paul. Paul was charming, the best looking of them all. I've all but lost contact with them, though we still send each other holiday cards. As for Salomon, he and his wife had had no children to play with Adolphe. Rose, Madame Salomon Reinach, was a doctor, and ran a children's home in Neuilly. She devoted herself during the war to treating wounded soldiers. In the early 1920s her husband Salomon himself pinned the Legion of Honor medal to her chest. I was at the ceremony.

So, as the only person of his age, I was the ideal accomplice for Adolphe, as Theodore no doubt realized. He enjoyed being with his nephew, but he knew only too well how much of a burden the family style of education could be, and the idea of him having someone to play sports with, someone ordinary, willing, and good humored, was far from absurd . . . One day he told Adolphe, who in turn told me, that I was certainly not his equal, and that he was going to need to forge some relationships in Paris; all that was required to annoy his uncle, Adolphe promptly declared, was for me to remain his best friend for all time. Theodore's ruse had succeeded.

When war broke out, somehow Joseph Reinach arranged for us to be assigned to the same regiment—it reassured everyone to know that Adolphe was, in a way, under my protection, I would be, after a fashion, his orderly, his aide-de-camp. I can still hear these words, spoken by a friend of the Reinachs; I thought of them so often after the attack.

Joseph was the only one of the three brothers to know true suffering: five days before his Adolphe's death, Pierre Goujon, second lieutenant (reserves) fell on the field of honor, in Méhoncourt. He too was born in 1875, and was called up at the same time as we were. Pierre was married to Joseph's daughter Julie, and loved by the whole family. We used to see each other from time to time. He was serious and fastidious, with a neat little mustache and the beginnings of a paunch. His father was senator for the Ain department; Pierre thought it was time to inject a little youth into politics and was elected a parliamentary deputy, also representing the Ain. He loved good food, and was very brave. Julie fell in love with him because he shared his family's passion for art. Renoir had painted his portrait when he was a child. They were planning to start a collection of modern paintings. Julie bought some beautiful works after his death in his memory. At her house I saw a magnificent Degas and a watercolor by Cézanne. Kindly, she purchased my first Cubist still life. She lent it out for my exhibition at the Jeu de Paume, when people were just beginning to know my name. She never remarried. Pierre Goujon was the first deputy to be killed in combat in 1914. He could have avoided joining up—he would have easily obtained a deferment—but he requested to join a regiment, the 123rd Infantry. He was wounded early on. He fashioned himself a makeshift dressing so as to quickly return to battle, and was shot dead with a bullet to the head on August 25.

Pierre might have hung some modern art in the bedrooms at Kerylos, after all, why not? The villa, without the war, would certainly have changed its appearance in the next generation. Adolphe would also have changed some of the decor, but in a different way. He would have brought in authentic objects from antiquity. What is a house where you can't move the furniture, can't put anything else on the walls other than what the architect has chosen, where the children feel like they're on show in their bedrooms, which are never the same from one stay to the next? I really believe that Theodore, in the single-minded pursuit of his vision, had never considered this. Adolphe did not suffer from it, at any rate less than his little cousins did, but that didn't prevent him from bluntly criticizing what Pontremoli had done. He would have preferred more accuracy, he wanted to know if we were in a house from Athens, or from Delos, or a wealthy villa in Asia Minor at the time of Alexander's successors. For me, Kerylos was simply a Greek villa. "Look at those terraces: do you think there was ever a similar kind of architecture in Greece? This house simply doesn't make sense!"

13

"BRING NOTHING FROM THE WORLD"

My first ride in an automobile was to Cambo-les-Bains, in the Basque country. At the last moment Madame Reinach told me there was a spare place in the car and that I should join them: in those days, taking a trip in a half-empty car was out of the question. It was extraordinarily exciting, the apotheosis of luxury, the chrome, the lacquer, the backfiring. And I was delighted to see the Basque country. I was going to meet a great writer, maybe even talk to him. I might buy myself a pair of the curiosities called "espadrilles."

In order to take one's place in society, one had to build a house: during the same period that Kerylos was being built, Edmond Rostand raised what was known as the "Basque style" to a palatial level at his house Arnaga, extending his fantasy with French gardens that were quite out of place there, an orangery that recalled Versailles, and a literary henhouse extolling the glory of *Chantecler*, a play that unfortunately was rather less successful than *Cyrano de Bergerac* and *L'Aiglon*. Fanny was rather mystified at my lack of interest in the engine and mechanics during the journey. Surely a child of the people must *dream* of engine oil.

I suppose there must have been as much gossip in Cambo-les-Bains—though perhaps a little less snark—as there was at

Beaulieu, during the three years the locals watched this architectural monstrosity being built. The Reinachs took an interest and were invited to visit. Rostand was a national treasure, everybody loved him. Today, at the entrance to Arnaga, visitors can read on a plaque a few lines of verse that I copied down and learned by heart:

> *You who come to share our golden light,*
> *And marvel at the glory of the ever-changing day,*
> *Bring nothing from the world, only your heart,*
> *And do not repeat what other people say.*

Everyone seemed to want their own dream house: in the vicinity of Nice and Monaco alone, there are a dozen extraordinary villas that have in one way or another made their mark on history. Adolphe scoffed at them all. Next door, on the Cap d'Ail, the Primavera was built in 1911, its fireplaces and furniture veneered with fake antique flourishes. I saw it just after it was finished, and had to admit that it was pretty, even if it lacked the attention to detail of "our" house. Some of these extravagant houses impressed me more than others. I visited many of them. They were nothing like the millionaires' villas along the Riviera, which architects produced on demand without much thought. The Camondos had their mansion in Paris, less outrageous than Arnaga, completed at the very beginning of the Great War. The Reinachs wanted to know everything there was to know about this project, with its faux Louis XVI style, both luxurious and tasteful, furnished with marvels of royal provenance and a miscellany of ducal treasures, a lesson in the history of furniture crossed with the Almanac of French Chateau Owners and the Who's Who of aristocratic families. I visited the Camondo house many times, delivering letters. One didn't have the impression of traveling back in time to the era of Marie Antoinette, which was all the better. These houses were like daydreams. Cahen d'Anvers, a banker, spearheaded the fashion for flights of fantasy that were both timeless in design and incalculably expensive. He purchased the grand but shabby Chateau de Champs-sur-Marne, renovated and improved it. His eighteenth century was flawless, whilst also managing to accommodate a telephone and portraits of the children by Renoir. The Camondos came from Istanbul, the Reinachs from Germany, and the Cahen d'Anvers family from Antwerp, as their name suggests. The three families were linked: the paterfamilias Moïse de Camondo, whom I knew, married Irene Cahen d'Anvers; this apparently unhappy union produced two children, Nissim, an aviator the same age as I, who was killed in action in 1917 at the age of twenty-five; and Béatrice, born two years after her brother. She married Léon Reinach, my Theodore's second son, who was born in 1893. Léon's mother, Theodore's second wife Fanny, whom I was so fond of, was an Ephrussi on her mother's side. This made her a cousin of Béatrice Ephrussi, née Rothschild, who built the famous villa on Cap Ferrat, a ten-minute walk from Kerylos. Spelled out like that, it all sounds rather complicated. What was striking was that Béatrice and Léon Reinach were heirs to the history of these four houses, Kerylos, Champs-sur-Marne, the Camondo mansion in Paris, and the Ephrussi villa on Cap Ferrat. But these large, extravagant properties didn't interest them: they loved music, animals, tennis, horses. They and their children, Fanny and Bertrand, were killed at Auschwitz.

Between 1905 and 1912, residents of Beaulieu could observe from a distance the construction initiated by the whimsical Béatrice Ephrussi. The Ephrussis and the Reinachs saw each other socially, though they were not the close relatives that the postman and the dairywoman believed them to be: Fanny Reinach's great-grandfather, Charles Joachim Ephrussi, born in 1793, the year that Louis XVI was beheaded, married twice. The elegant Charles Ephrussi, who may have inspired Proust when he created the character of Charles Swann, was descended from his son from his first marriage. His sister was Madame Reinach's mother. The wealthy Maurice Ephrussi, whose wife Béatrice liked nothing more than to sit in her vulgar pink salon sipping pink champagne, was descended from his second marriage. Theodore said there was only one interesting thing in the house: the wooden paneling, which came from various mansions that had been knocked down. The villa was a catalog of fragments from other houses. Theodore recognized an eighteenth-century door that had come from Balzac's house on Rue Fortunée. The great writer had bought many antique fixtures to impress Madame Hanska. Theodore loved the idea that in the middle of Cap Ferrat you could touch a doorknob that had once been turned by the author of *La Comédie Humaine*.

Back at Kerylos, in low voices, we all disparaged the splendors of the Villa Île-de-France, as it was called. Béatrice Ephrussi had decided her maids would wear bonnets adorned with pompoms, to give the illusion of being perpetually on a cruise. Right at the beginning of the work, when the ground was being leveled, I learned from the dairywoman that this rival villa was going to be truly monumental. It had blue marble, black marble, cherry marble, marble from Siberia and even from China, marble that looked like wood, imagine that! Everyone in the port talked about it endlessly. The notary said, "It truly is the ne plus ultra, a quite spectacular property." Everyone liked the Ephrussi villa. It was a strawberry macaron, sitting atop a raspberry macaron, reinforced with meringue and enriched with chantilly cream, with corollas of small violets made of marzipan and, all around, like spun sugar, fountains imitating Versailles. At Kerylos, after having once admitted that there were no fireplaces, only a forced-air heating system and palatial bathrooms, everyone learned to keep quiet, for fear of admitting that they did not know very much about how things should be done. I had a memory, from my visit to Arnaga to see Rostand, of a boudoir like in a fairy tale, with a painting of horses harnessed to a pumpkin taking a princess to the ball. Next door was Madame Rostand's bedroom, with a view onto flowerbeds, the flowers picking up the colors of the walls inside the house. From one villa to the next, all perpetuating the same enchanted world. I remember Theodore wondering what archaeologists in the year 4000 would say of the civilization of 1906 if the only traces they found were the houses of the Rostands and the Camondos.

What the people of Beaulieu were most curious about was how we lived at "Chateau Reinach." They wondered if the "fat Madame Reinach"—she wasn't that fat, but she was always wrapped in several layers of lace—wore Grecian sandals and walked around the house bare breasted, whether Monsieur Theodore pranced around, wearing his pince-nez, in a papier-mâché breastplate and a short skirt. I'm not saying that they might not, once or twice, to amuse the children, have organized costume parties. Quite possibly the costumes are still in a closet somewhere. But that wasn't at all the spirit of the house. The Greece of Kerylos was no masquerade; it was an attempt to recover the essence of beauty. Nothing less. I remember explaining that to the dairywoman. Similarly I doubt that Monsieur de Camondo, in his Paris mansion, ever put on a powdered wig to walk across Parc Monceau, or that the Marquis de Panisse-Passis, in his castle near Antibes, which he had restored beautifully after the small earthquake that nearly cost him his keep, dressed up as that ancestor of his who once welcomed Charles V and Francis I. But it made everyone in Beaulieu chuckle to imagine the Reinachs boarding their little boat moored down by the villa, draped in chlamyses and loincloths made of sheep's wool to protect them from the winter cold. They preferred to summer in the Savoie region, Theodore's electoral lands, if they didn't stay in Paris. In 1917, not long before her death, Madame Reinach disappeared into her furs. From then on at Kerylos, she was never seen without them. It is true that clothes could be a topic of conversation: the cousin of Napoleon III, Prince Plonplon as he was nicknamed, built a house in the style of Pompeii on Avenue Montaigne—there used to be an album of old photos of this curiosity in the library at Kerylos, it may still be on the shelves somewhere—and held gatherings where guests were invited to don classical costumes to read poetry and engage in other neo-Roman activities. For Theodore this was the decadence of the Romans. The Second Empire did not get a good press: the disastrous defeat at Sedan and France's humiliation were imputed to the excessive reveling of the period. Wearing ancient Greek and Roman costumes was seen as a kind of moral laxity. But Monsieur and Madame Reinach were wholly upstanding. Indeed, Theodore always stood when he wrote, just as in Guernsey the celebrated exile Victor Hugo, who by then had returned home with his liberty, used to stand facing the sea. As if behind him were the books he had read and before him those he was going to write.

14

MY FIRST PAINTINGS

Theodore insisted that there be no fakery. He used to say this constantly to Pontremoli. Everything in the peristyle had to be true, the huge stones, the massive beams, the bronze, there was no question of using plaster briquettes and hoping that at a glance no one would notice the difference. If everything were authentic, it would make everything that they invented plausible. The inner courtyard was the part of the house Adolphe liked best, the most true. He liked to set out a small table where he would sit and go through the notes for his first major book. He would watch the painters as they worked. He liked talking to them. The antefixes, carved palm decorations that elegantly punctuate the edge of the tiled roof, were copied from one found on the Acropolis in Athens. Gargoyles used for evacuating rainwater were sculpted into marble lion muzzles, with the triglyphs below, large squares of stone, according to the rules, separating them from the metopes, which were not carved into mythological figures but left white, so that the three lines of each triglyph would stand out in their purity. It would have been a vulgar mistake to carve every detail, to show off how learned they were and how much money they had. Theodore remarked one day to Pontremoli that if the house had been built on the other side of the Rhine, the brash, uncivilized folk would, doubtless, have chiseled every metope and painted all the triglyphs, with the result that they would have been all anyone noticed. At Kerylos the roofline of the peristyle goes almost unremarked—it only appears when, after a day of reading in the shadow of the columns, one lifts one's eyes up toward the sky and they linger briefly at the top of the walls. For nothing must interrupt the reader's focus.

Since I came in this morning I keep coming across all the elegant details that so pleased me in my youth. Three sides of the peristyle open onto the downstairs rooms, allowing a glimpse into their interiors, while the fourth is simply the other side of the entrance façade, leaving more room for the garden, and to enjoy the view over the bay of Beaulieu. The broad columns without a base are Doric. On the vestibule side are slender Ionic columns, with capitals that coil like reels of cotton. One of the most commonly repeated banalities in architecture studies, I once heard Grégoire explain to an attentive Ariadne, is that the Doric column, with its unadorned capital, represents virility, while the more graceful Ionic column represents femininity. Seeing her sardonic smile, he hastily added that he had no idea how true that was, but you read it everywhere. The ancients believed it, repeated it, but actually, said Ariadne, why might a woman not resemble a Doric column? She said she thought the painting by Cézanne of a cook in a blue apron was Doric. And why would the Ionic style not be used to describe the elegance of a young Zouave in a blue jacket embroidered with coils of red braid? That was the day that Ariadne showed me her sketchbook: the panthers and lions she used to sketch on Sundays at the Jardin des Plantes, the animals in motion, casting their hungry gazes beyond their cages.

Pontremoli made some sketches for the walls, but Theodore rejected them. They looked too much like Napoleon's cousin Prince Plonpon's Pompeian villa, dramatic scenes in intense colors unfolding against a red background. He wanted the frescos to harmonize with the Carrara marble. Tinted plaster, very diluted colors applied with a brush—the aim was to evoke the *lekythoi*, the tall Greek white-ground vases that he was so fond of. The whole would form an open, covered passageway, not very long, not very high, a cloister where he could walk slowly up and down, philosophizing in a low voice. Theodore knew that one thinks better when one walks, writes better when one stands, and that there was no need to feel shame in eating lying down, if that's what one felt like doing.

Having rejected Pontremoli's drawings, he didn't want to call upon a great painter, which would upset the architect. Ariadne and Grégoire suggested the names of two artists. Gustave-Louis Jaulmes, a young student of Victor Laloux—Pontremoli's first professor, to whom we owe the imposing Orsay train station that looks like a museum, just as the museums of that era looked like train stations. He excelled in ornamental pattern, waves traced with a steady hand, his palms seeming to sway because he preferred not to use a stencil, which gave them a certain flair and verve. Working with him was Adrien Karbowsky, who had been a student of Puvis de Chavannes, a man who had the habit of telling everyone that he was born in the year of the Great Exhibition in 1855, the one where Ingres and Delacroix were pitted against one another. A friendship immediately sprang up between him and Adolphe: together they pored over books about Greek vases and wondered what the ancient texts had to say about color preparation. Adolphe would call me over to look. Ariadne and Grégoire often took part in these discussions: together, like musicians in a small orchestra, they were reviving Greek painting. Greek writers bequeathed us descriptions of paintings, hundreds of artists, teachers and pupils, different schools, but no trace has ever been found. All we can do is imagine.

Theodore wanted to retain the style of the vases, but enlarged, as if they had simply been unrolled straight onto the walls. The subjects were to be simple, but original, and above all were to avoid the Trojan War. In a niche, to the side, there was to be a bust of a bearded Homer, with his eyes closed. The strangest scene is the one that shows the death of Talos, after the discovery of the Golden Fleece. The hero looks like one of those monuments that would be put up a few years later in every village throughout France, with a large cadaver in the center—that's the one that everyone noticed, though no one remembers the story of Talos, or even knows who told it. Alongside, Apollo and Hermes—or is it Dionysius?—are having an argument. The bearded god has grabbed the arm of the god of the arts to try and force him to loosen his grip on the lyre he is holding.

The frescoes on the lower part of the wall show stylized waves and a collection of Mediterranean seashells. I had been allowed to pick up a paintbrush, and these were my first attempts. That is the section I find most lovely.

15

THE LAST PAINTER OF ANCIENT GREECE

When Adolphe got married, at the age of twenty-five, it almost seemed fated. For years, Mathieu Dreyfus had been coming to see Adolphe's father; he would read the Reinachs letters his imprisoned brother had sent from Devil's Island. Adolphe and little Magui Dreyfus, Mathieu's daughter, had witnessed together all the twists and turns of the affair. I once found a poem he wrote for Magui when he was eleven, telling the story in his own way, rhyming "Dreyfus" with "Jesus." Magui was very pretty, with her round face, black hair and a childlike smile. Her private tutor was a wag: the famous Christophe, the pen name of a brilliant chemist called Marie-Louise-Georges Colomb, who created some of the earliest French cartoon characters, Firefighter Camember and the Fenouillard family. This gave her considerable prestige among children her own age.

Whenever she came to visit the Reinachs, she played a game where she pretended to be the humble yet verbose servant of another of Christophe's characters, Professor Cosinus: "The footbath you requested to aid your reflections awaits you, sir." Theodore used to beg her to perform it over and over again. Much later, she gave me one of the Cosinus books that had belonged to Adolphe, his name inscribed in purple ink on the frontispiece, with a dedication from Christophe himself.

All the Reinach clan supported Mathieu Dreyfus in his fight for his brother. They knew that everyone held against Captain Dreyfus the fact that he was too rich, had married too well, he seemed cold and aloof. That was what was said in the army too, and it took a long time for everyone in the village, from the notary to the dairywoman, to finally acknowledge that it was right that he be rehabilitated; the priest was one of the last to concede it, which the Reinachs were quite aware of, though they rarely mentioned it. "That man," Adolphe said, "shows Carthaginian levels of bad faith." Mathieu Dreyfus was a good deal warmer than his brother, and Magui took after him.

Magui and Adolphe spent hours together under the peristyle. They always knew they would live together. This is what the evening breeze murmurs to me as it stirs around the marble columns and the frescoes: my friend, the last of the painters of Greece, did not return from the war.

Because of him, and her, I began to criticize Kerylos. They dared to say out loud that the mattresses were uncomfortable, there were no clocks; they wanted to bang nails in the walls, repaint, there wasn't even a swimming pool, it was all very well being authentic from an archaeological point of view . . . I didn't exactly share Magui's criticisms. I was sure I wasn't going to end up spending my life among them all. I didn't know yet what I wanted to do. I lived on the Pointe des Fourmis as if it was an independent principality, my own private Monaco, but it was no longer enough for me. I didn't see many people in the village any more; I'd had enough of their gossip. But there were long periods when the Reinachs weren't there, and then I spent time at the Eiffel villa, with my mother, who was nagging me to get a proper job, and the domestic staff. Soon I couldn't listen to their stories anymore. In Beaulieu, people who had known me as a child must have found me rather stuck-up; the café owner asked if he was still allowed to talk to me, and I ended up retreating into the company of the postman, the bookish dairywoman, and the notary, who were all very fond of me and whom I found easy to talk to—apart from the fact that I could not bear the finely honed cruelty in the tone they took when they talked about Jews. The notary once said to my face, "This Reinach is the perfect example of one of those fine Jewish minds, quite brilliant, but who, ultimately, has contributed nothing." What he meant was that Theodore, Salomon, and particularly Joseph might in theory have ended up as famous as the greatest minds of the Third Republic, but that it would never happen. Did that mean that Kerylos was worth nothing at all? What about the books and the thousands of articles the three brothers had written, were they worth nothing either? And Adolphe, who by the time he died at the age of twenty-seven had published 180 articles? My fancy checked jackets and linen pants made me look like an affluent student and my mother said that my father would not have recognized me. I'm not sure that the thought pleased her. Now I took the train to Nice, I accompanied Fanny Reinach to the opera—in Monaco I discovered a world that no one in the Eiffels' kitchen could have ever imagined.

For centuries, archaeologists have dug deep to find and understand the past. Theodore's genius was to build in order to understand the past. He taught me, without actually saying it out loud, always to do the opposite of what people expect. Adolphe told me that you had to hold a paintbrush in your hand to have an idea of what painting in ancient Greece was like. When the painter Jaulmes mixed his pigments in front of us, scraped them on to his palette, he was an archaeologist, creating, inventing—it was a brilliant way of doing an excavation back to front. That was what interested Adolphe. Magui was no less fascinated. Adolphe's idea was to gather together everything that the ancient texts tell us about painting. His work was a summation, which I believe remains influential to this day. He had the very innovative idea of not only looking at the lives of artists, but of collecting together all the technical evidence. He had inherited a jumble of scattered sheets from a scholar who hadn't completed the project, and embarked on revising and annotating these texts. Even his uncle, the wise Salomon, who was himself perfectly capable of spending a year or two on some dry academic labor, tried to persuade him not to take on such a thankless task, but Adolphe crosschecked everything with enthusiasm and told me about the latest discoveries: in the ruins of ancient Demetrius some painted steles dated back to the Hellenistic era had been found entombed inside a brick rampart, offering a hint for imagining the paintings of the ancient Greeks. Decorated ossuaries were discovered in Sidon, and fragments of paintings in ancient tombs in southern Russia. Adolphe wanted to go and see them, but at the very word *Crimea* his uncle grimaced, and Theodore fell silent—I didn't yet know why. They had not shared every detail about their lives with me.

Unlike his uncle, who valued written texts above all else, Adolphe wanted to work with photographs of sites, for potential new excavations. He dreamed of setting off to search for Greek paintings from Macedonia to Egypt, convinced he would discover some. He told me he would take me with him and we would travel around the Mediterranean sweeping up images the likes of which these dusty old intellectuals had never seen. He was planning one volume on mosaicists, another on vase painting, and he would have written ten or twenty volumes on Greek art in ten years. That was his plan.

This great monument remained unfinished, and in the end, only his book on painting would be completed. When the war broke out, he had just begun to correct the galley proofs he had been sent from the printer. There were plenty of mistakes, misprints everywhere, for the typographers knew no Greek. The book was published seven years after his death at the front, with the help of the hundreds of index cards he had created.

I was moved to see the name of my friend resurrected on the cover of a book. He would have liked that. It was Theodore who completed the work; it was as if he were building a sepulcher for Adolphe, here, beneath the peristyle. With Adolphe, everything was premised on his enthusiasm. He used to borrow Monsieur Jaulmes's palette, help him grind crystals and measure out pigments. I saw how his eyes shone. He would sneak down to the scullery for some scorpion fish and come back up with a bottle of white wine.

Occasionally we went up to Paris together, to Rue Hamelin, to bring the mail and settle accounts, but the Reinachs' house in this beautiful neighborhood felt very foreign to me. Like the whole city, of course: my first trip up to the capital I got so lost that I got in a taxi and said to the driver, "To the station!"

My first courtesy call on that trip was to the Eiffel Tower. I was thrilled to see the elevator—I'd known for years how it worked and I wanted to cry out to the small group of Italians there with me that I was a friend of the remarkable inventor of this machinery—and at the top I spent hours trying to name all the monuments, spires, cupolas, I dreamed about a journey in a hot air balloon, it made me happy to be so close to the sky. Then I went down and made my way to the Louvre to lose myself among the Greek vases, thousands of them displayed on high shelves of dark wood. I sat down on one of the large benches in the center of the gallery and looked at all the visitors who weren't looking at anything. Mothers were explaining to their daughters that Zeus was Venus's husband, then they left the Louvre quite thrilled at having seen nothing at all. Middle-aged matrons sped past the Greek vases, and even the aging connoisseurs sat wiping their pince-nez. I went into the Apollo Gallery with its many treasures, and I too saw nothing much. When I spoke to Theodore about the painting by Delacroix, in which the snake, which looks like some prehistoric monster, is slain by the god of the arts, I didn't understand why his expression grew clouded. I thought he didn't appreciate Delacroix, or that he thought that this scorching image didn't correspond to what he loved about Greek refinement.

It was the words "Apollo Gallery" that seemed to displease him; he changed the subject and began telling me about the excavations at Miletus, how whatever was found there would belong to the museum, how the Rothschilds were financing the entire mission. He asked me if I had seen the Ergastines and I stammered. It was Adolphe who explained to me that it was the name of the most beautiful of all the marble fragments of the Parthenon frieze that had not fallen into the hands of the English, who had stolen almost all the rest. This fragment had been given to a Frenchman, and was now displayed in Paris: a cohort of young girls, their dresses falling to their feet, walking slowly, one behind the other, on their way to pay homage to the goddess of Athens. I didn't go back until many years later, and when I looked at this carving, trying to see it through the eyes of my friend Adolphe, I couldn't remember what he had told me. This is how it is: I forget the important sentences and I only remember the nonsense spouted by Professor Cosinus's servant. The Louvre, Paris, it wasn't for me: I needed the sea and the sun. Not that I felt the need to go back to my family, my uncles and aunts in Corsica—however much my mother insisted that I go more often, I just let her say it. I wanted to travel. I felt imprisoned inside the maze of Kerylos. Theodore understood. He too wanted to get away. One night there was a huge storm at sea, and I watched him, without uttering a word to anyone, open, one by one, every single window in the house.

PART TWO
ODE TO APOLLO

"By me, by my love, the Labyrinth opens . . ."

THOMAS CORNEILLE, *ARIADNE*

16

THE MOSAIC ANCHOR

My first expedition with Theodore and Adolphe was a sailing trip around Greece, before the house was finished, in 1904. This meant we were able to extricate ourselves from the conversations with the builders and masons, about which Theodore was rather less enthused than his lengthy discussions with Pontremoli—he wanted to be au fait with all the details of the design of his house, for it was his project.

At last I was going to visit Greece! I was beginning to know it well, without ever having been. While we were at sea, Theodore talked incessantly about the building work. My memories of this expedition are filled with images, views of the rooms being painted after the marble washbasins had been installed, designs for wooden towel racks and furniture for concealing the bidets. Sometimes, to show me what he meant, he would sketch them himself on the small forecastle at the back of the boat where we had our living quarters. The villa was becoming part of us.

The Reinachs traveled but gave the impression they never went anywhere. In a cabinet in the library, huge albums of photographs displayed their expeditions to Turkey, the Levant, Egypt. Where are they now? In heavy black leather bindings,

Salomon's travels got mixed up with those of Theodore, and the less frequent journeys undertaken by Joseph. They all piled up in the house. Even when he went away, Theodore never seemed to leave Kerylos behind. Souvenirs of his voyages were stacked here, in this ship of his. He loved to cry, "Raise the anchor!" and then recite in a loud voice the poem by André Chénier, "Let us go now, the sails are ready, Byzantium calls!" before falling back into his chair.

Today, I realized that this first trip to Greece was the great adventure of my life, though I had long forgotten it. I only recalled the beaches, the ruins, the anxieties of leaving, this morning, as I stood before the mosaics at the front door. As if I had never left Kerylos, as if this sailing trip had been no more than a dream, like the stories I made up for myself, where I pretended that I was with Dreyfus on Devil's Island or inside a rocket that was going to puncture the eye of the moon goddess. All the reality of my youth was deposited on the windows and walls of this house; everything I had seen elsewhere had remained a sequence of images glimpsed from the other side of the windows. The villa is a sphinx with claws. I too was immobile, even during my travels—and then all these tours around Greece, these departures, I made them with the Reinachs, I was never alone, never free. I only began to leave Kerylos when I decided to run away from them.

With their father, the three Reinach brothers had visited Germany, Switzerland, and Italy. I believe they had also seen the castles of England, and the brothers wanted to continue this tradition. An initial voyage was scheduled in 1902 aboard a ship called the *Niger*. I was not expected to be part of the expedition—I had barely arrived—but I heard plenty of talk about it. Monsieur Eiffel himself had said that he would join the expedition. In the kitchen people talked of Beirut, Damascus, Jerusalem, Crete . . . Except that there was an outbreak of the plague on board. Monsieur Reinach, believing in the virtues of hygiene, was in favor of going anyway: everything had been disinfected. But a lack of bravado among the others meant that he had to resign himself—and then he learned that the ship had been wrecked off the coast of Thessaly. I imagined myself captain, aged fifteen, saving everyone on board and being decorated by the president of the republic. When we finally left two years later, it was better: I was old enough to appreciate it.

On board ship, Monsieur Reinach became Theodore again. He liked to play like a child, something I had already noticed about him. He used to take me to the cinema with the entire family, and he was always the one who laughed the loudest. A projection was once organized in Cannes, which at the time was entirely unfamiliar with this new form of entertainment. At home, in Beaulieu, we knew about the Lumière brothers' invention. At Cap d'Ail their father had built three huge villas, one for him and one for each of his children, and everyone mocked him; Papa Lumière thought himself an architect and filled the houses with miniature columns and festoons everywhere. After the movie, Theodore explained with a learned air that the dialogue cards—white writing on a black background that narrated what was happening to the characters—were like the carved inscriptions of antiquity. We hadn't even noticed, all we had seen was the moving images. We made fun of him—which he rather liked.

We embarked upon the Île-de-France—a solid vessel that bore no resemblance to the floating palace that would bear this name between the two world wars—in April, which turned out very windy. I shared a cabin with Adolphe, we did our exercises on the bridge every morning. Between each port of call we would write and perform plays, or rather cabaret revues. I will never forget Theodore on the bridge, transformed into a stage, in front of an audience lounging on deckchairs, playing himself, the archaeologist. He didn't need to get dressed up. The other people he had brought with him were rather more serious: Monsieur and Madame Louis Merle, he was a mining engineer, the head of French aluminum, who had married the daughter of another industry baron, Albert Massé. So many names, so famous back then . . . They all appear in the pamphlet we published immortalizing our onboard exploits. The title was thought up by Theodore, and I don't believe any other members of the Institute ever got wind of it: *Herewego,* published "by a Society of experts and ignoramuses." *Herewego* was a play on the word Cerigo, the ancient name of Kythera, the isle of lovers, which we sailed to after our stay on Malta. For the show, Maurice Feuillet, an illustrator who had published his drawings in the satirical pamphlet *L'Assiette au beurre,* and *Le Figaro artistique*, designed Cretan-style costumes—who would have guessed that this cabaret compère who sang at the top of his voice would two years later become editor of the *Gazette des beaux-arts*? The story was of Homeric simplicity: an archaeologist makes land on Cerigo and finds an advertisement for Lombart chocolate and another for Dijon mustard. Theodore put on his pince-nez, frowned, and began reading.

Then he discovers some ancient sheet music, whose first notes appear to be "Come on, baby!" He complains a great deal about a certain Jason who insisted on reserving in his name all the cabins on the Argonaut. The vainglorious man pretended he was leaving with some friends of his to find some flamboyant golden fleece. Adolphe, his eyes made up like those of a Khmer dancer, swayed in his leotard in his role as the "Vasophore," a Greek servant who brought a huge krater of punch from which the half-reclining guests served themselves more alcohol with a ladle. Maurice Feuillet kept calling him back, shouting: "Over here, cupbearer to the gods!" I was slathered in green paint and told to stand on a pedestal: I was the statue of Heracles offered for the admiration of all. Alice Fougères appeared as a snake charmer, and did not dance only for her husband. Charles de Galland, who had not yet become mayor of Algiers, and who garnered the respect of everyone for his classical erudition, officiated as King Minos who understood nothing about anything. At the end they all left the stage together on "their petrol-driven ark," as though in a trance, intoning, "Bon voyage, Monsieur Dumollet," which Adolphe had translated into biblical Hebrew in my honor, for I was of course Heracles Dumollet.

Four years later, that same Adolphe became a member of the French School of Athens, and I have always wondered if he would have had this passion if it hadn't been for the *Herewego* voyage. He might well have turned his back on all his father's passions. Yet I watched him at archaeological sites, the most serious of everyone, taking notes on the thick invitation cards that he always used to stuff into his pockets rather than handing them over at receptions, and I imitated him, as far I could, sketching and photographing all the things I was interested in.

A few days afterward we had to cancel our visit to Delos because of headwinds. This upset Theodore, because he knew that there had been a recent discovery near the Temple of Apollo of houses that could be of interest to him for Kerylos—I add that to moderate the opinions a little of those who insisted that the villa in Beaulieu was a copy of the ones in Delos, which were discovered around the same time. All those people who knew nothing about it, those semi-savants—"the worst," as Fanny Reinach always interjected, and who enthusiastically feigned unwavering admiration of her husband—said that Kerylos was the identical copy of an ancient Greek house. Affecting great wisdom, they would add, foolishly, "Exactly the same as those discovered in Delos, where there are entire neighborhoods of them." The houses in Delos are smaller, less well designed, and they were only written and talked about just as the construction of Kerylos was coming to an end. Admittedly, the person who discovered them was Joseph Chamonard, a friend of Pontremoli, Grégoire, and Ariadne—who didn't accompany us to Greece—but to conclude that they were the sole inspiration for the house is to simplify everything. Were there music rooms in the Delos houses? The two-story houses were only discovered on the hill in 1904—after Pontremoli had sketched out his plans. He was delighted to discover that both he and the Greeks had arrived at the same conclusions about the layout of rooms, in particular the vestibules where the staircases were located. Delos confirmed what Theodore had found at Kerylos, rather than the other way around. The villa was open on all sides, and you could see the sea from every room, which was the opposite of what was unearthed in the alleyways of Delos. There was electricity throughout the house. How many porcelain light switches were found in Delos? And what about the hot water cylinder, that marvel of human genius!

The first time I spoke Greek in front of Adolphe and Theodore, there was a burst of laughter: the Cretans only understood half of what I was trying to say. The Greek spoken in Cargèse was so sullied with Corsican that it was like a foreign language. "I don't think anyone can interpret our interpreter," said Theodore. "Articulate more, less *iou*, more *os*, speak in simple sentences, we need you!" Adolphe laughed too. I was mortified. My mother had taught me her patois letting me believe it was the language of the gods.

After Valletta, we sailed to Chania, where we saw the beginnings of the museum where objects dug up during the excavations of the Cretan palaces were collected together. I didn't know at that point that Knossos was a folly quite worthy of Kerylos. The famous Arthur Evans, who would soon become "Sir Arthur," welcomed us to the ruins of this palace that he had decided was that of Minos, with the famous Labyrinth, porticoes, great halls, and horns of consecration. He treated Theodore as his equal. He was not an awkward intellectual like the Reinachs: he wore his shirt open, without a tie but with a beaded tie-pin at his neck, a beige linen suit with a waistcoat, a pink flower in his buttonhole, quite a different school of archaeology. He showed us the bedrooms, described the sumptuous bathrooms he was reconstructing—his concrete mixers were running at full speed. An army of painters from Athens, some of whom spoke warmly about the École des Beaux-Arts in Paris, the museums of Basel and Munich, were completing the fragments of frescoes that had recently been discovered. From a loop they constructed a face; two hooves became a great bull-fighting scene; an arm, a foot, and a neck were assembled to become *The Prince of the Lilies*—it was superb. Theodore wasn't fooled, and he had fun, over tea, seeing how they had avoided the classical style to return to the beauty of simple, primitive contours. Nobody was asking the fundamental question about truth and fakery. This was the invention of Minoan civilization, before our very eyes. Soon afterward, in Paris, women began wearing dresses inspired by Cretan fashion, without wondering if it wasn't in fact the Cretan frescoes that were inspired by their elegance rather than the other way around. In the throne room, Theodore sat and posed for a photograph that I still have framed in my house, which has survived all my moves and all my anger toward him. He is posing like an Olympian—he is ridiculous.

During the few days we spent in Cyprus, rather touchingly, he almost seemed to justify himself to me: "You know, Achilles, when I was your age, at school, where my father ended up enrolling us after all those years of home schooling, I hated sports. I hated the gym teacher who came once a week to the Lycée Condorcet—at the time it was still called the Lycée Fontanes—with a whistle around his neck in the courtyard that was once the cloister of a convent. A veritable agent of law and order. We called him the torturer. He had a stooge, the supervisor, who always used to say to me: 'Go on then, run away, go play ball with the others.' No one ever says to a young man kicking a ball, 'Go on then, pick up a book, go read with the others, look how happy Theodore is with his book, doesn't that make you want to do the same thing?' I found it terribly unfair. I think deep down that I haven't changed your mind. But you are made for sports, there's nothing to be done about it. We'll keep you anyway! Here, catch, it's a book!"

While we were in Cyprus, we visited Famagusta and Othello's tower, that monument to the glory of jealousy. Adolphe and I were not very sensitive to this emotion that drags a man down and leads him to crime, and still less seduced by Theodore's intolerable idea of having us translate Shakespeare's play in order to "clear the rust off our English." We slipped away to visit a few places that had nothing to do with archaeology. Then we sailed back to Crete; from Kalami, we went by mule to Phaistos, another ancient palace, more authentic and wild, because less invaded by British archaeologists. The site had been taken over by Italians, who yelled to each other from one low wall to another, drank a great deal, and didn't over-restore, which in my opinion was far better. Alongside the great spectacle of Knossos, Phaistos was a black and white movie. At the heart of this complex that had barely been unearthed, turtles were shuffling from one pool to another. The beach was glorious, the most beautiful I've ever seen in my life. At sunset I swam for three hours, as happy as a demigod.

In a storage area away from the main site, we were shown a terracotta disk that had just been unearthed, its inscription coiled like a snail, in a writing system that nobody recognized. Theodore looked at it cautiously, saying that it is never a good thing to find an object like this of which there is no other example—I did not pay much attention at the time, but he mentioned it again, furious, at the time of the painful Glozel episode that I shall have to recount as well. I could not help but wonder if he didn't suspect a hoax by the Italians.

He was very alert to trickery, though I didn't understand why. He said to me once, in a dreamy tone of voice that I can still hear, "A beautiful find, that is everyone's dream . . . You'll see, if you persist a little in the study of ancient civilizations . . . The discovery might come . . . Adolphe, I am sure he fantasizes about such a thing." The "Phaistos Disk" became wildly popular in Crete, and there were even key chains and charms made of it, but it still hasn't been deciphered—some people think it's a game of snakes and ladders. Adolphe took the time to copy out a lengthy inscription, a traditional kind, which he published. He was proud, almost as much as he was of our memories, which we kept to ourselves, of the disreputable houses we visited in Famagusta. One of our companions bought a fragment of a woman's profile, certainly authentic, for the Louvre. It's still there, and nobody knows that we owe it to the creator of the costumes of our wild cabaret where our greatest scholars shouted in chorus, "Come on, baby!" Whenever I talk about those sailing trips, no one believes a word.

On the voyage home, I was still doing pushups and Swedish gymnastics like a sergeant major, but I was also listening out for the voices of the gods. Kerylos was growing clearer to me. My Greek was improving, though I still struggled. I forced myself to memorize pages of Greek tragedy. We hadn't visited Athens. I wanted to. I was drawing better than ever, I tidied up my sketchbooks, my watercolor technique was becoming rather good. I had learned things that would be useful to me years later.

The mosaic anchor on the floor of the villa had been planned before our departure, and now it made sense. Today I look at it, enclosed within the dark red geometric lines of the tesserae that break the ground into a thousand pieces, and it reminds me of our travels. Humming tunes from *Herewego*—I had no idea they were still stored somewhere in my memory—I sketch it in this volume of my recollections. Theodore once explained to me that he'd had the anchor copied from some Greek paving uncovered in Delos in the House of the Trident, which had been written up in a scholarly journal, but he insisted on the fact that the original mosaic was located on the edge of an interior courtyard, "rather stupidly" on the main axis, while here it was better positioned between the vestibule and the great peristyle: the movement of the dolphin that wrapped around the anchor prompted guests to turn right, as though the house itself were in motion—and it signified that this was where he had moored his family. In his mind, it was clear: by placing the fragments he had chosen in places where they rang true, better than the originals, he had improved on the Greeks. According to Adolphe, the Kerylos anchor was placed in a location "that wasn't remotely in the Greek style." However according to Theodore, on the contrary, his anchor would have aroused the admiration of the Delos mosaicists, and nothing pleased him more. There is no billionaire today who would be capable of this combination of good taste, historical knowledge—he always found the perfectly apt, if entirely unexpected, recently unearthed quotation to illustrate his point in a conversation—and playfulness. He went on, apparently just for my sake: "You'll see, in a hundred years people will dare to say that neo-Gothic is an improvement on the Gothic, that the neo-Renaissance of the Eiffel villa is an improvement on the Renaissance, that Renoir's women are even better than Fragonard's, and that our Greek house is more beautiful than the houses of ancient Greece, and it will be true. Never forget, my friends, the archaeologists from the year 4000: we are doing this work for them!"

17

DREAMING OF THE THERMAL BATHS AT KERYLOS AFTER SPENDING SEVERAL DAYS IN A MONASTERY FROM THE MIDDLE AGES

Fanny Reinach concealed bottles labeled Coty or Guerlain in small boxes made of sandalwood. She whispered, "Naiads," which is the name that Pontremoli gave this luxurious room, built around an octagonal pool, with hot water faucets and steam vents, the last ancient baths built anywhere in the West to honor the naiads, those young women who loved swimming, surrounded by bearded tritons and gods crowned with fresh seaweed. Pontremoli procured fittings in Budapest and Istanbul and added technology worthy of the fastest locomotives. Today, none of it works anymore. I saw, glancing in briefly, cracks in the ground. I'm not even sure that there is still water. In the village, people gossiped that Theodore bathed there naked with Sarah Bernhardt, and I let them say it . . . The actress had long since passed the age of splashing around with members of the Institute.

In the early days, I did not use these facilities; I merely adjusted the temperature, ensured that the pressure was not too high, and disappeared while Madam Reinach settled in there to chat for hours with her friends. I was not worthy of such luxury—my mother did not think it very suitable at all to install a hammam in one's home. A young girl came from the new Negresco hotel to give massages. The small pool was designed so that people could sit upright in it, like in the mosaic baptistery discovered at Ravenna, except that here the decor was not Christian; there were dolphins, fantastical marine animals, a frieze of tiny waves. When everything was ready, I would leave a towel at the door, which meant that no one should enter. It was Adolphe who first dared to push me into this sybaritic cave—was Sybaris not the most famous Greek city in the world for the baths that softened the skin of its inhabitants?

It was late afternoon, the whole household had gone on an excursion, and we had done two hours of gymnastics and one hour of swimming. Adolphe turned on the steam, and we ended up like two Olympian athletes splashing about in the huge cistern, making salacious jokes. The ritual was established, and we accorded ourselves the right to steam once a week. Theodore approved; Fanny contented herself, laughing, with banning us from touching her ointments and summoning the masseuse from the Negresco.

After the war, the doctor advised me to do exercises in the water, to rehabilitate my legs. Naiads was at the end of the small corridor that led to Philemon, my bedroom. In the early days of my "affair" with Ariadne—what an awful word—when she came to see me every day, I surprised her. This is one of my fondest memories of love. The house was empty and she let herself in with her husband's keys, careful not to be seen by the caretaker—but she didn't find me in my usual quarters. I had left the door of the thermal baths open, and the scented steam was flowing out of the room. She understood the invitation; she undressed, left her sandals in front of the statue by the entrance. I saw her appear, naked, framed by the wooden doorway.

I believe that Theodore's project to see antiquity reborn was never more fully achieved than at that moment. Sitting in the water, facing her, I watched her step into the pool. White marble with dark veins, glowing in the light of the candles I had lit, projected warm reflections onto her skin. She threw herself at me, I closed my eyes, felt her body outstretched on mine. We made love without thinking of Greece, and I managed to completely stop thinking about the war. We stayed at least three hours in the heat, lounging by the side of the pool, holding hands, gently massaging each other, listening to the trickle of the water. That day I told her something I had never told anyone before: the details of the journey we had taken, Adolphe, Theodore, and I, into the most secret sanctuary of Greece, the holy mountain of Athos that still followed the rites of Byzantium.

At the back of the room, a mosaic-covered half-dome gave the room an uncannily religious atmosphere; it had an air of Venice's Saint Mark's Basilica equipped with a bronze soap dish. Ariadne asked me a lot of questions, and she dared to force me to talk about Adolphe, about whom I had been unable to speak since he had died. It was here, for the first time, in this place where he and I played as young men, that I was finally able to talk. Ariadne was intrigued by our secret sojourn in the forbidden place, where we were able to spend a few days. I told her that what we missed the most at Mount Athos, much more than women, who are not permitted to go there, were the bath oils at Kerylos, scented with iris. On Mount Athos we were treated like thirteenth-century paupers. We were fed boiled beans and lentils, made to sleep on mattresses in dormitories with thirty other impoverished people. We were woken up for endless Masses of which we understood not a word. Even I, trained in these rites by my mother, was lost. After a few days of this diet we were filthy, permeated with dirt and the smell of incense, stinking like old priests—horribly sanctified. We dreamed out loud, all three of us, under the vaulted ceiling of the Dionysiou monastery, of the villa's baths. I can still hear Adolphe: "What if we managed to bring the masseuse from the Negresco? Wearing a false moustache? Would the monks behead us? They might rather like it, the filthy old bastards."

We kept the purpose of the expedition secret. Adolphe and I let our beards grow. Before 1914, worldly men wore beards and mustaches; it was the servants who were clean-shaven. This detour through the Orthodox church allowed me to make headway in society: I kept my beard for two years, clipping it in the style of Edward VII. Adolphe kept his mustache, the one you can see in the last photograph taken of him in uniform. It was agreed that I would be the one who spoke to the monks, and to their leaders, the famous Hegumenos. I was not to tell anyone that the other two were Hellenist scholars—to ensure that we were not mistaken for traffickers in antiquities. The idea of being taken for a merchant horrified Theodore. Adolphe threw me a look and grinned within his freshly sprouted beard. I had recently found out one of the secrets of this family—the dairywoman, the notary, and the postman were not entirely wrong—and I now knew that they had been the cause of a huge scandal at the Louvre, though I continued to act as if the "Reinach affair" had never taken place.

Ariadne asked me questions about the secret monasteries. I loved that she liked the same things I did. I could teach her something. And I especially loved watching her when she asked me questions. I enjoyed explaining things to Ariadne, I wanted to show her Athos through my memories. Lying on my back, eyes closed, I talked to her as she stroked my hair. It was not easy to reach this wild peninsula, where twenty monasteries and an infinite number of chapels, not to mention caves where hermit saints lived, perpetuated an ideal of rustic and ascetic life. It is not Greece, it is not the Ottoman Empire, it is a republic of monks. In Athens people mocked them, saying it was wise to avoid bathing naked there in the mountain streams. Ariadne wanted details. But I saw only holy people there—no satyrs chasing young athletes. They had the features of Professor Barbenfouillis in those films by Méliès. They were unfriendly, even aggressive, convinced theirs was the only true faith. Before the Great War, Athos had not yet garnered the fame it has today, and there were no doubt many monasteries in Russia and the valleys of Romania where people lived like this, close to nature, cleaving to holy doctrines. In Cargèse I had long heard talk about such places. All the priests knew that there, where entry is "forbidden to any woman or female creature," faith remained as pure as it was at the time of the Virgin Mary, who, according to a passage in the Gospels disregarded by serious people, journeyed to this place and made her garden there.

This injunction against "any female creature" was a source of perplexity: the absence of animals laying eggs or producing milk restricted the clerics to a diet of vegetable soup, and they were plunged into anguish every time a mosquito, its sex uncertain, settled on the edge of a caldron. It was rather comical to be talking about all this after we had made love. Ariadne sensed that I wanted to talk about it. She stayed silent. She understood: what I was going to tell her was almost as important as our embraces. She liked seeing me back among the living, without the need for someone to help me, acting of my own accord—for her. She had a soft, clear voice I found utterly lovely, and a simplicity in her choice of words. She never stumbled, while I tripped over my words whenever I became emotional. I sensed that she loved me, and though everything around us was so complicated, these few hours were simple, in this lovers' half-light that enveloped us both. I was careful not to tell her that my spoken Greek still made people laugh, that the priests had little taste for my Ajaccio accent.

Upon our return to Saloniki after our stay in Athos, we went straight to the public baths, where we were massaged and perfumed, and slowly returned to civilization. Adolphe kept asking me if we still reeked, as we planned nocturnal excursions to houses of disrepute, while his uncle went to visit the synagogue and the old Jewish cemetery, as well as the great Roman gate and the basilica that dates back to the emperors of the Late Empire. The Jewish community of Saloniki was famous, and the renowned Monsieur Reinach was deemed worthy of a warm reception. One afternoon he took me aside and said, "Be very careful during your walks around the city; I don't want Adolphe to discover a passion for the Late Empire, that's the last thing I need! The arch of Emperor Galerius can exert a dangerously seductive appeal." Needless to say, I followed his advice to the letter, and we did not spend more than an hour on curiosities, whether Roman or Judaic. Moreover, as far as antiquities were concerned, only one thing occupied our minds: the discovery that we had made a few days earlier in a monastery on Mount Athos, of which we were so proud and so stunned we hardly dared talk about it to each other. That day in the thermal baths I told Ariadne my biggest secret, the one that Theodore would never now reveal, that Adolphe had taken with him to the grave.

I was the one who had organized it all: in order to enter the territory of Athos, a *diamonitirion* was needed, an ecclesiastical pass, signed by three Orthodox cardinals. I wrote a beautiful letter to my metropolitan bishop in Cargèse—I distrusted the worldly prelates of the Russian Cathedral in Nice—and we received his answer, written with a quill pen, informing us that three passes would be waiting for us in a village named Ouranopolis—"the gateway to Heaven"—on the coast of Chalkidiki. A border wall sealed off the sacred peninsula, which could thus only be accessed by boat.

We left from Marseille. The region of Macedonia was in turmoil, and when we arrived in Piraeus, the entire population was in uproar. I was worried that we would not be able to reach Mount Athos. I bought a newspaper and translated it aloud: the Greek army had attacked the northern provinces, which were still under the yoke of Turkey. Bulgaria, Greece, and Serbia had decided to liquidate "European Turkey" and divide it up between them. Greece, under the benevolent eye of Orthodox Russia, was eager to recover Alexander's first kingdom, whose population had turned on the Ottomans in support of the Greek soldiers. The Turks, who had begun with dramatic flourishes and a great brandishing of scimitars, had, to widespread astonishment, surrendered. Greece had succeeded in carrying out an entirely unexpected conquest, without igniting the Balkan powder keg. Adolphe mimicked the voice of his father, the redoubtable Joseph Reinach: "The formidable Balkan powder keg, upon which the great powers sit like students smoking cigarillos."

I didn't realize that I had, for the first time, mimicked Adolphe. Ariadne burst out laughing. She had forgotten he was no longer alive. I took her in my arms and carried on talking. Water from the gushing bronze spigot washed over me, and she didn't see that I was crying. I took a long moment before I spoke again. I gripped her two hands in mine.

On the first day of this second voyage to Greece, we went to the Acropolis. At last. I wanted to see everything. I wanted to embrace every passerby. I'd dreamed of it for so long. The site was crowded with modest houses and ruins from every era. At first sight, I was disappointed. Adolphe wondered whether one might inventory every chunk of stone and rebuild it. Theodore, standing on the stern of this great vessel, where years later young Greeks would raise the Nazi flag—I cut out a photograph, which I still have somewhere—recited a page of Chateaubriand that his father had made him learn by heart when he was ten years old: "From the summit of the Acropolis, I beheld the sun rise between the two peaks of Mount Hymettus; the crows which build their nests around the citadel, but never soar to its summit, hovered below us, their black and polished wings were tinged with roseate hues by the first radiant beams of Aurora; columns of light, blue smoke ascended in the shade along the sides of the Hymettus. Athens, the Acropolis, and the ruins of the Parthenon were colored with the most beautiful tints of peach blossom." I cannot help thinking, as I copy out this beautiful passage, of Elsie de Wolfe, the society decorator, who when she first saw the Parthenon exclaimed, "Oh! It's *my* beige!" She didn't quote Chateaubriand, but she was quite as ridiculous as Theodore. It didn't strike me at the time, I found it all very splendid, I was filled with awe and pride. I made drawings of caryatids and pretty nineteenth-century houses embellished with palmettes, their rooftops garnished with sphinxes and antique ornamentation—everything that Theodore refused to have at Kerylos, the papier-mâché and paste that would have its moment later on in the movies. On our first evening, we were greeted by fireworks: Adolphe told his uncle he always overdid things, he really didn't need to. It was Athens celebrating its victory over the Turks. The next day, we began our long journey by horse and cart along unpaved roads, with soldiers in astrakhan toques that would have been the envy of the sanctimonious ladies of Beaulieu, and troops in pleated skirts as white as the dresses Suzanne Lenglen wore on the tennis court. The entire population had come out to take control of the villages, and we were swept along in a triumphant march. It remained to be seen what would become of the monasteries on Mount Athos. The Ottomans had always respected the Orthodox religion and the independence of the peninsula, but how would the King of Greece's soldiers act?

Over the previous few years, Adolphe had taken several journeys alone, with the French School at Athens as his main residence. I hadn't seen him for a long time. Kerylos remained a base where he could withdraw and work. He sent me his first published articles, after which he started to write so much—adopting the graphomaniac habits of his family—that he stopped communicating with me altogether. He accumulated brief notes in scholarly journals, scattering to the winds enough to fill one or two books—that was all I could tease from him, and I don't think he cared at all what I thought about his research. Theodore had told me that Adolphe had barely arrived at the school in Athens, where his uncle Salomon had once been a resident, when he left again, fleeing the academic rigor and the opinions of his teachers—they knew that he had money, he was unpopular, he undertook travel at his own expense, never bothered with the necessary permits. The School at Athens is unique. Ariadne visited it once with the Pontremoli team; she briefly alluded to it, managing not to mention Grégoire's name. She painted a pretty picture: it was a library in the middle of a garden. Amid a great deal of excitement, the "Great Excavation" at Delphi—the excavation of the Temple of Apollo—had been planned there. An entire village had been moved, while in Paris, the parliament had voted a one-off subsidy—who would imagine such a thing today?—and a trade agreement had been concluded with the Greek government, anticipating, inter alia, that France would import I don't know how many tons of Corinth grapes every year. If only my mother had known the reason why so many recipes of the era called for grapes in such large quantities, in semolina, and all manner of desserts, even in the custardy *far breton*! All French children were required to consume the surplus Greek grapes for tea, in order that the most beautiful sanctuary in the world might be unearthed. It was for the honor of our nation. Olive bread was now served in all good homes. Meanwhile, the

Germans were scrabbling away at Olympia. Everyone spoke with immense respect of the French School at Athens.

A few years ago, I returned on vacation to show the garden to my children. The guardian opened the gate to me when I mentioned the Reinach name. He led us to the war memorial. I had found the names of all those I used to know on the memorial at the church in Beaulieu. But not that of my poor Adolphe. The words "God" and "Fatherland" are inscribed on the marble, as if not everyone had the same homeland and God. But his name is engraved at the entrance to the School at Athens. I saw the library too, which never closes. Young people work there day and night deciphering new inscriptions.

During this period, Adolphe wrote magnificent letters to his father from Egypt, in which he told him about his work but also about some other, secret, research that the two of them were hoping to undertake. For his book on the paintings of antiquity, he was analyzing some portraits that had been discovered in the area around Fayum, and he was still gathering all the quotations he could find by classical writers about the art of painting, even recipes for varnish. He had had the incredible epiphany, which surpassed his father's brilliance and his uncles' research, that to understand Hellenism he needed to travel to its borders. In Alexandria and Cairo he began surveys that would have occupied him for his entire life.

The librarian showed me an archive card on which was written "Notebooks left by Adolphe-Joseph Reinach." I didn't have time to look through them all. So that I could take something away with me, in a hasty scribble I copied out the first page that fell open, promising myself that I would come back to take notes on the rest: "Thasos. May 21, 1911. Went by boat this morning to Thassopoula. A rocky island with three promontories, mostly thorny vegetation overshadowed by a few olive trees and wild fig trees. Lots of birds and rabbits. We are going to nose around, there are so many legends about the treasures to be found there. At the end of the bay right next to the sea there's a hot spring. It's protected by a small house that opens straight onto the sea. It was built by a governor of Thasos who was doing a cure . . ."

In his letters—where are they today? The Nazis took everything when they came to Kerylos—he wrote mainly about something that the two of them had kept secret until Theodore began to tell me some of it on our journey by horse and cart from Athens to Saloniki: the real reason for our journey to this country without women. That morning, in Kerylos's thermal baths, I finally dared to reveal the secret to Ariadne, who could barely believe what I told her.

The truth is that Theodore had sent Adolphe to Egypt to realize the Reinach dream. He was going to make the crucial discovery that would relegate Schliemann's extraordinary finds at Troy and Mycenae to the rank of the feats of the past, and would make it clear to all, and for centuries to come, how great French scholarship was, and also, of course, a little bit about the part our archaeological school owed to the family. It had nothing to do with discovering the cities Homer sang about, or the arms of that Aphrodite whom guides at the Louvre still call the Venus de Milo—and who, according to Salomon, was an Amphitrite, a goddess of the sea. Adolphe Reinach went to Egypt to look for something better than vestiges of the *Iliad* or the treasures of Agamemnon, better than the Cretan Labyrinth and the temples at Delphi, better even than the ruins of Atlantis that Plato wrote about. He wanted to find the tomb of Alexander the Great.

That was what I loved most about this family: this mix of seriousness and folly, the way they became so irrepressibly excited about the most outlandish projects, from the safety of their "small house that opens straight onto the sea." Monsieur Eiffel could be like that too, when I'd see him exclaiming with delight, waving in his hand his weather reports or the plans for a new viaduct that he had been commissioned to design for some godforsaken region of Cochinchina. Something childlike remained unsullied within the spirits of these great men, and that's why, I think, they enjoyed talking to me: I was a child too, and I hope, even at seventy, that I still am. I was a child, a wounded soldier, and in my arms my Ariadne was also a child. Kerylos had become our plaything.

Ariadne, who had draped herself in a linen robe that one of the maids had forgotten behind a small curtain at the back of the room, sat down to listen to me in the golden glow of the apse. She looked like a delicate statue. I plunged down under the water again and then came up and kept my eyes on her as I told her the whole story. Since ancient times, no one has known where the tomb of the conqueror was located, or even what it looked like. "But," Adolphe had written, excitedly, "if anything remains of the paintings by Apelles—the greatest of all Greek artists, the favorite of the master of the ancient world—the only place they could possibly be located is in his tomb." Apelles painted a portrait of Campaspe, Alexander's favorite, and had the misfortune to fall in love with his model. The conqueror, delighted with the painting, gave him the young woman as an exchange, which was noble and beautiful, but also gave people plenty to ponder regarding Alexander's tastes. Adolphe had jotted in the margin, "Campaspe's nakedness was not unusual for the era. Anaxarchos, one of Alexander's courtiers, always insisted on being served by a beautiful naked young girl." He underlined another passage a little further on, an anecdote told by Pliny the Elder: "Alexander talked a lot about painting, though he lacked any knowledge. The artist discreetly encouraged him to hold his tongue, telling him he was provoking a great deal of amusement among the young boys who ground his pigments."

The conqueror died in Babylon. A huge funeral cortège brought his body back to the Mediterranean. The generals who inherited the mantle of his empire quarreled over his corpse. They spirited the hero away and everyone thought that he had returned to his father and his ancestors in Pella, Macedonia, or that he had been buried in Athens or Delphi, or that he had been placed in a large carved sarcophagus like the ones Theodore had studied at the new museum in Istanbul. Most likely he was laid to rest in Egypt, near the oasis of Siloam, where the oracle of the god Amon had spoken to him and told him that from henceforth he was now equal to the gods.

Finding Alexander's tomb was the holy grail of archaeology. Except that, since it was a grail, my beloved Adolphe did not find it. At least not in Egypt. He began mentioning it less often in his letters and writing more about pigments and paintbrushes. He stopped dreaming, became serious and methodical, not always the best methodology. But his uncle Theodore did not stop dreaming; impatient and restless, he became a long-distance researcher. He thought the answer was as likely to be found in books as in the desert sands. He had the most up-to-date German atlas, a large volume, always open on his desk; he experienced Adolphe's expeditions from his bedroom.

One autumn day, late in the afternoon, he found it. In his bathroom on the second floor Theodore stood up in the carved marble bathtub copied from a Roman tub, which, according to my mother, looked just like the gravy boat she always saw at her mother-in-law's. He let out a cry and yelled my name. I was in the gallery that ran the length of the master bedrooms, folding towels. I ran to him. He was standing up, completely naked, covered in foam, splashing water all over the red and ocher wall paintings, laughing and shouting in Latin, *"Proh! Pudor!"* then Greek, "*Eureka!"* then he sat back down in the water and said, "I know where it is! The tomb. We have to go, we can't tell anyone, we can't say where we are going. Guess who gave me the solution! What a genius. Actually, he wants to come with us, he says he's still strong enough."

"Who? Go where? We're going back to Greece?"

"The one who figured it out is that very model of a modern man, our neighbor, your friend Monsieur Eiffel."

"But he's eighty years old!"

"He's a genius."

"He's in no fit state for the roads of Greece . . . "

"It's his idea. He found it. A streak of light, the lightning rod at the top of his tower."

"He can't come with us. That would be utter folly."

"He told me the other day as he was smoking his cigar that the Greeks must have buried Alexander at the top of a high mountain."

"It can't be Olympus, that is reserved for the gods."

"The other peak, in Macedonia, at the heart of the kingdom of Philip II, his father and all his ancestors. Mount Athos, Achilles, does that mean anything to you?"

And that is how we ended up taking a small boat from Ouranopolis, headed for Kharies, where there were mule tracks and boats to take us up to the monasteries. Fortunately Eiffel listened to me and did not come with us—he would have died along the way. Theodore found it hard walking in the sun. Adolphe had no real idea of where to begin our search. He told me to go and ask one of the monks in the harbor—who looked like the priests in Nice I hated so much—if there was anywhere in Athos where one could pray to Saint Sisoes. What plan was he hatching? The monk, who was very old, thought for a moment, and said, "Dionysiou." It was good timing since a felucca was about to set sail for there. All the other monks were in a state of great agitation: they were reading the newspapers that had been brought over in our boat. Two Greek gendarmes were also on board, speaking to the Kharies authorities, confirming that an entire regiment was on its way to liberate Athos. Adolphe explained the situation to us: the Turks had always left the monks in peace, while the Greeks terrified them. These twenty monasteries are the hidden Vatican of Orthodoxy. The Russians wanted to get their hands on the priests by pretending to protect them and the Bulgarians too. Theological disputes had been fanned to divide the twenty communities—the debate that year was about the name of God, was it or was it not divine. Everyone had an opinion, the supporters of the Bulgarians were busy trying to drive out the supporters of the Russians, and it was just at that moment that the Greek government troops arrived unexpectedly. We thought no boats would be allowed to leave, and that the Greeks would block the ship we had spotted containing the hidden food supply of these backward monks, in the diabolical form of boxes of fresh-laid eggs. But the Reinach uncle and nephew each had a secret weapon: In passable modern Greek, Adolphe announced to our new friend the priest, who suddenly developed an obligation to accompany us, that he was ardently devoted to Saint Sisoes, an Egyptian hermit. Theodore handed over several tickets to the captain. I felt like I was in a Jules Verne novel, standing in front of Captain Hatteras or Professor Barbicane.

That same evening, after signing a register, downing some raki, and admiring the frescoes, we were all three given beds in a large dormitory, in the heart of the sacred, filthy monastery of Dionysiou. On a cliff overhanging the sea, it looked like a drawing by Gustave Doré, a fantastic citadel made of huge blocks of stone, a stack of floors that seemed ready to tumble onto the rocks below, with a studded wooden door that had remained unaltered for four centuries. Ariadne closed her eyes.

I will remember the peacefulness of that first day until the end of my days. The view over a nature unchanged since the Middle Ages, which had never known modern roads, plantations from the Americas, the messy jumble of buildings. There had been a question, after the death of Alexander, as to whether to transform this sacred mountain into a colossal recumbent statue in his image. Was that not proof that this was where his tomb must be? No one had ever searched for it, which was the most inexplicable thing. The third tip of the Chalkidiki peninsula, this trident sinking into the sea, had become heaven on earth for the few monks who established monasteries there like the Coptic ones in Egypt. It was inaccessible, but we had managed to reach it.

In the middle of the night, we heard a dull hammering: the monks being called to prayer. I think I still hated them just as much as when I was twelve years old. It really was very ironic: to have made me cover so many miles so that I should endure, years later, one of those Masses that I had so loathed as a child. We went, we sat in the darkness and we watched. I almost fainted in the swirling incense, in front of paintings that rippled in the light of the church candles, at the moment when the Hegumen, the abbot, appeared, dressed in white and holding a huge staff. I understood that was how the Byzantine rulers, and the Roman emperors before them, must have appeared to the people. Adolphe claimed that certain rituals of Delphi and the sacred mysteries of Eleusis had been passed on to Rome, where they continued to be celebrated in the bowels of the Palatine Hill, and from there they had survived into Byzantium—and after the sack of Constantinople, the holy traditions, relics, precious paintings, and the true faith stretching right back to the depths of time were kept secret here in this rocky place, hidden from the world, facing the Greek sea, only for us.

Beside the church where the monks prayed—I said I thought they were hideous, hunchbacked, obese, some looked like they had the evil eye, though Adolphe told me I was exaggerating—there was a room adorned with frescoes opening on to a cobbled atrium. Adolphe and I looked at the paintings, one after the other. We came upon one in a corner showing a hermit with a long beard leaning toward a skeleton that was rising up from his grave. Before him, a crown of gold. It was the sepulcher of a king. Two names were written there. For the monk, "Sisoes," for the skeleton, "Alexandros."

Had one of the desert fathers, the solitary monks who established churches like the one at Bawit, near Siloam, where the French mission in Egypt was now excavating, discovered the tomb of the conqueror? Better than that: had he exhumed his body? Had these Coptic priests—if not my brothers, my not-so-distant cousins—dared to profane the most sacred thing on earth, the burial place of the noblest of all men? All my childhood hatred was flooding back. Adolphe told me that my reaction was ridiculous, that Egyptian hermits could hardly be held responsible for the priests of Nice. I told him they were a band of looters, thieves, scavengers.

That night we dreamed that Alexander's body had been brought to Athos. Two hours later, we were awoken by the wooden drum announcing another Mass. Adolphe grumbled, regretted not having brought the works of Voltaire with him, and then convinced us that we had to leave for the veneration of the relics. Among the relics that Dionysiou gloried in were some objects in a silver chest, the most sacred because they had belonged to the Blessed Virgin. After the visit of the Magi to the manger, the mother of God, prescient and wise, had kept behind a little gold, a little incense, a little myrrh, and these "gifts of the Magi" were still here, she had brought them with her when she had decided to end her days on Mount Athos. We were allowed to admire them, the first Christmas gifts in history, shown to us by a mumbling assistant of the Hegumen, laid out on a small table in the center of the catholicon, the main church building in the monastery.

All of a sudden we heard a great commotion: the Greek police had stormed the courtyard. The monks ran outside, leaving us alone in the church.

I was seized by a moment of madness. I opened the cupboard that contained the relics, not to steal, just to look. Adolphe seized the one in the middle, a golden crown. "That looks very ancient indeed," he said. Peering closely at the filigree olive leaves, braided and delicately worked, we saw on the inside a distinct inscription: "Alexandros."

A rowdy mob of soldiers entered the catholicon. We had to show our passports, explaining that we were from an allied power. We were treated with respect, but that same evening we found ourselves back in Ouranopolis, escorted on a military boat.

It took me a little time before I dared open my coat to show my two companions, caught between excitement and horror, that I had brought with me the funerary crown of Alexander the Great. I despised the monks for hiding this extraordinary object and keeping it away from the eyes of the world; I had taken it back from them, it was justice. I had robbed the Orthodox Church and avenged myself of everything my mother had made me endure. I was euphoric.

Now we had an extraordinary clue to help us locate the tomb, which might even have been right there beneath our feet when we were standing before the fresco. We would have to come back. That night I saw in a dream the map of Athos laid over that of the Pointe des Fourmis: it was almost the same shape. The crown went through the formalities of the border crossing hidden beneath a pile of shirts in Theodore's cabin that the customs officer didn't even glance at.

Ariadne was spellbound by this escapade. I felt that I was growing in stature in her eyes. I wondered what would happen if she decided to leave Grégoire. She never ended up living with me. But that day, I thought, "Why not? A new life."

Theodore and I bade farewell to Adolphe, who returned to Athens to spend a little time with his professors, who were complaining that they never saw him.

On the boat returning to Marseille, Theodore remained locked in his cabin. I wondered what he could have been thinking about. I never saw the crown again. But when I think about it, it belongs to me. I was the one who found it. I discovered it. I stole it.

In Naiads, Ariadne, my naiad, clapped her hands and took off her robe to join me in the water, to embrace me, fashion a crown for me with her hands, open her eyes wide as she stared into mine; to tell me that I would always be her hero, her Achilles, hers, only hers.

18

THE LIBRARY

"You mustn't disturb your father, you can go into the library later. Walk around the back of the house if you want to go down and swim with Achilles." Every morning Fanny made sure that her husband was left in complete peace when he sat down facing the sea to write, having first spread out over the table the engravings he was focusing on. Folios of illustrations of Greek vases from the museum in Naples and the English catalog of the Parthenon sculptures sat open on the lecterns. The library was the room inside the labyrinth that was the most difficult to leave.

In the early days, as I watched it being built, furnished, stocked with beautifully bound books, although everyone kept saying that I was free to go in whenever I wanted, I never felt entirely comfortable. All the rooms in the house had words inscribed on the door: some had a Greek name paying homage to a mythological figure, others translated their function. But on the door to this room there was no specific name; the Greek word βιβλιοθήκη was the same word in French, *bibliothèque*, a term that remained unaltered and proved that we were still Greek. It took me a long time to make this simple observation. In this room I experienced hours of suffering, hours of study that drove me to despair. It was so complicated. I used to think to myself, "And people are surprised that such a language died out!" And then one day, at the end of a week of dreadful exercises, Theodore said to me, "There you are, you've got it, you see."

I hesitated to go into the library today. I walked through the door and rushed—almost ran—straight over to the windows to look at the view. I shouldn't have; I collapsed, exhausted, into one of the chairs. I'm a broken man. I can't go on much longer. I usually manage to hide it, but I have no stamina any more. I do three strokes of breaststroke in the sea and I can't carry on. I am the antiquity now: I have no arms, no legs, no color left; I could be on display in a museum, like my paintings. It has been a long time since I have had any desire to read. I took a few deep, slow breaths, to recover a little, and looked around. I closed my eyes, opened them just before I fell asleep. I took out the special Royal Wedding edition of *Paris Match* from my camera bag and leafed through it in a state of absolute exhaustion, then dozed a little. I've brought with me the strange anonymous postcard that inspired this return to Kerylos. Is the stylized wreath an allusion to Alexander's crown? Or is it merely a victory wreath for the Olympic Games? They are taking place this year in Melbourne, and the emblem looks a little like this . . . I wondered if perhaps one of the Reinach grandchildren wanted to play a joke on me, or one of the dairywoman's nieces or the pastrycook's daughter. The girls used to be friends of mine, they always teased me for my airs and graces, maybe they were still at it, or perhaps they just wanted to see me again. Tonight I am going to have dinner by the sea, in plain sight, in case anyone wants to speak to me . . . I shall prop the postcard on the table in front of me.

I wanted to film a little here, but I haven't been able to. What's the point? I barely managed to do more than push open the door of the thermal baths to glance inside. I would have liked to film the octagonal cistern and the little dome, but somehow I didn't dare.

Fanny Reinach rarely went into the library; she had her own books that she stored in a large chest in her bedroom. Her particular passion was theater. She was the one who got me interested in Rostand. She loved to read aloud. To her the verse was a kind of music. She claimed that Thomas Corneille's plays were much more beautiful than those of his brother Pierre—what she was saying, obliquely, was that the "elder Corneille" was not the great one, just as the greatest of the Reinach brothers was not Joseph, the oldest. She teased her husband, asking him what might have happened if there had been three Corneille brothers, if there had been a Theodore Corneille. She had several beautiful editions with eighteenth-century bindings of one of her beloved Thomas's tragedies, *Ariadne,* whose action took place on the island of Naxos, where Theseus abandoned her. I learned the soliloquies, for a performance in the garden that we never managed to put on—no one else shared Fanny's love for Corneille the Younger. She even went so far as to claim that he was the author of all the plays attributed to Molière: "There are fakes in literature too, and extremely talented forgers, there's a whole book to be written revealing the names of all those who were the true authors of so many famous books. There are no doubts about the Reinachs though. They are too disorganized. For my sins, my husband writes all his books himself, built his own house, made his own babies."

In early 1913, after our return from Athos, Theodore planned to write an account of our discovery, which he hoped would be published by the end of 1914. Of course it never saw the light of day. Fanny, who by then was seriously ailing, spent several weeks resting in the sunshine at Beaulieu. She died three years later. He never came out of mourning. He never again mentioned the Saint Sisoes fresco and its open grave. One evening in the army encampment, no more than ten days before his death, Adolphe said to me, "You know, our crown—he stole it from us, Uncle Theodore! He will never give it back. I have not seen it since. All I know is, it is somewhere in Kerylos. He's hidden it. We shall take it out to celebrate our victory. It will go to the Louvre, it will be our golden revenge, revenge against the assassination of our good name . . ."

I have no idea what he did with Alexander the Great's crown. It must still be here, somewhere within these walls. Why did Theodore not want to make the discovery public? Did he have doubts about it? Was he hoping to keep for himself the possibility of further excavations on Mount Athos, hoping that he, like some contemporary Sisoes, would be the one to unearth the body of the king? Or perhaps he thought that the book should have been written by Adolphe . . . I even wondered if he might have placed the sacred wreath upon his wife's head before he closed the lid of her coffin.

Theodore was a solitary man who used to force himself to be sociable, to hold his own in conversation with his beloved Fanny's friends. He also knew better than anyone how to keep his own counsel. Left alone with his research, he would have needed nothing more. He had no interest in real life—except that one day he decided he wanted a house, not any house, so that his family could see the world in which he really lived. He must have thought that stones could be touched, bedrooms entered, beds slept on, plates eaten off, and that this entire world, come forth from his mind, would help his wife and children to live like their father did, or at least to understand him. The house entertained him, but it served this purpose too: it made exterior and tangible everything that was buried in the staircases, the rooms paved with tesserae, the painted galleries, and the immense library inside his head.

Though he may have had to force himself to play the paterfamilias, looking after his guests' well-being was also, obviously, a straightforward manifestation of his fundamental generosity of character. He always said that kindness is the greatest of all the virtues. Perhaps it was also a cure he had invented to withstand life. I only understood this much later, thinking about it far from Kerylos, when I saw my own children doing well at school. A dunce like me, who became a good student by dint of great effort, didn't instinctively think of such things. At the local school, it wasn't that I was bad or mediocre. I was absolutely hopeless. I got everything wrong all the time in chemistry, I dropped Latin early, English was unpronounceable for a Corsican, I couldn't understand what mathematics was about any more than how water came out of the tap. Students at the top of the class are often somewhat solitary, it's common knowledge, no one likes them, they're left on their own, they irritate everybody. Theodore was the top student in the whole of France. Every lycée gave out prizes, gold wreaths, piles of red books tied with broad ribbons. For him it was a hundred times more glorious and unbearable: in a way, Theodore was still the seventeen-year-old boy who stunned everyone when he was awarded the largest number of prizes ever handed out in the National Schools Competition. If he had had high hopes of coming top in Latin at Lycée Condorcet, of one day becoming best friends with the boy who came top in Latin at Lycée Henri IV or Louis-le-Grand, he was obliged at this point to drop the illusion. He was like a species apart, a white duck, or, worse, a blue duck or a yellow duck: the strange creature, even among the swans, that everybody stares at. He had to make an immense effort to have a life beyond family life, friends other than his brothers, to love, live, commit to an existence in which he must always have known there would not be many people he could talk to. A large building project is an excellent conversation starter.

The National Schools Competition has been in existence since the reign of Louis XV; Victor Hugo was a laureate—his subject in physics was the somewhat implausible "theory of dew"—as were Baudelaire, Évariste Galois, and before them Lavoisier and Robespierre, Turgot, Calonne, and Rimbaud, a superb student, outstanding at translation. In his first year of rhetoric, Theodore was awarded first prizes in French oral, Latin verse (Baudelaire was awarded only second prize), Latin translation, Greek translation, geography, and English, second prize in Latin oral and geometry, and a certificate of merit in history—a stimulating little wake-up call. The following year, by now specializing in philosophy, he received first prize in French composition—the queen of all subjects, he always used to say, the one that writers win, that Michelet was awarded—chemistry, and English, and second prize in Latin composition, history, and mathematics. He beat Salomon, who had not picked up as many.

When Theodore used to talk about this in front of the family, it was unbearable, especially for his children. His father used to say, his German accent still quite pronounced, "My sons are the most gifted students in the whole of France," with a stress on the word *whole*. The National Schools Competition still exists. Just before the last war, I clipped a photograph from the newspaper of a young woman standing in her kitchen who had won all the prizes in Latin and Greek, the first girl ever to pass this intellectual driving test. The Reinach brothers would have loved her, I'm sure, like the little sister they never had. They would have tied ribbons in her hair.

Theodore had a deep affection for his friends Eiffel and Fauré: he recognized in them both the solitary child who draws bridges in the margins of his schoolbooks, the musical prodigy with perfect pitch, an exceptional memory, and a host of ideas quite unlike anyone else's—who, in order to survive, understands instinctively that the first thing to do is to not draw attention to oneself.

On the library walls, in the glow of the rising sun—according to the recommendations of the Roman architect Vitruvius, a library must be oriented toward the east—are the names of his only childhood friends: Euripides, Aristophanes, Archilochus, Sappho, Pindar, Aeschylus, Sophocles, Herodotus, Homer, Hesiod, Thucydides, Plato, Aristotle, Demosthenes, Menander, Archimedes. Each name held for Theodore memories of joyful times—and of solitude. The topmost inscription on the wall declares: "Here, with the orators, the scholars, and the poets,

I designed a peaceful refuge for the contemplation of beauty, which is immortal." No first editions, no rare tomes, nothing but books for research and a few of those tall, illustrated volumes that cost a fortune.

It was in this room that he gave me the first edition of a dictionary he had just received, written by a teacher at the Lycée d'Orléans, a modest, scholarly man whom he knew a little, Anatole Bailly, an associate member of the Academy of Inscriptions and Belles-Lettres—a formula that always sounded to me like an administrative post at the court of the Emperor of China. The idea that one might be acquainted with the authors of dictionaries in real life had never occurred to me. He explained that this doorstop might prove useful to me—it was very well done, even if he had spotted the odd imprecision—since I spoke neither German nor English. Adolphe had learned Greek with dictionaries compiled by Liddell-Scott and Wilhelm Pape. Monsieur Reinach was very emphatic about the fact that we would soon be able to hold our own without the help of the *Rosbifs* and the *Fridolins*.

I ended up rebelling against it all. It's all so easy, this rhetoric, brilliant, fascinating, and seductive, when you're rich. I was furious with him for squirreling away Alexander's crown. My mother had taught my brother and me that we had to study things that would be "useful" to us later in life. It took me a while to grasp what that sentence really meant. It's a little like when an insurance salesman says, "in case you get into an accident," rather than, "when you die." The formula "Study something useful," really means, "Study something that will earn you money," which is no less obscene than the insurer's euphemism.

Theodore used to quote *Cyrano de Bergerac*: "No! No! It is far more sweet when it is all in vain." And I listened to him, which very nearly led me to disaster. By the time I was thirty I still didn't have an occupation. He had stolen my youth. I was no good at anything. All I had harvested was books.

A friend of the Reinachs, passionate about Celtic languages and old Irish, told them how, when he was leaving for the trenches, he had searched for a copy of Homer to take with him. He realized that the only decent, well-produced editions with the Greek text alongside were in German. The Reinachs were fighters. Such a thing was intolerable to them. The consequence of this, so I was told, was that in 1917 the celebrated series of bilingual volumes now used by every student first appeared. Theodore observed this indulgently, though he needed no translation, and he actually preferred the small English editions that he could carry around in the pocket of his English jacket. The French translations, with Athena's owl on the cover, were a huge help to me. At last I could access the marvelous world at the heart of domestic life at Kerylos: I understood Aristophanes, I read his tragedies, I thrilled to *Antigone*, and recited Oedipus's woes out loud.

I have forgotten nearly everything now. I never open these books anymore. One evening, a few months after our return from Greece, here in the library, I plucked up the courage to ask a question alluding to Alexander's crown. I wanted to see it again. I asked Theodore, out of the blue, if he thought he would ever write the book. I quoted Baudelaire, so that he would understand that my interest in "this beautiful diadem, so dazzling and clear" was above all that of a poet.

I had overstepped the mark. He dismissed me with a wave of the hand. I saw from his expression that I had offended him. His small eyes appeared even more sunken and shadowed than usual. He set down his new spectacles alongside one of the tree-shaped bronze candelabras, from which dangled opals that imitated the gentle glow of oil lamps. In the tone of an exiled king he said simply, "A crown? Who would believe me?"

19

A SCHOLARLY CONVERSATION IN THE FRONT COURTYARD

One morning a statue appeared in the Proauleion, the entrance hall that opens out from the vestibule. A great man of antiquity leaped in a single bound out of a wooden crate stuffed with straw and scraps of fabric, bearded, draped, majestic, sandaled. No one dared utter a word. Fanny Reinach stared with astonishment at this white giant, then declared that they would have to get used to him:

"When you marry a Reinach, you have to be prepared for statues to turn up like this. I would probably have chosen to put him in the garden, myself. We would have watered him during the summer. I'd have preferred someone less austere for the entrance hall. Have you forgotten this is a vacation house? I was not even consulted. Apparently my opinion is worth nothing. Well, I shall hang garlands of flowers around his neck."

It was going to be the first thing visitors would see as they came through the red front door. Theodore, with the air of a magus making a prophecy, lowering his voice and speaking with restraint, explained to Fanny how this serene figure, with perfect features and one arm draped in fabric, was one of his first victories. That was the reason he was important to him. A battle won.

They were addressing one another using *tu*, the familiar form in French, which happened rarely. They were having a minor altercation. I often listened at their door: when they had something pleasant to discuss they always used *vous*, the formal form of address, even when they were alone. They hadn't noticed me in the gallery that overlooks the library, sitting cross-legged like the famous Egyptian statue of a scribe in the Louvre. I eavesdropped on the entire conversation. It was like being at the theater. I always liked to listen to them talk; I found it enthralling. From my hiding place overhead, through the large bay window I could see the calm sea extending all around us. "The thing is, the original statue, in the Lateran Palace in Rome—this is a copy, of course, which I commissioned—is held by the gentlemen of Berlin and Munich to be a statue of Sophocles. They think they see in his stance the poise of the tragedian, the author of *Antigone*, *Oedipus Rex*, *Oedipus at Colonus*, *Ajax*, represented by the scrolls that you see at his feet."

"And what *extravagant* sandals!"

"*Scandalous* sandals, indeed! One German scholar even presumed to write that such sandals are typical of a tragedian, as if anyone knows what kind of sandals old Sophocles wore! As if there were sandals for tragedians, and sandals for comic authors! But in fact, when the sculpture was dug up from the ruins of Terracina, the ancient city of the Volsci . . . "

"Please, spare me the details."

" . . . and then when the count Antonelli gave the statue to Pope Gregory XVI—in 1839, not even a century ago—it *had no feet*."

"You mean someone smashed your Sophocles's feet? That would indeed be poetic justice."

Theodore explained that an Italian sculptor, whose name, as it happens, we know, a certain Tenerani, had taken it upon himself to restore the feet. "It is to him we owe these elegant sandals, the likes of which are unknown on any other statue. A pure invention, which would no doubt sell well in the boutiques of Menton. Nowadays such a creative artist would never be allowed to appropriate a statue and reconfigure it to his own taste, but this kind of thing happened again and again over the centuries. One day all the arms, feet, and ears that you find in museums everywhere will have to be removed. They will be packed away into little boxes and stored in museum reserves. Antique fragments are highly prized, they must never be meddled with. Imagine someone giving the Venus de Milo back her arms!"

"Your brother Salomon would rather like that. Did you see the creature he wanted to introduce to us? She's playing an orphan on stage at Châtelet. She's the Venus de Melodrama!"

"Can you not be serious for two minutes?"

"Of course. Anyway, if they say this is Sophocles, that must mean that they know what Sophocles looked like. Are there any pictures of him? Your marvelous German scholars must have thought of that . . . "

Theodore was surely delighted at how clever he was to have married such a quick-witted woman. In his storyteller's voice, he told her about a bust in the Vatican with a damaged inscription, on which it was just about possible to make out *ocles*, not even *phocles*, and definitely not *Sophocles*. This inscription had also been repaired by a heavy-handed restorer in order to bestow an illustrious but bogus identity on the figure. The resemblance was vague, even if the beard was similar. Archaeology is a precise science: everything must be constantly queried, examined, compared, one must arm oneself with all the reference books and almanacs such as the ones his esteemed brother Salomon wrote, the fundamental basis of this work. It is like a police inquiry. You must identify the suspects, which is not a straightforward task given that these people died 2400 years ago. It was clearly in the Germans' interest to say that it was Sophocles. A great literary figure, so beloved of those pompous oafs; Hölderlin translated Sophocles, Germany adopted him as one of their own. And thus, *voilà,* the crime benefited the country." Theodore was proud of lampooning the Germans with the story of the fake sandals. Yet just as the dear doctors of Berlin were the first to claim it was Sophocles, the poor, scorned, spluttering French specialists had such respect for the erudition of those boors that they repeated it in book after book. Even though the statue could just as well be Diocles or Empedocles . . . Theodore concluded his lecture with a laugh: "A bearded man whose name ends in *ocles*, it is not as if there is any lack of them in the agora."

"He looks as if his arm has gotten caught in his cloak."

"That is the classic pose of a fifth-century orator, it symbolizes that he has not wrought any trickery."

According to Theodore, the power of a philosopher's oratory and countenance had to be enough to persuade. Gesticulating only began in the fourth century. It was not until several years later that statues of orators began to show them waving their hands around. In his peroration entitled *Against Timarchus,* Aeschines, who maintained the traditions of the fifth century, mentions a statue on the island of Salamis of Solon the Athenian legislator, "with his arms inside his clothing."

"When I came upon this reference, I jumped up, you can imagine—I immediately drew a connection with this statue."

"It comes from Salamis? You mean the original one does? But I thought you said it had been dug up in Italy?"

"The one from Salamis would have been in bronze. With such a famous historical figure as Solon the Wise there would have been a good many marble copies in circulation right up to the Roman era."

"Do we know what Solon looked like?"

"We do have one portrait of him. Here, you can see it in this book. All the pieces of the puzzle fit together. A head kept in a museum in Florence, this time with an unequivocal inscription, 'Solon the legislator.' See, they look like the same man."

"Well, it's a man with a beard who looks somewhat carried away, but from that to say that it is the same man . . ."

"I am employing the same principles as Monsieur Bertillon: focus on what does not change in a face over the years, the distance between the eyes, the relationship between the base of the nose, the mouth, and the chin. Look, they're exactly the same. I've measured them. The Sophocles of our German friends is in fact Solon of Athens, one of the seven sages of Greece."

"Please don't ask me to tell you the names of the others, I beg you."

"I pulled off a decisive victory over those oafs in their spiked helmets. But that does not mean they are going to give us back Alsace and Lorraine. They simply keep going, writing more and more articles attacking me. Well, I am standing firm. And now every day when I arrive home I shall see him, the image of the man who gave us democracy, the greatest Athenian of all."

Theodore had never wanted to have a "collection," where the crown would have had pride of place. That was not his style. His wife was a little regretful because there were so many delightful, eclectic collections in her family and among her friends. The Bischoffsheims bought Rembrandts and Goyas. The Rothschilds were unbeatable; beautiful things seemed to find their way to them effortlessly. They could have filled Kerylos with authentic antiquities, tall glass cases displaying vases and rows of bronze figurines—they certainly had the means, like the Count de Camondo with his eighteenth-century furniture and dinner services. Theodore observed, smiling, as the Cahen d'Anvers family and their cousin Béatrice Ephrussi accumulated all sorts of lovely objects. He didn't like living surrounded by ornaments; it made him ill at ease. He liked museums. He had grown up in Saint-Germain-en-Laye, where his brother was now the director of the Museum of Antiquities, and he believed that the treasures of the past must be accessible to all. He was not a collector—he liked to be able to sit down heavily in a chair without fearing that it would break—but it was primarily because of his republican principles. The Marquis Campana, who collected Greek vases, ended up being convicted of fraud and sentenced to the galleys. The Duke of Aumale built a chateau at Chantilly to house his treasures, and he was quite clear from the start of the construction that it would be a museum open to the public. The time of princes and great connoisseurs was coming to an end: every child in France had the right to visit museums, the galleries of the Louvre were opened up for lectures held in front of great works of art, allowing everyone the opportunity to advance, discover history, learn to love beauty. The museum was the future, the cement of a great nation, enlightened through knowledge and moral rectitude. Kerylos was intended to be neither a gallery showing authentic works of Greek art, nor a museum. It was his home. It was for the pure pleasure of a passionate connoisseur, and also a tool for an even greater understanding of ancient Greece, about which he had amassed a fine collection of books, but which he wanted to comprehend from within. He explained to his beloved Fanny, as they stood looking at Solon's sandals: "If I work hard enough, I hope I will, eventually, be able to enter the minds of the ancients, to understand them, by making the architecture of their language mine. Kerylos is my Trojan horse that will help me gain access to the interior of their citadel." And so Theodore brought only a few works of art to Beaulieu: he purchased a fragment of a painting from Pompeii, but solely because he wanted to study it closely; at auction, he let the Louvre acquire the most beautiful piece. He had no interest in commissioning sculptures. It was too easy to spot a fake Greek goddess, with her resemblance to a garden nymph. It is a question of patina. He did own a few reproductions of sculptures.

When the Charioteer of Delphi was discovered beneath the sacred path that traverses Apollo's temple, he wanted to own a copy, so that he could study the fine drapery, elegant features, and tranquil face of the charioteer holding a pair of reins in his hands. He displayed this statue, in his eyes more precious than any other, in the library. According to Plato, man is a coachman steering two horses, one a handsome and noble beast, the other a rebel.

20

SUNLIGHT ON THE FURNITURE

The furniture in the library was, to my twenty-year-old self, the most beautiful in the whole world.

Pontremoli designed the pieces as he went along. One day he gave me a couple of sketches for tables, wonderful to behold. It's not easy to furnish an ancient villa. In Greece, apart from caskets, chairs, and beds, there was little furniture. Fanny Reinach drew up lists of what she needed and Theodore amused himself thinking up ideas for them. A dressing table? A chest of drawers? A small desk for keeping up with correspondence, where his wife could sit in the morning and reply to invitations? A little bell on the table? He took note of everything. He was making it up as he went along.

I sometimes went up to Paris, to the Faubourg Saint-Antoine, to check on the progress of the furniture, which was being made in Louis-François Bettenfeld's workshop. Bettenfeld crafted solid furniture from carefully chosen wood: lemon from Ceylon, wild olive from the Mekong Delta, plum from Australia, tamarind from the Indies . . . Pontremoli wanted inlays of mother of pearl, ilex, ivory, subtle touches of mahogany, nothing too elaborate. It was like watching Ariadne's watercolor palette, the way she layered colors, waiting for the flat tints to dry before dabbing on a touch of purple or emerald in just the right place. Rays of sunlight pierce the curtains and sweep over the furniture, sketching new and unexpected lines, making me think of her, her delicacy, the way she explained everything to me so that my illustrations would be less dry and precise.

To have style is rather easy; to invent a style is more extraordinary. Theodore's directives were straightforward. That requires talent. He knew what he didn't want. He wanted to avoid any variation of neo-classicism, a return to Grecian style as has been practiced for centuries. The warmth and pale wood of Austrian Biedermeier furniture could be kept; the main thing was to forget the Empire style, in spite of its straight lines, and the gracious style of Charles X. He wanted simple forms, occasionally broken up with turned feet, bronze scrolls, or huge nails, to give an impression of asceticism and refinement. The furniture in Kerylos is quite unlike any other. It was the kind of furniture that before the First World War people looked for, but didn't find: imposing, solid, practical, comfortable, and elegantly crafted. Like the house, measurements were calculated in Athenian cubits and feet, the measurements of the Greeks—there was no question of using meters and centimeters. The most extraordinary pieces, in my eyes, were the chaises longues where Theodore liked to lounge and read, the fruit of a guilty romance between the English deckchair and the starkly virile Roman chair portrayed by David in his prerevolutionary paintings. When, several years later, I came across Art Deco furniture, I detected a family resemblance to those chairs: as is so often the case, it is by reinventing the past that one catches a glimpse of the future.

Cerberus died of old age. Theodore, for whom these daily walks were immensely important, replaced him with a watchdog called Basileus. At last the villa would be guarded—one might have suspected that, on our return from Athos, Theodore wanted to dissuade prowlers and burglars. He did not dare ask Pontremoli to design a kennel, even though the architect hadn't forgotten even the most trivial objects for the bathrooms—but those were for humans; it would not have been seemly to ask him to make something for the dog. The caretaker enjoyed the task, nailing together several planks in the shape of a temple with a pediment, designed according to the animal's dimensions so that it could lie down comfortably inside. Theodore himself picked up a paintbrush and wrote *Basileos,* which could mean either the dwelling place "of the king," or the kennel that belongs to Basileus. This folly, enlivened with small columns, sat proudly beneath the peristyle in front of the entrance to the library.

The books were hidden away. Theodore arranged them in wall cabinets, trunks, and behind the curtains in the gallery above the library. It was unthinkable to display modern bindings; he wanted people to imagine scrolls, as numerous as those that had been found in the ashes of the volcano at Pompeii, in the Villa of the Papyri. Theodore was a genius. He didn't flaunt quotations like his brother Joseph. He didn't bludgeon other people with his knowledge. Joseph, when he read about a discovery in the *Journal des savants,* would cry, "Well now, this is absolutely extraordinary! I shall have to write about it!" One day, during lunch, Fanny Reinach burst out laughing when she heard this familiar phrase. Joseph didn't understand, but he fell silent.

Theodore, rather than responding to my question about the golden crown, took down from a shelf a volume published by Hachette, the translation of a dialogue attributed to Lucian of Samosata, who composed dialogues with the dead and voyages to the moon as if they were true stories. He hastily assured me that this was not the work of the great poet himself, but probably of a certain Leon, one of the academic philosophers, about whom nothing more is known.

"It is called *Halcyon, or the Metamorphosis*. Look."

I have since got hold of another copy. I remember reading to him:

"'What voice is that, Socrates, a good way off from the shore? How sweet it is to the ear. I wonder what creature it can be, for the inhabitants of the deep are all mute.'

"'It is a sea fowl, called the *kerylos*, or Halcyon, always crying and lamenting. It is very small, but the gods, they say, bestowed on her a recompense for her singular affection: while she makes her nest, the world is blessed with Halcyon days, such as this is, placid and serene, even in the midst of winter. Observe how clear the sky is, and the whole ocean tranquil, without a curl upon it.'

"'This indeed is, as you say, a Halcyon day, and so was yesterday; but how, Socrates, can we believe the tales you spoke of, that women can be turned into birds, and birds into women? Nothing seems to me more improbable.'"

According to myth, the halcyon built its nest upon the Aegean Sea. The seven days that precede and the seven days that follow the winter solstice mark the period when the seas are flat, everything is calm, and, according to legend, the halcyon's eggs were protected. During those days of calm between two storms is a time of quiet, for doing nothing, thinking about nothing, eyes wide in the light of the day.

21

THE MORNING WHEN THE MOST ANCIENT MUSIC IN THE WORLD WAS HEARD IN THE OIKOS

As the day turns around the house, the sun travels from one sundial to another. The first overlooks the peristyle, the other the gardens, each one inscribed with one half of a single phrase composed by Theodore: on the side where the sun rises is carved, "I designed this monument for the sun, in twelve parts, six facing the Levant, six facing the Zephyr," and on the other, the side of the setting sun, "so that everyone, seeing the wall from afar, knows the hour of work and the hour of rest."

The pink curtains—the same shade as Homer's dawn, Fanny used to say—which I saw being hung after they were delivered from Lyon by the embroiderer Écochard in large cardboard boxes, have faded to ocher, the washed out color against the pale whitewashed walls like a sepia photograph left too long in the sun.

At Kerylos, I liked to listen. On evenings when the house was empty, it creaked like an old sailing ship: wooden doors swollen with damp, bronze curtain rings agitated by the wind, beams shifting; sometimes I could even hear, over the sound of the waves, the cries of the birds perched on the roof tiles.

By contrast, from the terrace at the top, the Bay of Beaulieu looks like an animated maquette, but without any noise: the boats returning to port, the swimmers and walkers in the far distance, the little train chugging silently through the palm trees with its tiny cottonwool plume.

All the sounds of Kerylos composed a kind of silence. Today they are here again because the house is empty, the murmur of ghosts as they cross each other's path. The sounds that remain when no one is left—and Ariadne's clear voice. I pine for her still.

At the heart of this silence is the piano, the most famous object in Kerylos; even those who were never invited to visit the Reinachs, but who wanted to suggest they were on familiar terms, used to talk about it, the only ancient Greek upright piano.

Because all the furniture in the house was designed in the pure Hellenic style, Fanny Reinach grew desperate during her first winter there, thinking that she would never be allowed a piano. Her cousin Béatrice Ephrussi, in her neighboring villa—whose comforts Fanny would laud out loud to annoy her husband—had all the pianos she wanted! Fanny reproached her husband for depriving her of her greatest pleasure, of stifling the thing she loved, of sacrificing her on the altar of his archaeological obsession—she even threatened not to come back to Beaulieu. She needed those hours at a piano, no doubt, as an escape. Then Theodore realized that she wasn't joking, her face grew hard, she shut herself up and wrote letters all day. And one fine day in 1912 she saw the instrument arrive, with, in Greek letters, the words *Pleielos Epoiesen*, "Pleyel made it," inlaid in dark wood against the pale lemonwood, an idea her husband had to make their literary friends laugh when they saw the inscription. Folded up and closed, it looked like a sort of tall chest. It would be opened in the evening, revealing the invisible keyboard as the sheet music was taken out. Obviously Fanny would have liked to arrange family portraits in silver frames on top, but she understood there were limits.

She liked to play with the window open. In the garden, where I could listen without being seen, I heard Ravel's *Waltz*, and Debussy's *Six épigraphes antiques*. I liked one section in particular, "For the invocation of Pan, god of the summer wind," and another, more mysterious, called "For a grave without a name." I think of Adolphe whenever I hear that piece. I make no distinction between thinking about him and praying for him. I think of Léon too, Fanny and Theodore's son, a musician who might have become a great composer—two names without graves.

I could sing quite well, but I only ever learned to play the harmonica, and that not very well. I had so many things to learn, I didn't devote the necessary time to music. Madame Reinach loved Bach, his sarabandes and fugues. She had charming ideas, poetic and unexpected; she would take on a dreamy air and say, "How I would love to go to the Congo and play this piece in a village for some little African children," and her husband would smile, because he loved her.

When Theodore himself sat down at his "Pleielos," he played riotous pieces, like the carillon from Offenbach's *The Grand Duchess of Gerolstein*, which would cause quite a stir among the bathers down on the rocks. *Orpheus in the Underworld*, of course, was one of his favorites: he loved Public Opinion's main aria, and the Infernal Galop, better known as the cancan. Sometimes I would hear him singing in his bathtub, "When I was king of the Boeotians . . . " The line he especially liked in *The Grand Duchess of Gerolstein* was, "And we, what luck, we are three!" which he often sang, reminding the assembled company that there were only two Montgolfier brothers and two Goncourt brothers, unlucky for them. He could have become a pianist, a virtuoso even, he could resolve any technical difficulty, just as he might have become a chemist or a mathematician: that was why he always chose pieces from comic operas, as a way of mocking himself and his multiple talents. His slender fingers raced over the keys as he beat time with his feet. On the wall, among the motifs in light relief that contrast with the painted details, is a depiction of Ariadne's nuptials, after she has been abandoned by Theseus on Naxos, then seduced and saved by Dionysius, who consoles her with wine, festivities, folly, centaurs, and music. Eros is pouring perfume over the head of the young woman. It was inspired by a famous vase in the museum at Orvieto. The stucco artist applied it to the wall in less than a day. I turn my head: there is Ariadne, standing with Grégoire on the terrace, applauding, my Ariadne, enraptured, so lovely, her hair loose around her shoulders. I have the feeling she is watching me, surreptitiously.

One sunny morning Theodore invited me into the music salon—with its perfect proportions, barely large enough for all the family, there was certainly not enough room to hold the small concerts that he so loathed—"Listen closely, Achilles, I am going to play for you the earliest music of humanity. No music older than this has ever been found. It is the Delphic hymn to Apollo, which I managed to decipher. There are not many things I am proud of, but this, yes: enabling people to hear the sounds of ancient Greece. Gabriel Fauré, a friend of ours, as you know, arranged the hymn and played it on this very piano—you weren't here, you must have been in Nice, at school. Since then I have transcribed another piece, less lovely, slower. There were some mistakes in the notation that I was wrong to correct; they were, perhaps, after all, the fantasies of this musician of antiquity whose name we shall never know."

I was still a young man with no culture, but I found this Monsieur Reinach, who claimed, with the aplomb of some marvelous mandarin, that he had managed to correct the spelling errors of the ancient Greeks, quite incredible.

"Listen to them both, and tell me which one you prefer. The first was played in the Grand Amphitheater at the Sorbonne, during the first International Olympic Congress, after the games were revived. You know the frieze by Monsieur Puvis de Chavannes, *The Sacred Wood*, with all those pretty girls in nightgowns? I showed you a reproduction in one of those books that my dear brother Salomon writes for young ladies—and older ladies—who attend the École du Louvre. Have you heard of the Olympic Games? They are very new and very old. You are a consummate athlete, you ought to take part, you might even win a chocolate medal. I saw the Baron de Coubertin seated in the front row, weeping when he heard it, tears dripping into his mustache."

I was intrigued by this story. I asked him how he had managed to decipher such ancient music. He explained that no one knew why, but in the chiseled inscription there were symbols that appeared above certain letters. He realized that this was the Greek way of writing musical notation before musical scoring was invented. Much has been written on the subject, but he approached the problem with a fresh and uncomplicated perspective. I was fascinated.

I listened as each note rose as if a temple were being built before me. The music was beautiful, solemn, full of mystery. I played it on the harmonica that night, looking out at the sea. I wanted the sea to hear this music that it had heard two thousand years before, to hear it respond with the crash of waves and wavelets, for neither had the sea changed. I detected a similarity between the music's slow rhythm and the Corsican songs of my childhood, intoned by the mountain people at wedding Masses, before the statue of the Virgin, just as the harp used to be played for the victorious Athena on the Acropolis. The second or third phrase was particularly lovely, and I could have started it over ten times in a row, like a snake charmer.

I will never forget the first time I heard this music. I walked over to the window, opened it, and looked out toward the horizon, listening to each second of the hymn to Apollo. When it was finished, I asked Theodore to play it for me again. He did.

I found the second hymn, though very lovely, more repetitive, more rhythmed, like a ritual dance, perhaps more real. Fauré hadn't altered it at all. I had been an avid reader of Theodore's book, *Greek Music*, which, he said with a malicious little smile, would be useful to two sorts of people: musicians who knew a little Greek and Hellenists who knew a little music, two categories of whom there were not very many at all.

I met the famous Gabriel Fauré here, in 1919. He had been to Monaco to perform his composition *Masques et bergamasques*, in the pretty little chocolate box in the shape of an opera house built by Garnier, and afterward he came to perform his pieces in the Oikos at Kerylos, surrounded by stucco masks recalling those in the theater of Pergamon. Fauré was a charming old man, fond of art, and sculpture in particular—he was married to the daughter of Emmanuel Frémiet, the man to whom we owe the statue of Joan of Arc riding her horse on the Rue de Rivoli in Paris and, scaled down, upon many a Catholic home's mantelpiece. Fauré, the son of a schoolmaster from Pamiers, had done very well for himself. The Countess Greffulhe, taking herself for Ludwig II of Bavaria, made him her domestic Wagner, though he was not very Wagnerian at all, in spite of a piece he wrote called *Souvenirs de Bayreuth*. Like many great composers, he was hard of hearing. He insisted that every compliment he received be repeated. Theodore much admired the score of his opera *Pénélope*, and requested that he arrange several abbreviated sections for the piano. Fanny had been dead for two years, and I think the music must have helped him hold on to his memories of her.

I don't recall if Pierre de Coubertin, the founder of the modern Olympic Games, ever came to see the Reinachs at Beaulieu, or if I caught sight of this pontificating personage at the Reinach mansion in Paris. I've never understood why he was so indulged by everyone, the beau monde especially, with his Boy Scout ideas that culminated in a eulogy to the strongest, the humiliation of the hopeless, for whom "the most important thing is taking part," and the exaltation of physical strength. In ancient times, the Olympic games were also the occasion for contests of poetry, song, and drama . . . His gimcrack games would have horrified the Reinachs, if they had taken a closer look at what the prophet of the "modern Olympic games" wrote, but they were so naïve, sometimes, my great men. Hitler understood, he saw straight away how he could exploit the so-called "Olympic ideal," and vulgar supermen in singlet tops and athletic gear.

22

ALL THAT REMAINED OF PERICLES IN THE BIG KITCHEN (WHERE AT LAST WE DARED TALK ABOUT THE GOLD TIARA OF SAITAPHARNES, KING OF OLBIA)

What became of Ariadne? I looked for her for a long time. After my injuries, Adolphe's death, my forced leave, my convalescence at Kerylos, I returned to the front and fought right up to November 11. I was still in uniform when I heard the trumpet sounding the ceasefire, three days after I received another shrapnel wound.

In 1918, not immediately in the wake of the Armistice parade but two or three weeks later, I was still in Paris, left arm in a sling and medals on my chest. I could not get Verdun out of my mind. It was said at the time that "everyone went through Verdun," and I would think: apart from those who had already died. What I had seen did not seem real. I thought about it all the time; I tried to give narrative form to what I had experienced; I read what was written about it in the newspapers; I forced myself to say that it was like the Battle of Marathon, so that it would become an episode in history; I forged an account that I could bear to tell. At night, the real images returned.

One day I was wandering the streets of Paris, not knowing where I was going, when I found myself at the Louvre. I sat down in the Cour Napoleon, at the foot of the statue of Lafayette. On one of the doors in the courtyard someone had scrawled in white paint the word *Victory*. I went inside. I wanted to see, poised atop her stone steps, free of her anti-bombardment defenses, my statue with her wings spread wide. But before I got to the Winged Victory of Samothrace, I found myself at the postal station of the Louvre—that glorious Parthenon of the Third Republic, where there are more pretty girls walking up and down than you can see on Phidias's friezes. There was a directory hanging from a piece of string. Inside it I found the address of Monsieur Grégoire Verdeuil's architectural practice. He even had a telephone number. He denied himself nothing.

I noted down his details so I could go and stand on the other side of the street from his office, to try and catch a glimpse of Ariadne, perhaps try to talk to her, understand why she had decided, quite out of the blue, to cut ties with me. We had been so happy, had that frightened her? I wanted to tell her she had nothing to fear, I would be a discreet lover, I wanted to talk to her without knowing quite what I wanted to say, I wanted her not to forget me, to know that whatever happened, I would never forget her. It took me weeks to pluck up the courage. It's always the same: I let too much time go by before allowing myself to love, to learn, to hate . . . I'm afraid to rush toward the very thing I want, afraid of getting hurt, being disillusioned, causing sorrow.

When it came to the affair of the Reinach tiara, though I could have pieced the story together quite easily, in the end it took me several years to find out all the details. This episode was the hidden face of Kerylos. I first heard about it in the one room that was never shown to guests, the kitchen: with its modern tiling and stovetop worthy of the Ritz, its indestructible burners and spits that looked like complicated watch mechanisms. It had a cold room, enormous serving trolleys, metal sinks; it was a whole new world. My mother often came by, filled with admiration, to gossip with sweet little Justine, who still cooked for me rather more than was reasonable.

In the kitchen, Pericles had abdicated. And Aspasia too, his mistress and servant, who must have cooked him up many a delicious treat. There was no question of being satisfied with some traditional Spartan broth, or with olives, garlic, bread, grilled lamb, and sheep's cheese with honey, as though this were the Parthenon. Monsieur and Madame Reinach's chef came from Paris. Justine deferred to his orders. After Madame Reinach had been for a swim, she would clamber back up onto the rocks where she was served four grilled cutlets: that was the sporting diet recommended by the omniscient Coubertin.

The secret of the tiara was like an enormous roast that Adolphe drew out of the oven in front of me, not realizing that it would turn my world upside down. I wrote it all down in a small notebook that I still have, with a meticulousness worthy of Adolphe, who was incapable of leaving out a single detail. He told me about the scandal one morning after he came down to the kitchen in his flannel dressing gown followed by Basileus, carrying a pile of books and humming the ballad of the King of Thule from Gounod's *Faust*. I can still hear him enunciating every syllable of the chorus, "a vessel of chiseled gold." I was wearing espadrilles and beige linen trousers, having already spent an hour in the water. I served myself a second cup of coffee to keep him company.

The drama, as he recounted it to me, took place in 1896, the year of the first modern Olympics, and an otherwise excellent year for the family. Salomon had just been elected to the Academy of Inscriptions and Belles-Lettres. He was advising the Louvre regarding the acquisition of a unique gold headpiece. At 200,000 francs, the price was not insignificant. The Saitapharnean tiara, made in the third century before Christ, was the most beautiful piece of ancient Greek gold work ever discovered, an exceptional find. This tragic, sorry episode took place just before my arrival, and I have often wondered if that was what they were talking about in hushed voices in the Eiffels' garden, that famous day when Theodore recruited me. Perhaps I promised him a breath of fresh air at one of the worst moments of his life. Often some long-ago incident can only be properly understood many years later. It is undoubtedly the case that during that period, the "tiara affair" must have been the focus of a great many family conversations. I even wonder if he had not taken on the project to build Kerylos as a way of trying to forget the blasted Saitapharnes. Adolphe talked in the empty kitchen, knowing that no one would overhear us.

He told me how the tiara, on a scarlet silk cushion, was given pride of place at the Louvre, surrounded by the other treasures of the Apollo Gallery, the French Tower of London. Between the display case, where the Regent Diamond blazed alongside other huge diamonds bequeathed by the kings of France, on which was carved in large capital letters RF, for "République Française," and the tall cabinets displaying carnelian ewers from Louis XIV's bedchamber and snuffboxes belonging to Louis XV, was a small vitrine. The whole of Paris wanted to see it.

In a few days it was more famous than the papal tiara. All the newspapers printed photographs of its intricacies. Even Marcel Proust left his house to go and gaze upon it, presumably wearing his legendary fur-lined overcoat, arm in arm with one of his friends.

At the top of the tiara a stylized serpent yawned; between a frieze of foliage and a band of tiny images of a hunt, scenes from the *Iliad* stood out in subtle relief. Achilles sitting on a chair, with basins and vases at his feet. Ulysses drawing toward him the beautiful captive Briseis, her head veiled, behind her a procession of servants and birds. A bearded athlete holding the reins of the deceased Patroclus's horses and, on the other side, the funeral pyre of Achilles's comrade-in-arms, made of huge tree trunks, on the shore of a wind-tossed sea where a dolphin swims. Boreas blowing into his conch shell, Zephyr carrying a lowered torch. An urn standing ready to receive the hero's ashes. Achilles, inconsolable at having witnessed Patroclus's death, holding up his arm in a gesture of farewell. In the photographs it looked splendid, it was as pleasing an object to me as the little lead soldiers of my childhood—the first clue that might have alerted me. Adolphe leaned toward me to point out all the details on the large photograph that he had gone to fetch from his bedroom.

His elbows resting on the oak table as he showed me the picture, he grew almost as impassioned as when he used to talk to me about the Dreyfus affair. At the beginning, many people found it hard to remember the name, "Saitapharnes," instead calling it the "Olbia tiara," after the archaeological site on the shore of the Black Sea. Engraved on this sublime object made of pure gold, beaten, hammered, and sculpted, was the inscription: "The Council and Citizens of Olbia honor the great and invincible King Saitapharnes." Pericles, Demosthenes, Plato, those are names you can remember, but this name, Saitapharnes! A few people understood it to mean that it had belonged to the Farnese family, thinking that the tiara came from the Villa Farnesina in Rome. Some even said it was the antique tiara that had belonged to Pope Paul III, born Alessandro Farnese. Not everyone can know the names of all the Scythian kings.

The newspaper *Le Figaro* commissioned a series of articles from Salomon Reinach in which he recounted the exploits of the satrap of Olbia and described his regal headpiece as demonstrating the barbarian chief's love for Homer's epics. Adolphe had kept the articles. The tiara was fashioned during a period of antiquity that in a way resembled our own 1900s: the Greeks knew their glory days were behind them, the Parthenon was old. Other peoples existed beyond the borders of their world, who also loved gorgeously wrought precious metals, exotic fur, and jewelry. The Greeks had learned to admire the Persians, their enemies. They knew, deep down, that the peasants and the goldsmiths of the Black Sea were stealing their motifs and their poems to decorate their helmets and their shields, that they would soon be vanquished, but they also knew that they had conquered their fierce victors first.

That was Adolphe's interpretation. It made the tiara seem even more seductive. The tiara of Saitapharnes was an object that came from the border, the border between two eras, between two worlds, and it had surfaced at just the right moment. For

Joseph, Salomon, and Theodore, who had held it in their own hands, this fragile headpiece, pliable, dented and covered in light scratches, was the most beautiful object bequeathed to us by the ancient world.

23

A FAKE FROM ODESSA?

In the Mollien wing of the Louvre, in the meeting room of the Committee of National Museums, all of educated France had gathered for the first public appearance of this object.

"Most of the time the committee members don't come to these meetings," Adolphe told me. "Everything is decided by a small group of people, with a specialist in eighteenth-century furniture or Renaissance painting come to plead the cause for his acquisition. But that day the rumor of this treasure had spread like wildfire, and they were all there in the white wood-paneled room. There was a flurry of questions. This Saitapharnes, who was he? We already know of him, Uncle Salomon replied. His name has been verified. Uncle Theodore explained that an inscription, published in 1885 in Saint Petersburg, mentioned the Scythian king. What about the shape? Like a pointed bonnet? It is very similar to a headpiece discovered in the Ak-Burun barrow, near Kerch, in 1875 . . ."

That day, the consulting committee was unanimous, and electrified. Someone said that the British Museum had expressed interest. It was expensive. On April 1, 1896—"Your birthday, Achilles!"—a memorable session was held in the Institute building. Héron de Villefosse presented the masterpiece to his colleagues from the Academy of Inscriptions. A little skeptical at first—it was so beautiful!—he had quickly recognized the object's significance, and how important it was that it didn't leave France. Two academicians, both newly elected, who perhaps wanted to make themselves popular with their new colleagues, advanced the necessary sum, half each. The first was Salomon. The second was a very prominent man, an architect and member of the Academy of the Arts called Édouard Corroyer. He was the man who restored Mont-Saint-Michel, who gave it an arrow and a gold archangel brandishing a sword over the shoreline. He invented a Middle Ages that was perhaps not entirely historically accurate, but which became so popular that most people now believe it to be true. His genius was to have given a recognizable silhouette to the island monastery, which until then did not have a clearly defined shape. There had even been an onion dome in the eighteenth century, on top of the medieval bell tower! The Reinachs knew and liked the great historian. Corroyer had a maid, filled with good cheer, called Mère Poulard; Adolphe remembered her well. He adored this woman, who would chatter away as she beat the eggs for her omelettes. He said to me, "She won't make her fortune with her biscuits, but she loves what she does, she loves her hens, and she's even quite fond of the tales and legends of the Middle Ages. She has served dinner to Clemenceau and the King of Belgium; you can't imagine how worldly she is. I must take you to Mont-Saint-Michel, you'll like it, it's so gaudily inauthentic, worse than this place." All his uncle Theodore's friends seemed to come from a different era, as though they were escapees from some fantasy of centuries past, except Eiffel, who came from the future and extolled the virtues of "progress." Mère Poulard would have been surprised and flattered that she was being talked about in a Greek villa on the beautiful French Riviera.

The entire region of Olbia, Adolphe told me, was a goldmine of archaeological treasures. Excavations had been taking place there since the 1830s. The discovery of the Kul-Oba tomb stunned the West. In Russia, the finds were a cause of great pride. It had long been thought that these barbarians, mentioned by Herodotus in Book IV of his *Histories*, had invented nothing, that they were unsophisticated, without culture, knew nothing of the poets, lived in huts made of branches; and now suddenly these trophies had emerged, weapons, gold earrings, a sophistication that merited the word civilization.

The Hermitage museum was festooned with this treasure, all unearthed in Crimea. Under Napoleon III, war had made all those melodious names—Sebastopol, Odessa, Alma, Malakoff—familiar to the French, but conflict had interrupted the excavations. Hence the pillages, illicit business, and a trade in antiquities that eluded the grasp of curators. Theodore owned books in which the marvels in the Hermitage were reproduced, new pages in Greek history, unknown to historians until then. It was hardly surprising then when two dealers in antiquities called Vogel and Szymanski turned up in possession of the tiara, a necklace set with huge gemstones and crystal pendants, and a pair of earrings, all, they claimed, from the same grave. They had commissioned a mahogany display cabinet. They even had a shred of fabric from the inside of the tiara, discovered with it in the tomb. They knocked on all the doors of cultivated Europe. In Paris, they met with a man, somewhat brusque but with a considerable reputation, Monsieur Héron de Villefosse, a shrewd connoisseur of the art of the ancient world. Theodore had also been informed.

The first to express doubts was the great professor of the history of the art of the ancient world at the University of Saint Petersburg, Wesselowsky. The curator of the Odessa Fine Arts Museum went one further. He pronounced it a fake, and declared, as if he knew all about it, and with undisguised contempt, that the creator of the object was a "Lithuanian Jew."

The great Furtwängler spoke next. He was the most celebrated of all the German archaeologists. His museum, in Munich, was the most splendid, his authority considerable. He did everything to shatter the pretensions of these naïve, idle men, who thought they knew everything there was to know about everything, these amateurs: the Parisian archaeologists.

The ingenuity of the forgers had reached an extraordinary peak; they were sometimes even cleverer than the curators. In Europe, from England to Russia, fakes were on the rise, and with them the market in counterfeits. Everyone knew that Crimea was not only a land of unauthorized excavations, but also a region where forgeries abounded. The backrooms of Odessa were known to everyone. The Reinach family, who had cousins there, could not have failed to get wind of them. Of all the French scholars, they were the best placed to know about it all. In the big kitchen Adolphe stood on the table, belting out "The Calumny" from the *Barber of Seville.*

24

NIGHTTIME IN THE PERISTYLE

"I talked to one of Furtwängler's assistants," Adolphe said to me. "He told me that literally everyone was laughing at us. They were damn well informed in Munich."

"Bloody Krauts, they have spies everywhere."

"It turns out the forgers all worked in the same place, a place called Ochakov, a small town on the Black Sea, not far from Odessa. The network was well known: the Hochmann brothers, grain merchants turned antiquities dealers, would commission goldsmiths to work on beautiful collector's pieces, copies of objects discovered in tombs. The worst thing was that my poor uncle knew all about it—he even wrote about it in 1893 for the *Archaeological Revue*! I've got the article somewhere."

"Which does not mean that the tiara is not a magnificent piece."

"As beautiful as this house, you mean? There's nothing authentic about this big ornament, except maybe the bronze rivets along the side, which make it look like it might have had a chinstrap. The rest is just a mishmash of antique forms, beautifully executed, but the whole thing is modeled on a template, all drawn from illustrations that we are quite familiar with. They are all here in the library, I'll show you. That horrible Furtwängler's attack was finely honed, don't you think? This allegedly ancient tiara was, according to him, '*ein wüstes Sammelsurium*,' a crazy hodgepodge, a trumpery, a whimsy, a bird with two heads."

How had Theodore and his brother Salomon failed to suspect anything? To them, the engravings that had served as models were additional proof of authenticity. Furtwängler drew attention to one particular detail that had struck no one else: didn't the family of Reinach's wife also come from the Black Sea, in fact from Odessa itself? Surely she—or one of her relatives—was acquainted with all those little Jewish goldsmiths beavering away in secret? At the very least the international traders who had signed secret agreements with them . . . Was it not by selling grain harvested on the Ukrainian steppes that the Ephrussi family had built up the fortune that they spent in Paris, with all those chic people, their new friends? Furtwängler saw immediately how the trap would work. It needed no more than a flick of the finger for the whole thing to collapse, for the entire edifice of international Jewry, who had become erudite in a single generation, to sink into the abyss, he would get them all, he would make them eat dirt. Theodore's primary enemies were not barbarians but scholars, his colleagues. I had never imagined that.

The ordeal lasted far longer than was rational. Adolphe stood turning the massive, empty spit, miming greed, basting an imaginary hen with an empty ladle, as he described what happened next. There was the poet of old Montmartre, a tramp really, who in 1903 caused a commotion at the Louvre when he stood before the tiara and cried out, "But it is I who made it, the famous crown of Semiramis!" The story appeared in all the newspapers, and made Theodore frown. Soon the editors started receiving letters. One, from a jeweler, triggered a cataclysm when it was published. He said he had been born in Odessa but had lived for many years in Paris, and was well informed regarding the activities of the forgers of gold treasures in his native Crimea. He named a well-known counterfeiter. The man was, in his own way, an artist, a creator of antique jewelry one might say, largely unconcerned with the distinction between real and fake. His name was Israel Rouchomovsky.

The Reinach brothers' defense, backed by the entire French academic establishment, was precise and well argued. Héron de Villefosse wrote a detailed response to Furtwängler's accusation. Other specialists focused on the inscription. Nothing betrayed a forgery better: this one was perfect in terms of grammar, and the shape of the letters conformed to everything that was known about practices in the region at the time. Salomon, speaking in his own name, though one sensed that he was also speaking for his brother Theodore, was convinced he would have the last word. "Frankly, another campaign of this type and the opinion of Herr Furtwängler will no longer count for very much." Then he added, "The natural fate of beauty is to provoke slander."

But the piece had already been taken down from display. Charles Clermont-Ganneau, a member of the Institute and professor at the Collège de France, was charged with carrying out a definitive expert assessment. This was worse than the graphologists' analyses of the "note" during the Dreyfus affair. This scholar owed nothing to the Reinach clan. He was well acquainted with the arts of the East. He should have been able to produce an objective response. Theodore and Salomon did not doubt for a single second that he would do anything other than come out wholeheartedly in their defense. The affair was brought up in the Chamber of Deputies, and even the foreign press took an interest. The saga of the tiara delighted the journalists who traded in gossip. Caricatures were made, like the figurine of Theodore, a lorgnon perched on his nose, wearing a gold dunce's hat—he found it in a novelty shop. Wisecracks circulated about Rashumovsky, Tripatovsky, Machinovsky . . .

Nonetheless it took several weeks for the rumors to reach the ears of Israel Rouchomovsky. He was a perfectly decent man who was not expecting this kind of notoriety. When he realized that he had been paid 1,800 rubles—he calculated that was the equivalent of 5,000 francs—for a piece that was later bought for 200,000 francs, he wondered if he shouldn't head straight for Paris. He was afraid. Afraid that the Russian authorities would throw him in jail. In the Odessa Jewish community, everyone knew you had to keep your head below the parapet. He knew, deep down, that he had been making fakes. But because he was an observant Jew, respectful of tradition, of the laws of God and of the empire, he had never considered them as anything other than works of art inspired by the craftsmen of the ancient world, the glory of the region and of all Russia. Visitors from abroad liked to buy these reproductions of archaeological finds. All the aristocratic ladies wanted to wear jewelry like that worn by ancient Greek princesses. He loved his work, his family, his colleagues. He cared about his honor. He had been passionate about ancient art since his childhood at his father's house in Mozir, south of Minsk, where he decided he would rather become an engraver than a rabbi. His wife bore him several children. He had not always had the means to live well. One day he met the Hochmann brothers, heaven-sent men ready to pay him in silver. When he got wind from an old newspaper of the Montmartre poet's bizarre claim he was furious. No one was going to take credit for the Saitapharnes tiara as long as he lived! He alone, the finest of all Greek goldsmiths, was responsible for it.

Theodore was still convinced that the tiara was authentic. He was going to fight for it. It was all he thought about. Salomon, on the other hand, was beginning to have doubts. Theodore had the idea of writing to his uncle, of using the members of his wife's family who still lived in Odessa. The Ephrussi network in Odessa was still powerful. He wrote to the uncle that they had to find this "Razumovsky" immediately. The response was negative. All that the name evoked for them was Beethoven's Razumovsky Quartets, nothing else.

For years, every night in Kerylos's interior courtyard, Theodore would go over all the details of this storm. It went on for years, and he was taken by surprise at the surge of violence from every direction that he had entirely failed to see coming. The red tip of his cigarette glowed in the darkness. He had loved the past, he had loved his contemporaries, had been a parliamentary deputy representing the Savoie region, the people had granted him a morsel of their sovereign power, he cherished Plato's Republic and Athens, he believed in France and in liberty, he loved his wife, his children, he was contented, surrounded by his books, and when he looked out to sea from this rock, lines of verse from Homer came unbidden to his lips. He was the best of what this century had produced, and he knew it. Nothing had prepared him for this public humiliation. He was no more prepared for such ignominy than Dreyfus had been. He had never imagined that he and his family, devoted to art of every kind, to study, and to other people, could have provoked such hatred. Léon Daudet took to joking in literary salons about the winner of the "National Schools Circumcisiopetition." Disgrace carried the day.

Theodore learned from the newspapers that the goldsmith from Odessa had decided to come to Paris. At what moment did my dear Monsieur Reinach begin to wonder if he had, perhaps, made a mistake?

25

"I HAVE, OCCASIONALLY, BEEN MISTAKEN"

I found myself standing facing Grégoire Verdeuil. He was in shirtsleeves, stooped, thin, his eyes ringed with fatigue. His office walls were covered in architectural drawings. "Ariadne?" he said. "She wanted to avenge all the abandoned Ariadnes of literature, opera, art, sculpture, so she abandoned her husband. I thought you knew. I even wondered if she left me for you."

He was very open with me. Ariadne wanted children. They didn't have any. Was it he or she who couldn't? He blamed himself. He thought she must have fallen pregnant with someone else's child, and hadn't dared tell him, or had gone off with the father. He had no proof for any of this. He imagined it all and tortured himself with it.

Once the thought that a child might have been conceived in the steam bath at Kerylos, or in some other room—we made love all over the house—had stolen into the labyrinth of my unhappiness, I could not get it out of my mind. I had been sure that it was because she loved me like she had never loved anyone before, but now I wondered if the frenzy of the days we spent together was the passion of a woman desperate for a child. Had she conceived a child? It was possible. But she would have told me. We would have run away together to Nice, to Naxos, anywhere. Or maybe—and now I was torturing myself—she did have a child, but with a different person altogether, neither Grégoire nor Achilles.

She disappeared without leaving a note, without any money, without threats or anger, and she never contacted me again. Whom did she go with? Whom did she know, apart from me and her husband? I realized I knew nothing about her; I had never asked her anything about herself. Arrogant little fool that I was, I never wondered if she might have had other lovers, if she was lying to me as well; all I saw was our love, then I suffered from her silence, but it was because of my own hubris.

"I couldn't bear working for the Reinachs any more," Grégoire told me. "By superstition. Something about them invites betrayal. You must remember the story of the tiara." The last time I saw Ariadne she was leaving for Paris, and I asked her, as a kind of provocation, if she was meeting one of her lovers there. I smiled as I said it. "But I don't have any other lovers," she replied. How happy those words made me. But there was too much pride—call it stupidity—mixed in with my happiness. Instinct told me I could trust her. I never asked her anything about her family, the sister she was so close to, her friends, who perhaps were not so fond of poor Grégoire. I never worried about Ariadne. I thought only of myself. I never looked at her drawings as anything other than gifts for me; I never acknowledged she was an artist, that she had an unusual talent, that perhaps she even wanted to be a free woman. I told Grégoire I knew nothing. He looked me in the eye as we shook hands. I hated him and I pitied him.

Adolphe told me that he had heard early on about the arrival of the goldsmith from Odessa, impatient to proclaim his pride at having executed the masterpiece that was on display in the Louvre. He submitted himself to a barrage of questions. He was interrogated five times in a row, once locked inside a room with paper and pencils. He had to describe the object, draw it from memory. He had brought photographs with him showing the tiara, but without the dents that made it look like an archaeological find. His story was that two strangers had come to his workshop bearing books and templates. He was able to describe in great detail these well-known books by experts and academics. They told him that they had been commissioned to make a gift for a professor from Kharkov. They said nothing about a forgery.

Doubts persisted: perhaps he was a pathological liar? They put him through a test that left no one in any doubt. He was locked up inside a building opposite the Louvre, the Paris Mint. For one week, Rouchomovsky found himself in the finest gold workshops in the world. He was allowed no contact with the outside world. He created fragments in gold leaf: an ornamental motif and a small beaded border, like the one on the tiara. Then he began the real work. I was troubled when Adolphe, who was as meticulous as Joseph, his beloved father, was in his interminable articles, told me: "He made a sleeping Ariadne, accompanied by a small goddess of love playing with her veils, an erotic scene, and a head of either Themistocles or Pericles, in profile, that looked like a large hallmark. His Ariadne was beautiful. It was all very well done, but bore no comparison to the tiara." Had Adolphe seen me looking at Ariadne? He was quite capable of having understood long before me that I was in love with her, and that she would fall in love with me. I shall never know. Rouchomovsky asked for a large sheet of gold leaf. In a few days he produced a fragment with three bands of decoration, arranged in tiers, and part of an inscription.

"A slice of the tiara, like a piece of melon," said Adolphe, "It was a terrible day for the family. June 6, 1903. Impossible to continue arguing, at the risk of destroying ourselves through our obsession. We had lost our Dreyfus affair: Rouchomovsky proved beyond doubt that he was the creator of the Saitapharnes tiara."

Theodore wanted to carry on the fight. What if it wasn't entirely fake? If a part of the object in the Louvre was the real tiara? Did he still really believe this was possible?

In March 1903, sixteen-year-old Adolphe clipped a report from the newspaper: "In the wake of new information regarding the authenticity of the Olbia tiara, and serious doubts expressed by Monsieur Héron de Villefosse, the curator of Greek and Roman antiquities requested authorization from the Ministry of Public Instruction and Fine Art to remove said object from the museum galleries until further expert opinion has been obtained. This authorization was accorded immediately."

Rouchomovsky remained in the city, which he liked very much and where he had become quite a celebrity, discovering the glory of being an artist exhibited in Paris. He succeeded in convincing everyone of his honesty. The 1,800 rubles that he received for the tiara helped make his case: a decent price, for a nice piece of work, but quite implausible for a genuine antiquity. Nor was it the derisory sum that buys someone's silence in a counterfeit transaction. He began to make it known that he had some pieces he would be willing to show, a rhyton for drinking wine, in high Scythian style, a pectoral, a relief on an embossed disk showing Achilles and Minerva. At the Academy of Fine Art, a prankster started the rumor that Rouchomovksy had been nominated for one of the chairs of engraving that was waiting to be filled. At the 1903 Salon of French Artists, where he was awarded a medal, he was one of the highest profile artists to take part. He showed his masterpiece there: a skeleton in a tiny sarcophagus, as exquisite as the Fabergé eggs that were all the rage in the Russian court.

"Everyone knows this story except you, my poor Achilles. It's incredible how well they kept it from you. You aren't curious enough about the world around you. The tiara tarnished our family, and now it is being handed down to the next generation! In the November 1909 issue of *La Revue Blanche*, Apollinaire wrote a piece about art forgeries. He talked about the tiara. You must have read the Arsène Lupin story *The Hollow Needle* that was serialized that year in the newspaper. You remember? How we loved it! In his secret hiding place in Étretat, the gentleman-burglar had the real Saitapharnes. That's what is written, the tiara, it's Lupin who has it!" Adolphe stood on the table and laughed. The dog yapped at his feet, like in a play.

Theodore was deeply wounded. The attacks were directed at him, his family, his wife's family. The anti-Semites had a field day and he was horrified. He began spending more time alone in his office. He even avoided his friends: he read in their eyes that the names of the Rothschilds and Camondos would be remembered by posterity for their important donations to the

Louvre, while he was going to go down in history as the man who had cost the museum a fortune. He published incessantly. Everyone admired his books. In 1908, his name was cleared: he was elected a member of the Academy of Inscriptions and Belles-Lettres, finally joining Salomon there.

"We lost against those who hate the Jews, we lost against the Germans, can you imagine? They were all right and we were all wrong," said Adolphe. After that how could they ever look again at Furtwängler's compendium, his *Griechische Vasenmalerei*, on Greek vase painting, that Theodore used to spend hours reading, the sun playing over its pages. Salomon Reinach had begun an immense catalog of Greek sculpture, to stymie Furtwängler's research—Furtwängler was everywhere they looked. They loathed the man, because he was German, but they also admired him, because he was a great scholar. The library at Kerylos, the holy of holies, contained his entire oeuvre. They had placed the devil's tablets in their holy ark. He had trampled all over them during the Saitapharnes affair, while they continued to quote him politely in their own writing, even after his death in 1907. That was how they were. The three brothers were convinced that the tiara was authentic, because it was covered in motifs that Furtwängler had written about, proof of the great respect they had for him. He had no such scruples and called them ignoramuses and imbeciles, even though he had before his own eyes the very images that had inspired the forger. Adolphe told me that when he was at the French School at Athens, he saw a letter on the director's desk from his uncle Theodore, which ended with the words, "I have, occasionally, been mistaken."

Among the pile of records I have in Nice is a recording of Beethoven's seventh symphony conducted by Wilhelm Furtwängler. I had no idea, when I found it at the record store, that he was Adolf Furtwängler's son. I caught it on the radio: "Son of a great scholar and architect who led excavations at Aegina and Olympus." The presenter said that his best recordings were made during the war, but that there was no way of judging this anymore, since the wax molds had been expropriated by the Soviets. He mentioned a recording of the Seventh, made in November 1943, and an *Ode to Joy* Furtwängler conducted on the occasion of Hitler's birthday for an audience of wounded soldiers and leaders of the Reich. I was horrified. Reinach and Furtwängler both had a musician son. Léon Reinach was several years younger than Furtwängler's son. November 1943: the month that Léon was deported. "Furt," as my musician friends call him, must have offered a public apology because he makes recordings now with Yehudi Menuhin. I might buy them, but I'm not sure I could bear to listen to them.

The summer of 1914, Adolphe told me about that lost battle, and went even further: "That tiara was made for us, that's the worst part of the story. It came from the very edges of the Greek empire. Look at the places where my uncle led excavations, all those huge sites about which he wrote so many articles: Myrina, near Smyrna, that's where the statuettes were found; think about the islands, Thasos, my favorite, Imbros, Lesbos, facing the Turkish coast; on the other side there's Assos, where Aristotle was born . . . He went to Carthage, to Djerba, then to Odessa. But he sidestepped Athens and Sparta—he never went there. Did you notice that, Achilles? During our first voyage to

Greece, we didn't see the Parthenon. You were so disappointed. You know why? Because we, the Reinachs, we are Bohemians when we travel. We come from the margins of the Great Book. That's what we like, the mysterious city-state of Olbia, the steppes where Scythian horsemen rode, the kingdoms of Sudan, the monasteries on Mount Athos. Not Athens."

All Adolphe needed was to listen to his father's flamboyant and interminable perorations: he spent his time talking about democracy, fatherland, invoking the great men of the revolution who had brought equality, secularism, and brotherhood to France. Essentially, between 1789 and 1889, from the revolution to the Eiffel Tower, it was a new century of Pericles—while the brothers came from a barbarous tribe from the forests on the other side of the Rhine, who settled in French cities and ended up more Athenian than the Athenians, who felt like Romans in Rome, but who continued to appreciate borderlands. The Reinachs admired Alexander, they romanticized him, because he was from Macedonia, a rustic who raised horses, he was educated by Aristotle, and became the greatest of all the Greeks before dying at the very furthest edge of the empire. They liked the men who succeeded Alexander, the distillation of heroes and tyrants, Demetrius Poliorcetes, Eumenes of Cardia, Seleucus Nicator, Antigonos Monophthalmus, so many fabulous names, and Ptolemy Soter, who wanted to blend the heritage of the Pharaohs with the ideas of the Greeks.

That's why they got the tiara so completely wrong: it was everything that they liked, original, unique, and composed of quotations. They liked Hellenism burnished by the East, the Bible, Carthage, barbarians, the shepherds who brought mare's milk to Ovid when he was in exile on the banks of the Euxine. Adolphe told me that there is a painting of this somewhere by Delacroix, which Baudelaire praised to the skies.

"This is my heritage, Achilles. This is what I want to do: study how Greece spread across the whole of the Mediterranean, how it wasn't simply a miracle, but a protracted phenomenon, it didn't just bequeath us the Acropolis, but also, more importantly, all those forgotten temples, houses in composite styles, like ours, the last one to date. You feel it, don't you, that there is something Gallic about Kerylos. You can sense the influence of the tribe of the Parisii, the tribe of people gathered around an iron temple that points a thousand feet into the sky, with elevators in every corner. Every other archaeologist has gone to Attica and the Peloponnese; I shall go to Palestine, to dig in Jerusalem with the most modern techniques. I shall go and live there—why not, it's my land, though Papa and my uncles would be horrified to hear that; they have no other fatherland but France. I shall go to Crimea, I shall go to Africa, with my aunt Fanny and her piano—we will put it on wheels—that's how I shall carry on their work, and avenge them. Why must beauty always be pure? I want to display masterpieces born of amalgams, hybrids, conjunctions of different things that breed rare and unexpected artifacts. I want to go to Afghanistan, to see what happens to Greek and Roman sculpture when it rubs up against the art of India."

He thought he had his whole life ahead of him. His mustache was growing thicker and he was cheerful, serious, solid, clear-sighted, able to talk about his background and his family of marvelous visionaries in the same caustic tone that he used about himself.

He spent his life reading and writing. One of his cousins was like him, young Bertrand, the son of Léon and Béatrice; he was passionate about cabinet-making, intrigued by the mechanism of an eighteenth-century *table à la Bourgogne* made by Jean-François Oeben that could be transformed into a low church chair or a desk with a shelf, which I always admired at his parents' house. He wanted to become a craftsman and he had real talent, he was brilliant with his hands. I remember him playing with the dog he adopted. Poor, murdered Bertrand. The Germans were great humanists too—they loved the arts of antiquity, had admired Greece for centuries, they translated Plato—none of which stopped the Nazis from becoming executioners. That is the other reason why I have for so long hated to hear about those things that I once loved, that were part of my youth. It must be why I paint white and yellow squares on a blue background, a few geometrical shapes that are impossible to interpret, paintings that people like, I hope, that they remember, are perhaps even moved by, that they can linger in front of, could live with in their homes every day, even if they know nothing.

26

THE CLOGGED HEATING SYSTEM

In May 1920 I was passing through Paris. I stopped in front of an art gallery. The painting I saw in the window made me want to start painting again. It had been several months since I stopped drawing; I hadn't been able to do it anymore. I forced myself to stop thinking about the daughter or son of Ariadne—it was too unbearable—and I chased away the image of Ariadne too, whom I had been drawing obsessively from memory. It was killing me.

I went inside. That day I met Kahnweiler, who told me about Picasso; three months later, he sold my first painting. I liked Picasso straightaway, I understood him, Picasso the Cubist as much as the Picasso who painted bodies of monumental women. He reminded me of what Adolphe had said about his family, the way Picasso combined classical rigor—that of the academic masters that Theodore had brought to Kerylos for the peristyle—with the art of African masks. A little barbarity, a kind of primitive force, was what was needed to brutalize and bring the dusty plaster casts to life. That's what I learned at Kerylos, where I never dared show any of my paintings. I surprised them all during those years: a rough mountain peasant polished up with a bit of Greek grammar. I owe it to Adolphe more than to

Theodore. They invite betrayal, all of them, Grégoire told me, advising me to flee, as he had fled—"There's something about them." There you have it, I betrayed them.

It took me one week to decide to become a painter and to forget all about classical inspiration. But I don't disavow any of it, the paintings in the church in Cargèse, what Eiffel taught me, the Pointe des Fourmis, the frescoes on Mount Athos, my drawings of Ariadne naked. I created my own alphabet from it all, have inscribed my own clay tablets. Today, I exhibit alongside Braque, Picasso, Juan Gris. I suppose I wanted to shock the Reinachs, with whom I no longer have much of a connection. I find collectors who buy my work and a gallery in Nice exhibits them. I won't say any more, it's all in my catalogs anyway. When Picasso began to paint nymphs with pale thighs and boys playing panpipes, I realized that my revolt against Kerylos had been perhaps a little naïve, but I carried on. The master, the great Pablo, told me to my great surprise, when we met for the first time at Kahnweiler's house, that he had always dreamed of Greece. He's always been very generous to me, and owns several of my paintings.

After my early success, I moved to Paris. I still went to see the Reinachs from time to time. I bought books. And now suddenly here they are again, all my friends, so old now.

Sacrilegious thought: they were ignorant. They didn't read novels; they said they were a waste of time. I would have liked to go to the bookshop in Nice and buy a Giraudoux or a Morand, something by André Gide or Valery Larbaud, but I didn't dare because I was afraid of what they would think of me. They missed out on all the great writers of their time, one by one, stayed loyal to Demosthenes and Thucydides, and when they wanted to frighten themselves, they read their friend Rostand or one of Corneille's brother's forgotten plays. What might have happened if Theodore Reinach had invited Cocteau to visit Kerylos when he was staying on the coast at Lavandou with Georges Auric and Raymond Radiguet, when Radiguet was writing *Count d'Orgel's Ball*?

It's unimaginable. Cocteau would have rather liked it, he would have turned up with his drawings of the Sphinx, perhaps he would have thought up Oedipus in *The Infernal Machine* in the 1920s, they could have talked about Sophocles and Euripides. But no, my poor Theodore would have quickly decided that he was wasting his time listening to this worldly illusionist, and he would, with his exquisite manners, have politely shown him the door.

One day, about a year after Theodore's death, I bought a fat book. I didn't know what it was, but I was taken by its white cover and blue lettering: *Ulysses*, by James Joyce. I read it in confusion, without understanding it, though I was entertained. I thought it was going to be a modern adaptation of the *Odyssey*, which it is in a way, but it's a hundred other things as well. Theodore would have liked it, there was something of his spirit that I recognized, the art of laughter in books. I thought it was a comedy, a cabaret. I skimmed through some chapters because I didn't understand a thing; I read every word of the brothel scenes. And then I began to underline entire passages. I still have it, it's legendary now, and my first edition is worth a lot of money.

On page 150, a professor with owlish spectacles speaks. I imagined the delight of the three brothers if they had read it:

"I teach the blatant Latin language. I speak the tongue of a race the acme of whose mentality is the maxim: time is money. Material domination. *Dominus!* Lord! Where is the spirituality? Lord Jesus! Lord Salisbury. A sofa in a westend club. But the Greek!"

A few pages on is a pastiche of a play, with stage directions in italics, in a schoolboyish humor that is very Reinach: *"Bloom explains to those near him his schemes for social regeneration. All agree with him. The keeper of the Kildare Street museum appears, dragging a lorry on which are the shaking statues of several naked goddesses, Venus Callipyge, Venus Pandemos, Venus Metempsychosis, and plaster figures, also naked, representing the new nine muses, Commerce, Operatic Music, Amor, Publicity, Manufacture, Liberty of Speech, Plural Voting, Gastronomy, Private Hygiene, Seaside Concert Entertainments, Painless Obstetrics and Astronomy for the People."*

Greece continued to live, though the Reinachs had no role in it. Ariadne and I shut ourselves up in the house to draw, to draw each other. The evening that I turned on the hot water faucets in the thermal baths, she posed for me, naked, in the position of Ingres's bather, in front of one of the great slabs of tiger-striped marble. The drawing looked a little like a Picasso, though at the time I had never heard of him. I loved Ariadne's neck, her damp back, the tilt of her head. A preparatory drawing for a painting that I never finished, I never even sketched it, for this house was constructed to live out love affairs that never happened, for writers who were never invited, for artists who didn't appreciate it until it was too late.

Back then all the artists were flocking to the Villa Noailles, in Hyères, which was the height of fashion in 1925. After my first exhibition, my paintings furnished me with a passport to this world. It took me a while to enjoy the Roaring Twenties; I had been badly wounded, I thought it was all over, so I did not plunge into this new era right away. Picasso I came to know in more recent years, after the Second World War. Whenever we meet we embrace. People do not dare approach him; he is very intimidating. After the Liberation I began again from scratch. I became the most radical of abstract painters. Now I make minimalist art. More and more collectors are buying my most recent paintings.

Meanwhile, I still have not found my treasure: Alexander's crown. I decided that I had to unthinkingly obey the anonymous postcard's tacit injunction; taking it home with me is the only real reason for my return. Or perhaps I am lying to myself and I wanted to see all this one last time. Nothing prevented me from trying to find the crown the day I came back to the villa after the Germans looted the house. But I didn't dare. It's taken me years to dare. In the adventures of Arsène Lupin there's always a moment when the hero finds himself with an hour, not a minute longer, to locate an object. Instead of beginning methodically, with the tension mounting, he sits down on a chaise longue and smokes a cigar. At the last second, he gets up, adjusts his monocle, and goes straight over to the hiding place. I fear I don't have that level of expertise. I'm an amateur. There are so many potential places to stash something away in this house: all the rooms have false ceilings concealing beams and secret hiding spaces. I know where the trapdoors are in the system Pontremoli invented for keeping the rooms cool in summer and warm in winter.

I had one idea left. The huge hot water balloon that Theodore was so proud of. He showed it triumphantly to Eiffel to prove that he really was the last of the Greeks, the most modern of men.

I descended the staircase to the laundry. The basement was full of old trunks holding clothes and toys—nothing had been moved. The Germans hadn't touched a thing down here. The furnace was where it always was, painted white, with a lever and wide steel pipes. Hot air used to be pumped out from here and sent around the house, imprisoned by the marble.

I wondered if under the cover there might not be enough space to conceal a box with the conqueror's crown inside. The hot water system doesn't work very well anymore, which hardly matters since Kerylos is now a summer palace. I couldn't unscrew the large metal disc, all clogged up with limescale. I tapped the tank, which sounded full. I didn't have the strength. It would have to be taken apart, sawn into rings. If the last treasure of the Macedonian king really had been hidden there, it must be wedged right inside and I don't know if it would even be possible to get it out. Pontremoli had warned me that the whole system needed to be serviced and the tank emptied every two or three years; it was done in the early days, then forgotten.

I still occasionally see Pontremoli, the dear man. He's not in good shape, and I think he senses he is going to die soon. He has received every honor, not that he cares. I don't know if Prince Rainier invited him to the wedding, though how apt it would be to have the creator of the Monegasque architectural style sitting in the nave of the cathedral. But probably nobody thought to invite him, and anyway he is too frail to go to such occasions.

He has one particular obsession. He can go on about it for hours at a time, in an utterly scathing tone as if he were lecturing his students at the Beaux-Arts: he detests Le Corbusier. He says that if one were to listen to this prophet, this dictator, this man who knows nothing about history or the major architectural movements, about ornamentation or formal restraints, of which Kerylos is in a way the most beautiful and simple expression, this man who knows nothing about the art of living in a beautiful house, everyone would end up living in rabbit hutches. Pontremoli is tireless on the subject. He sees that young architects are drawn to Le Corbusier, considering him to be the successor to the master builders of the Parthenon and Chartres. But every time he hears that, the old lion awakens and flies into a rage: "'Corbu,' as they call him, is an opportunist, a schemer, a friend to all the Vichy clique, a bloody Swiss man who's only good for building prisons—he should have ended up in one himself . . ." I have not dared to tell him that I am going to visit Le Corbusier in his little cabin in Roquebrune. He lives there as if he were on a boat, a naked, barrel-chested Diogenes, an old wise man with whom Monsieur Reinach would have had lots of lively disagreements. His monk's cell is the most beautiful 150 square feet imaginable, with the sea and the trees right within reach.

27

ECHOES IN THE GARDEN AND AMONG THE ROCKS

Theodore and his brother Salomon were, in everybody's eyes, the brothers behind the Louvre's purchase of the most expensive forgery in history. When at last I understood this, it shed new light on the saga of this family. I sat down on a bench outside the front door and gazed at Beaulieu stretching out before me. I thought about what must have happened. Kerylos had been built after years of vilification, defamation, expert assessments. All their enemies, a great pack of mediocrities, crawled out of the undergrowth. Years later, I went with one of my girlfriends to the Nice carnival, trying to distract myself and forget Ariadne. Long after I would have thought that the scandal had become a distant memory, I saw a float with the tiara fashioned out of lemons, and an effigy of Monsieur Reinach wearing a large pair of spectacles and a ball and chain around his ankle, alongside the director of the Louvre in a pair of pajamas. Everyone was still talking about it: it was a curse, their crime, how unjust it was. Happily, the headland of Kerylos was a miniature version of the Athos peninsula; they could just close it off and the villa became an inaccessible cloister.

Theodore had wanted calm, the Mediterranean, music, and a not too large garden. In front of the house he had placed some statues, but not too many. He didn't position them on pedestals overlooking the sea so that they could be seen from a distance—not because he was afraid of what people might say, but because he preferred them this way. His statues are set back, close to the house and almost hidden among the trees. They are copies of bronzes discovered at Herculaneum, bought at the archaeological museum in Naples. There is one I particularly like, a young woman with regular features and white enamel eyes, adjusting her cloak and hitching it up onto her shoulder. Just beyond her a faun dances among the tea roses.

The neighboring houses vied with each other, with their French parterres and their English gardens. Béatrice Ephrussi combined the two; the genius Rostand was unable to choose between them at Arnaga. Theodore contented himself with choosing plants that he liked, sowing them here and there and leaving them to grow. The gardener came once a week, and was instructed to do as little as possible. The Pointe des Fourmis gradually began to resemble a real Greek island. I don't know whose idea it was to put down gravel, and I imagine someone comes to kill the weeds now as well. For Theodore there were only flowers, of all kinds, in all sorts of colors, and, in a corner, herbs for the kitchen.

We used to work out in the garden. I fixed a rope to one of the bars over the portico and we did our exercises every morning, with the children. Basileus barked like the devil. Fanny's chambermaid, who was a little scared of him, missed Cerberus. I never thought of myself as living in a museum. This house was a folly, a considered work of delirium, but above all, it was an act of optimism, proof that one could travel back in time, just like resetting a clock, and resist the outside world. I have not visited all the Greek-style villas in existence, but I don't think they installed ropes to stretch their limbs, or allowed plants of all kinds to grow wild. I would like to visit the Villa Stuck, in Munich, which I have heard is beautiful, if a little dull. I have been to Corfu, where I visited the house called the Achilleion, its slightly naïve Greek decor invented for Empress Sisi, with Achilles's chariot painted, disturbingly, in the style of a Viennese café. The Empress of Austria's villa—she would have been quite capable of putting up parallel bars and croquet hoops—later became the home of the Kaiser, and his ghost seemed still to haunt the place, guarded by young soldiers dressed like foot soldiers from the battle of Marathon. In Bavaria I visited the Glyptothek, in Munich, built by King Ludwig I to display the statues discovered on the island of Aegina, where, in a field of wildflowers, the most beautiful temple was found, dating to before the Parthenon. There in Munich, where ancient pediments had been restored in a slightly heavy-handed manner, the galleries were painted blue and red, faintly echoing the pompous study sheets made by the students at the École des Beaux-Arts in Paris. Apparently Ludwig I—foreshadowing his descendant Ludwig II's follies, the fairytale castle, the miniature Versailles, the Wagnerian forest sanctuary—built himself a Roman villa, the Pompeiianum, but I have never seen it.

These extravagant white elephants were nothing like Kerylos. Theodore appreciated subtle colors, pale walls juxtaposed with marble; he wanted butterflies and bees, ladybugs and beetles, to settle on the stones, a subtle symphony, nothing like the aggressive polychromy that was all the rage in the nineteenth century.

He preferred Debussy's version of antiquity to that portrayed in Verdi's operas, with their trumpets and cymbals. His house would have fit in India or Japan.

My whole world changed, my whole life, my environment, I traveled and went to war, I matured rapidly. I had to be agile. Today, sitting on a red bench in the garden, I thought back to the age I was, to the person I was, to the paltry things I knew—it is all so hard to believe. I murmured some lines by Mallarmé, lines that no one ever told me to read, I found them for myself:

Nothing, nor ancient gardens mirrored in the eyes,
Shall hold back this heart that bathes in waters its delight.

The trees are overgrown, the soil has been dug up to plant idiotic new bushes, the bees and butterflies no longer come in such numbers, swimmers climb up onto the rocks, passersby can walk all the way around the peninsula, coming through the underground gallery that remains open day and night, hardly the kind of place where someone would hide a treasure. This is not the place I dreamed of.

Adolphe loved this garden that was allowed to grow wild. He loved its modest proportions, so unlike the parterres and fields of La Motte-Servolex. He didn't like the Reinachs' large chateau in the Savoie region, with its muddy English-style bridle paths. But many people thought Villa Ephrussi and La Motte-Servolex better reflected material success than Kerylos, which resembled nothing else.

Fanny Reinach had a chambermaid who complained endlessly: she didn't like the house, it was too hot in summer, too cold in winter, the beds with their leather webbing weren't comfortable, all those straight lines, it was all so austere. She didn't dare say that she didn't understand how anyone could have spent so much to build it. There was couch grass growing outside the front door. Her mistress was too proper to put up with her husband's caprices. When you think of all the things Madame Ephrussi has done, now there's a fine lady who built a proper palace, its fountains even more fabulous than the ones at Versailles, because they are by the sea! She ventured: "You know what would be pretty, if Madame liked the idea, would be a rose garden, with arches. I saw a flowerbed filled with dahlias in Nice, on the Promenade des Anglais—just think what lovely bouquets you could make." She was only happy when the family decamped to the mountains, to the Savoie that Theodore had fallen in love with. He had bought a property near La Motte-Servolex, a charming village surrounded by cows and sheep, an array of cheeses, and during the years he was creating Kerylos he was also modernizing his "chateau." The result was a horror.

La Motte-Servolex became a neo-Louis XIII iced cake, an indigestible fondue, a ghastly subprefecture surrounded by fields. It had more than fifty windows, mantelpieces, corniches, pediments everywhere; it was the apotheosis of excess. The architect was called Louis Legrand, and the long-running joke in the family was that no one was ever going to talk about the age of Louis Legrand. Several years after his death, the family decided to donate the chateau to the region. But Madame Reinach's chambermaid loved everything about it: the mountain air, the fluffy eiderdowns, the huge grates, the delicate rococo furniture, the fringed curtains, the plush upholstered armchairs.

One day she ran away from Kerylos, brave woman, and left a note in which she didn't even ask for a reference for another job: "I can't stand your house any longer. I don't want to work here anymore. I hope Madame is not too angry with me." They soon found someone else to take her place.

Theodore was happy at La Motte-Servolex, as if, from time to time, he grew tired of Greece. I found him in good spirits there, in his four-poster bed, surrounded by bourgeois furniture, relaxed, reading aloud the regional newspaper that he financed, *Le Démocrate savoisien*, which adorned his silver-plated breakfast tray every morning without fail. Over the mantelpiece there was a play on words in Latin: *Servo lex*, "I serve the law," the motto that every parliamentarian had to adopt, except that it wasn't even kitchen-sink Latin—it should have read *Servo legem*. He loved this silly little schoolboy joke, he was very proud of it. Was he trying to impress the locals? He was a different person there, an opulent potentate, a satrap in his satrapy, the Republic personified, all perfectly suited to this Louis XIII style. He was a democrat who acted like an aristocrat and became a tyrant, a lover of Greece who was agoraphobic, a monogamous man who was a seducer, a sophisticated museologist who was taken in by forgers, the creator of Kerylos who slept so well surrounded by this appalling decor. Basileus ran free in the woods, happy as a hunter.

"Do you think that we're obsessed with nobility?" Adolphe asked me. "I always found it quite absurd that Adolf Reinach, whose name I share—without an *f* at the end though, thank goodness—went to collect his baron's title in Italy. My father's first cousin, Baron Jacques de Reinach, who changed his name from Jacob, saw himself in competition with the Camondo and the Cahen d'Anvers clans—that's the snobbish side of the family. The Cahens became counts and changed their name to Cahen d'Anvers because they were pouring money into Italian royalty. The Camondos became counts in 1860, the year of Theodore's birth. And that's not to mention my cousin Viktor von Ephrussi! They wanted to be like the Rothschilds, that's what I think. The "Baron de Reinach" was actually my grandfather, because Papa married his daughter you know, we are like royal dynasties, we intermarry, did you know that I am half noble, I am Reinach y Reinach, Reinach squared. It's all completely ridiculous."

Nobility, as far as he was concerned, meant having the right to do everything differently than ordinary people. In his family, they all managed that quite well, not to mention the pleasure they took in not doing things to please other people, and their disdain for idle chatter. Kerylos was a manor house without a single pack of cards; there was no embroidering around the fireplace, or boredom dissipated by charades and board games, no suicide on the way home from the casino—an invention that brought the suffering and febrility of the aristocracy within reach of the merely wealthy.

I always wondered what the parents of the three brothers must have been like. I did find out in the end, but there too the history of this lineage, without being a secret, was not a topic of conversation. Hermann Reinach's family was originally Swiss—from the town of Reinach—and went to Germany in the eighteenth century. He was born in Frankfurt. His grandfather, from Mayence, served Napoleon and his brother Jérôme, King of Westphalia. These souvenirs of empire pleased Adolphe, there was something thrilling about it, adventure, the elegant cut of the hussar's jacket. Hermann Reinach came to Paris under the July monarchy. From his beginnings as a courtier he ended up branching out and setting himself up as a banker, becoming involved in the world of politics. Theodore told me that his father was a close acquaintance of Thiers, and indeed, Joseph gave the little bespectacled man a good place in his anthology of French oratory, one of his more successful books. I think they admired him, their family owed him a great deal—though for many people, Thiers was the man responsible for violently crushing the Paris Commune.

Little by little the pieces of the puzzle were falling into place; it had taken me a while, but now I thought I could put the whole thing together. The Reinachs made good investments, in the Spanish railways and other innovations, and they were wealthy and discreet, living in their large house in Saint-Germain-en-Laye. Adolf was Hermann's twin brother, the father of Baron Jacques de Reinach, who committed suicide at the time of the Panama scandal. Hermann had a beautiful house that testified to his great wealth, a minute's walk from the birthplace of Louis XIV, on the royal esplanade in Saint-Germain-en-Laye; it is still there, you can't miss it. There is even a plaque on the house today, I believe.

At his death in 1899, I read in a newspaper I found in Theodore's bedroom, Hermann had amassed a fortune of fourteen million gold francs. An enormous sum, abstract—at least for me, a Corsican shepherd. For the three brothers it meant that money would never be an issue. They had a private income from stocks and shares and property, which allowed them to devote themselves to serious things, politics, the Louvre, which interested them more than hunting—the passion of Béatrice de Camondo, the wife of Theodore's son Léon—and joining the Jockey Club—something that appealed to that dilettante, Proust's Charles Swann. A similar thing occurred in a family of German bankers, the Warburgs, whose eldest son was passionate about the study of art history: Aby Warburg, it was said, exchanged his birthright with his brothers not against a bowl of lentils, like Esau in the Bible, but against the promise that during his lifetime his brothers would buy him all the books he needed for his studies.

In the Reinach family, the banking vocation had died out. The brothers kept their eyes on their well-managed fortune while devoting themselves entirely to the allure of true wealth for those who have everything: books. I took a while to understand: for my mother, who was poor, the daughter of people who were even more impoverished, money was the only thing that mattered. She would doubtless have been happy if Theodore had landed me a job in a bank instead of giving me grammar lessons. She would have loved if I had married one of those daughters of millionaires who accompanied their mothers on visits to the Reinachs. The cost of the tiara was irrelevant to Joseph, Salomon, and Theodore; money meant little to them. They were denounced for their greed, the way this scandalous acquisition had contributed to the ruin of France. Their fortune, which they were only distantly involved with, collapsed between the wars. I've seen a new generation of Reinachs boast that they always travel third class, because "when you have a book in your hand you are comfortable anywhere." This lack of interest in money is the result of three or four generations of great wealth. Adolphe was already like that: "This garden, Achilles, is all I need if I want to get some fresh air and look at the sea, do a little exercise, listen to the piano through the open window. Do you find orchids chic? This fashion for black flowers, dreary tulips, blue hydrangeas forced to grow in slate. In Papa's house in Paris that's all there is, in Sèvres vases—he has no taste. Uncle Theodore pretends he has no time for the garden, but you can't imagine how much he loves it: he forbids cut flowers inside the house, and he is absolutely right. Papa thinks it makes him look like an elegant, worldly man to have orchids on the mantelpiece. But we don't need these relics of the nobility, these salons for old dowagers or the little court of swooning young pages who follow the old Empress Eugénie whenever she comes to Menton. Did you know she is still alive? Nobility is science, arts, letters, Rostand's panache. Do you think I'd be any good at writing plays?"

And he jumped off the parapet, made three balletic leaps on the stones, and dived fully clothed from the top of the biggest rock, all the time watched by Madame Reinach's chambermaid, who threw up her hands and then ran to fetch him a towel.

28

THE ART OF DINING LYING DOWN

A day like any other, during the last war. The shelves in the dining room knocked down, smashed plates all over the floor. It was raining in the courtyard, in front of the frescoes. I didn't linger there.

I was the first to go in, I happened to be in the area, a few days after the house had been looted by the Nazis. The caretaker had rushed to Nice and asked me to come to the house right away. The dairywoman's daughter—a beauty who was going to find herself facing a lot of problems after the Liberation—had already warned me over the telephone.

I swept everything up, the pieces of plates and bowls that could be salvaged, anything that was still intact. The villa had been turned upside down, but not destroyed and not emptied. They had gone through all the closets. All the papers had been taken away. The worst wreckage was in the dining room. I picked up the shards one by one, instinctively, respectfully, because I didn't know what else to do.

Ariadne always admired these plates and bowls when she was invited with the Pontremolis for dinner in the Triklinos. Theodore had wanted to avoid copies. He couldn't see himself eating meals out of fake Greek vases. Those in museums are often ornate pieces, luxury objects, offerings to be placed in graves. He imagined everyday Greek tableware, the kind that potters took out of the kiln and then perfunctorily daubed with a few garlands, the Greek equivalents of the ones discovered in the ruins of Pompeii and Herculaneum.

There are several cupboards in the kitchen. I went downstairs but the Germans had emptied them out as well. There was nothing to save. I pocketed a little shard. In the same way that they had chosen different woods for their color, perfume, and density, from countries that the ancient Greeks hadn't known, they had taken inspiration from Korean potters. The ceramicist had elected to use stoneware rather than terracotta, sometimes adding a little kaolin. His pieces used limited colors to complement the palette of the house: beige, ocher, and black, simple and elegant.

In the dining room, daybeds suggested that they took their meals lying down. One was higher than the others; it was, according to the classical Greek way, reserved for the master of the house. For effect, it was perfect, but I never saw Theodore perching there. He used to sit facing his wife at one of the little tables, the woven leather daybeds serving simply as decoration.

The dining room, with its offset angles, was, to his eyes, perfect, because it was too small for large festive meals. I decided not to bother poking around the ceiling with its flaking blue paint, and I couldn't see anywhere that could serve as a hiding place in this room. The pictures on the walls, copied from those in the museum in Naples, suggest easel paintings, which already existed in ancient times. The Germans had left them hanging on the walls. I peered closely at them, lifting each one by one:

behind them there was only plaster. I took the few remaining plates and dishes down from the shelves for the pleasure of looking at them, holding each piece in my hand, feeling the slightly rough surface.

In the Triklinos, my principal memory is of the person who had the biggest appetite, who liked to stay at the table the longest, Salomon. He had two scholarly passions. Beside his articles, his enormous notebooks, and his indexes—his greatest joy, his treat, was doing the index for a book, a task that he refused to delegate to anyone else—he liked to write the kind of books that anyone could understand. I liked that very much, because he tried them on me first, in the form of long after-dinner conversations, and he always gave me a copy as soon as it was published. I have kept them all, dedicated to me in his lively handwriting. He published short, well-written digests, written in the tone of a discussion between friends, that one could carry around in one's pocket, and they were very successful. The best known was *Apollo*, with its green cover decorated with a gold coin in relief, which told the story of art from cavemen to modern American sculptors. He also wrote *Cornélie, or Latin without Weeping*; *Sidonie, or French without Suffering*; and *Eulalie, or Greek without Tears*, my favorite. These books ought to have been handed out in all the schools in France, and perhaps if they had been, we wouldn't be where we are today. I—the person who ended up intentionally forgetting everything I ever knew about Latin and Greek—wonder now if the people who know nothing are having the last laugh. For Salomon, a scientific truth was one that could be explained. The course he taught at the Louvre was very popular; he used to tell us about it over dinner at Kerylos, describing the oppressed women of the world sitting in the first row, drinking in his every word, while he sat preening himself in his pulpit, like the cockerel in the lower courtyard. Joseph laughed, not realizing that his brothers teased him for the same manner, the way he had of bringing into the conversation the tall silhouette of Léon Gambetta, whom he had worked for as a top advisor. Occasionally, when he came down to Beaulieu, he would go to visit Gambetta's grave in Nice. I once heard him say in this very room, "the great minister," as if he had a partridge in his mouth.

One day, in my presence, Joseph and Theodore brought up the subject of Salomon's affairs; in lowered voices they described his relationship with the scandalous Liane de Pougy, who was not accustomed to erudition but who never erred in matters of great wealth. Salomon, permitting himself a fling with the most intelligent of the demimondaines, had brought the Reinach clan into the closed circle of those who ruin themselves for disreputable ladies, from Ludwig I of Bavaria with Lola Montès, to Count Henckel von Donnersmarck with La Païva.

Eiffel often came for dinner in the Triklinos, and, using his aches and pains as a pretext, he would immediately lie down, sighing as he was served a haunch of venison or some iced delicacy. He always seemed to me to be both incredibly young and terribly old: he was born in 1832, at the beginning of the reign of Louis-Philippe. His father, Alexandre, whom he used to tell me about, had been an officer in Napoleon's Grande Armée. Monsieur Eiffel was also called Alexandre, as Theodore liked to remind him, pointing out that he was Greek too in his own way, but everyone else used his second name, Gustave. When

I was thirteen or fourteen he was always traveling, even though he had been told to rest in Beaulieu: he wanted to know the results of his meteorological laboratory at the top of his tower, he wanted to position a wireless transmitter there, he was conducting experiments in aerodynamics and he claimed that he would be able to study the law of free fall from the top of his 984-foot tower better than Galileo from the top of the tower of Pisa. He told the coachman, the cooks, the chambermaids, my mother, me, my little brother, that the Eiffel Tower would soon be used for everything: it was going to light up Paris, become a military observatory, a beacon for dirigible balloons, it was his obsession, his fixation—he wanted to die safe in the knowledge that his monument would live on.

And I, at fifteen, had the luck to see them together in this room. I compared them, of course. On one side the brilliant engineer who had built himself a house worthy of the Renaissance, overflowing with crystal and silver, on the other the man who embodied ancient history and had turned instinctively toward purity of line, simplicity of form and central heating. On the one side, stone balustrades, on the other metal balconies, as if the two men had swapped places. "My dear old Eiffel, you were right, before your time!"

"And you, young Reinach, you understood that ancient Greece is the future, whereas I, thanks to my dear father and mother, never learned Greek, and now it's too late."

"Well, do you think I studied your pneumatic problems?"

"Reinach, you are too modest, you won the prize for physics in the national competition. You wrote, I seem to recall, on Archimedes's screw and Pythagoras's theorem."

These after-dinner conversations went on for hours. Never with any ill will, the conversation rarely focused on people; they preferred to talk about what they had read. They had memories of books the way other people recall stories of hunting and fishing, or love affairs. After dinner they would go and sit in the Andron to smoke and drink cognac, while the women settled in the Oikos and opened up the piano.

On our return from Athos, a lunch was held here, with Eiffel, who wanted to hear about it all. I was invited. I heard Theodore lie, while Adolphe and I remained silent: we had not found anything, it was a false lead, Alexander's grave was not there. He described the monks' filthy food, their Masses in the middle of the night. Eiffel joked, "If I had been there, I would have looked harder! You thought you didn't need my services, that was a great shame!"

As the years went by I found myself less and less able to bear being at these meals, but if I do not write about them now there will be nothing left but a handful of dust and a few broken plates.

29

THE ANDRON, WHERE THE REINACHS ENTERTAINED KINGS ON STORMY NIGHTS, AND WHERE THESEUS FOUGHT THE MINOTAUR

A party at Kerylos was not a frequent occurrence. The house was visible to all from the beach, but few had ever visited, simply because it wasn't very accessible. Some evenings the house was lit up, but it was impossible to hold large receptions there. The largest room is the Andron, in ancient Greece the part of the house reserved for men, although the Reinachs permitted women to enter. I was allowed to be involved when gala dinners were held there, and I helped move the heavy furniture and set up round tables with vases of flowers, to stunning effect: the red marble, called "peach blossom" marble, harmonized with the fabric on the doors, and candlelight reflected in the silver vases glowed against the south-facing windows that looked out onto the sea. Serviettes embroidered with the letter *R* were emphatically not Grecian: they were the same ones used for republican banquets at the family chateau in La Motte-Servolex. Theodore refused to allow the library to be used for these dinners, although that would have meant more tables could be laid and more people invited: no impious guests were permitted to enter the sanctuary.

The Belgian King Léopold II once attended a party here, looking extremely smug about owning the colossal Villa

Leopolda a short walk away. Theodore was entirely unmoved by his presence. He had known more than a few kings in his time. Several had been his guests at the house, and he would welcome them humming, "Here comes the King," from *La Belle Hélène.* King Gustaf V of Sweden thought the garden would have been improved with the addition of a tennis court—tennis was his passion—but they would have had to invent one worthy of the Olympics, a challenge that Pontremoli had failed to take up. George I of Greece borrowed some ideas from Kerylos to render the royal family's residence, the Tatoi Palace, more authentically Greek. The president, Armand Fallières, on vacation in Monaco, was keen to visit out of democratic curiosity. He greeted Basileus, who barked ferociously as he always did, as an equal. He asked if his name was Argos, Odysseus's dog who was the first to recognize Ulysses upon his return to Ithaca, and the assembled company chuckled appreciatively at this witticism—which it wasn't, really. In his strong accent of the southwest, he demanded to know every last detail about the gratings that separated the Andron from the peristyle—he was the grandson of a blacksmith. Theodore congratulated him in front of everyone for the decision to move Zola's body to the Pantheon, and they discussed whether Captain Dreyfus, too, might one day take his place in the temple of great men.

I saw few members of the Institute at these parties: Monsieur Reinach was perhaps a little unwilling to show his fellow academics what a man of means he was. He bequeathed the villa to his colleagues with the idea that they would continue to nourish its spirit, but he wanted his children to be able to continue to visit. It was what Justine the cook called a "donation on condition that the juiciest part of the fruit was retained," and evidently the best solution.

During King Léopold's visit a huge storm broke out. Rain began to fall, all the doors were closed, and the storm grew stronger and stronger. I was an extra in a white jacket, and my job was to ensure that everything ran smoothly. The king stood up, made one toast to the Reinachs and another to Pericles, then requested that the windows be opened. The guests were invited to go outside to watch the roaring waves and the lightning in the night sky, as if it were a performance. The house proved that it could withstand a storm. All the guests in their evening dress were soaked, the women's gowns looked like rags, it was like a ceremony in Africa for the return of the sun; mesmerized, the guests stood around the white-bearded sovereign, who looked like Poseidon and was pretending to control the elements. I have glorious memories of that night. A kind of lunacy had taken over the house. Seeing this room again, I can barely believe such scenes ever took place. Everything is so quiet now. Arrayed on console tables along the walls are bronze and plaster statues from the Naples archaeological museum, where they have been making copies for tourists for over a hundred years. One shows Alexander on horseback. I picked it up and inspected it—perhaps the horseman's gaze was directed toward a slab of marble that would slide open. I found nothing. My first thought had been that the Andron would be the most appropriate place to hide Alexander's crown. But I found nothing this afternoon. What if the Nazis had found it? Perhaps they had taken not only the Reinach papers but the crown as well? There were enough brilliant scholars in their ranks who might have imagined it crowning their terrible Führer, after he became master of the whole world.

There is one other possible hiding place, the throne, the always-empty chair, reserved for the ancestors. Pontremoli's design is majestic and light, and Bettenfeld surpassed himself in its construction. I have always wondered if it was Homer's throne—I could imagine his ghost seated upon it, bathing in the adulation of all the great writers who came after him, like in Ingres's painting, *The Apotheosis of Homer,* which looks rather like a school class photograph. Adolphe, as a joke, used to call it Achilles's chair, and he showed me a photograph of the painting by Léon Bénouville, *The Wrath of Achilles*, in which the hero, looking very fierce, sits naked and draped in a large white sheet. It was he who gave me the idea, later on, to sketch Ariadne in this chair. As soon as we became lovers she wanted to draw me all over the empty house. She kept Grégoire's keys, and whenever she could she would come and find me here at night, during those weeks when the house was ours. I made her sit on the throne, she was so graceful looking, nestling there against the armrests. I outlined her figure in my sketchbook without taking my eyes off her. She insisted, "No, you have to sit there, Achilles." I never loved Kerylos as much as when I looked at her drawings. She showed me the place I thought I knew better than anywhere else in the world—rooms that I could have drawn with my eyes closed—as if I were seeing them for the first time through her wide eyes. She showed me the embroidery on the russet-colored curtains: Pontremoli had given instructions to the seamstresses to change the reels of thread from time to time, so that the colors would never all be quite the same, depending on the dying lot, to leave something to chance, so that nothing would be too regular. I had never even noticed. What would Theodore have said if he had surprised the two of us naked in the dining room, in front of this ancient altar, with our sketchbooks and colored pencils in our hands?

My old body is deformed, I'm frail, I feel weak. I kept all our drawings, and I was right to. My grandchildren will surely wonder who this handsome hero was. I haven't written anything on the back. I hesitated to undress in daylight in order to pose for her, but she insisted. In her first drawing of me she erased my scars. I asked her to do another one, this time with all my scars, and she kissed me and tore the first one up. Whoever finds these pages will see the most beautiful woman in the world. I never framed our drawings, though I ought to now. For years, when I was still searching for Ariadne, I wondered if she had kept the bunch of keys, whether sometimes she was tempted to come back to the house, which in a way belonged to her too. Perhaps the reason I used to go back when I knew no one else would be there was because I dreamed that she might have had the same idea, that I would bump into her in the Andron, as if she were waiting for me there. But fate was not that kind to me.

For the first time, standing in front of the chair that I couldn't bring myself to sit on, I wanted to cry: I pictured Ariadne's body, myself facing her, here, so many years ago. I put out my hand into empty space, placed my palm on the wood, my lips on the armrest. This was where she had sat. How had I let her leave, how had I never found her, after Grégoire told me that she had disappeared? Where is she now? For years I have refused to think about it. But here it's no longer possible; grief seizes me like a kind of madness.

With some difficulty, I moved the imposing chair out of the way and began tapping my fingers over each stone tile to listen for one that sounded hollow. Nothing. Sitting on the floor, it occurred to me that I would never find it. When he was designing the windows in this room, Pontremoli studied Italian palazzi: he wanted the tiling to resemble vaguely what was done in Rome in the sixteenth century, and he put in bronze hinges and latches, interior shutters. It wasn't Greek, but it looked "historic," and at twenty I found it very beautiful. Today I found it gloomy, and it did not stop my tears.

The conversations I used to hear in this room took on a different meaning. I used to tell her what they spoke about. According to Pontremoli—and Reinach said he was right—it was not that there was a rupture between different eras, but that each period overlapped with the next; something of the fortifications at Troy and Mycenae could be detected in the shape of the Acropolis, some of the structures of its monumental doors survived in Orthodox monasteries, the houses of Athens and Delos had influenced the architecture of houses in the Mediterranean under the Roman empire, and the riads of north Africa and Andalucia, and one can see their traces in the palaces of Felix Arabia: even when the barbarians have destroyed everything, enemies have burned everything, sprinkled salt, every era men have rebuilt from memory, adapting, simplifying, transforming, finding new ideas. What mattered was that this chain had never been broken—and in a certain way, that was their greatest idea, that Greece was still here among us, even if we were not always able to see it.

The house altar stood at the other end of the room, with its inscription, "to the unknown god," although this room had never been used for any religious rite. That was the Reinachs' true religion: one god, who had made the world, but whom we do not know. A channel had been carved in the marble, for the blood to drain away after an animal was sacrificed. I doubt it was ever used for that purpose. I can't imagine the cook coming up to the marble-clad Andron to cast a spell on a chicken according to rites determined by Orthodox priests. I passed my hand over the front, perhaps it would trigger a mechanism inside. Too obvious, I suppose. There was nothing there, no trace of a hiding place.

The mosaic in the middle of the room shows the Labyrinth: Theseus fighting the Minotaur. The postcard is still in my bag. I managed to find the strength to get down on my knees, but no stone shifted, no trapdoor sprang open like the one on the heraldic fireplace in the Chateau de Thibermesnil, nothing appeared to have been designed by the architect to conceal a secret. The only secrets here, I thought, were those rare moments of joy in my life that left no trace other than the absurd wounds that I came back to awaken. Why did I want to suffer anymore, when I have my children, my grandchildren, my paintings, my life, elsewhere and otherwise?

The crown must have been in Theodore's bedroom the day of our return. He would have unpacked it from his trunk, but then what happened to it? Did he plan to return it to the monks of Dionysiou? Was he really so afraid of rekindling the tiara scandal? I was losing myself in the geometrical labyrinth, staring at the ax striking the neck of the man-beast. The design of the floor in the Andron was like one of the false leads that Theodore was so fond of. Ariadne said, "See, you don't even need a string to escape from the Labyrinth. You just need to be methodical." The Kerylos labyrinth is too easy. It is not to Theseus's credit that he is about to kill the Minotaur.

This morning I sat on a café terrace and read a long article in *Paris Match* about the new festivals springing up along the Côte d'Azur. One photograph showed a jazz club in Juan-les-Pins, the Minotaur. In front of the entrance three starlets posed in bikinis, along with the proprietress of the establishment, a playboy, and a saxophonist. Behind them was a large painted sign—it's hard to believe—showing an exact copy of the Kerylos labyrinth. It's so famous, this house—as for the Minotaur, for everybody else, it's become synonymous with Picasso.

30

ATHENA ON THE STAIRCASE

Fanny Reinach used to place vases of old roses in the Amphithyros, the hallway that led to the staircase going up to the Reinachs' private quarters, and the scent bloomed among the curtains, the marble, the beams, the paintings of ships that hung on the walls. The children used to race down the stairs two at a time. I loved this hall, dominated by a bronze-painted Athena wielding a lance beside a pierced brazier diffusing pinpoints of light that summoned the atmosphere of a temple. Theodore had placed another brazier at the top of the stairs in front of a small statue of Hermes; the staircase became shadowy and mysterious when they were lit and we scattered incense paper over them. Was Fanny aware that this helmeted statue, a reproduction, fit one of Furtwängler's hypotheses? What had motivated her husband to put it there, where everyone would see it, almost in homage to his great rival? It was like a permanent "Remember you are mortal, and fallible," whispered in the ear of a triumphant general at his moment of triumph at the Capitol in Rome. Theodore, like a good little Spartan who had learned how to suffer, liked the fact that a fox, hidden beneath his tunic, was constantly gnawing at his belly.

The Greek statues had made him dream; the fact that he possessed one that had been restored according to a German hypothesis, a plaster Athena that it was immediately apparent was unlikely to be genuine, was also, perhaps, the kind of irony he liked. The three brothers, at various ages, had dreamed of making great discoveries. This Athena was the goddess that none of them had found. They knew Greek culture better than anyone, better than Furtwängler. For so many years they had believed it would be logical and legitimate if antiquities were to reveal themselves to them—and yet their only major discovery was made by me. In 1878, Joseph, aged twenty-two, had been the first of the three to travel to Greece, never doubting for a minute that the first hole he dug would reveal a statue to rival the Venus de Milo. In reality that first trip lasted two weeks: he went to Athens, Mycenae, Corinth, and the Bay of Navarino, ending up at the Trieste opera house, where he saw *Tannhäuser*, and then Venice, still in pursuit of Wagnerian myths. From all this he had managed to extract enough for a book, his *Voyage to the Orient*, a youthful lapse that even his brothers teased him about. In Greece he met only politicians, for that was already his true passion. Theodore told me how he too, at twenty-two, had been obsessed with the Venus de Milo. The Marquis de Rivière, who gave it to Louis XVIII, was a simple man with his hands full: he didn't know a great deal about anything, yet it fell to him to have the pleasure of bringing to Paris the most extraordinary of statues. Salomon said that she had similarities with the artistry of Phidias—he published this in *Apollo*—but Theodore thought she was from a later date, after Alexander. He was right. Before I became devoted to the Victory of Samothrace, I too was a young man besotted with the Venus de Milo: Adolphe and I used to try and draw her with arms to see what she might have looked like. It started innocently enough, we drew her with a trumpet, a mirror, a palm frond, then, unsurprisingly—we were only sixteen or seventeen—we'd invent horrors that we destroyed as soon as we drew them.

Theodore always wanted to make one of those discoveries that is due to genius rather than to chance. Maybe he thought my innocence would bring him luck. Schliemann, the fat provincial Kraut, excavated what he thought might be the site of Troy, and he landed on it, and then Mycenae, where he found the gold mask of Agamemnon. He felt his way toward treasure with the instincts of a fool. The photograph of Madame Schliemann wearing jewels dug up during these excavations made Madame Reinach laugh; she said that Theodore and his brothers were completely incapable of bringing anything like that out of the ground for their wives. Theodore parried by telling her about the fake Greek house that Schliemann had built himself in Athens, a great big meringue decorated in the spirit of Pompeii. He found it funny that the ceilings were painted with plump putti prospecting for archaeological finds and deciphering inscriptions. Theodore asked his wife which she preferred, the ridiculous Schliemann palace or the Villa Kerylos.

At twenty-two, in the same frenzy for discovery, Theodore, who had just qualified as a lawyer at the Paris bar—around the same time that Salomon had left Paris for the French School at Athens—left for Constantinople. He was overwhelmed with admiration when he saw the Hagia Sophia. He made no great discovery, but was merely happy to admire these famous places. In the library at Kerylos, he showed me the large round metal hanging lamp fitted with candleholders and discreetly electrified,

"We don't really know what lanterns would have looked like in antiquity, so I showed our architect a few photographs. This must remind you of something, no? You are Orthodox, are you not, in a way?" He didn't tell me immediately about his intended voyage to the Greek monasteries—he had not yet decided it would be to Athos, and he was contemplating going instead to the Meteora monasteries or to Mystra. I didn't tell him that I have detested the Orthodox religion since I was a child. He must have wanted to study me a little, to be sure I wasn't deceiving him. One day, standing by the statue of Athena, he suddenly turned to me and said, "I was so happy when I first saw the coast of Thessali, from on board the *Latouche-Tréville*. So, to reward you for your progress, I am going to take you with me on a trip. It would be a terrible shame for you to lose your modern Greek." The idea that he might try to learn modern Greek seemed not to have occurred to him. For him, the language that came second after archaic Greek, for its beauty and its nobility, the language of philosophers, poets, and orators, was French.

One day, not long after I arrived at Kerylos, I heard Theodore and Gustave speaking German on the little pointed outcropping I called the Tarpenian rock, and I was afraid. I only understood years later. Eiffel used to remind us at every opportunity that he was born in Dijon, but his family's real name was Bönickhausen, they came from the Rhineland, a region called Eifel, from where they had taken their name. This was fairly widely known in Beaulieu, and the notary used to say that Eiffel too was Jewish—he wasn't, I knew that he and his family were Catholic, and had been since the dawn of time. Though he was a believer in science only, I saw him at Mass several times. I had no idea he spoke

German, and that day I was utterly taken aback; his parents' generation must have still spoken it at home and he remembered it. As for Theodore, half the books in his library were in German and he spoke it as well as he spoke French.

At Beaulieu, the rumor spread among the more reactionary local families that Eiffel had made money from shares at the time of the Panama affair, with the complicity of the Reinach family, because they were "coreligionists"—although there wasn't a word of truth in the story. The day I overheard them speaking German, I think they were having a slightly bawdy conversation that was not suitable for children's ears—the priest's housemaid saw it as proof that the two rich men were spies in the pay of the Kaiser.

Archaic Greek is a language that takes a long time to learn and a short time to forget. Today I can still read a few pages, but I have to stop all the time to look things up in my old Bailly dictionary. Like Latin, I remember almost nothing: the other day, with my grandchildren, I stood dumbly in front of the inscription on a sundial. Occasionally, entire pages of grammar come back to me without warning, absurdly. I would never have thought they were still there somewhere in this old head of mine. It took a good six months for the rules about accents to stick. They are not particularly useful for translating texts, but I wanted to learn to write archaic Greek as well. The first time Theodore gave me five simple lines to translate, he gave me minus thirty-five out of twenty. I lost all the points just because of the accents, all of which I put in the wrong places. I was extremely proud when I managed to get zero. I can remember a few scattered, intimidating rules, having spent weeks of my life, bound like a prisoner to my little table in the library, reciting and then applying them. Take the word oxyton: if it has an acute accent on the final syllable, it is paroxyton, proparoxyton, perispomenon, that is a circumflex accent on the final vowel, properispomenon, and barytone, when there is a grave accent on the final syllable. But as soon as you start using declensions and conjugations, all the accents move. I learned the rule—one among dozens of others—for when the vowel of the penultimate syllable has to have an accent and if it is long, this accent will always be a circumflex if the vowel on the last syllable is short. In the declensions, when the final long is accentuated, the direct cases are oxytons and the oblique cases are perispomenons. In an average aorist, all the imperatives are perispomenons. How did I not go mad? I forced myself, it was a question of honor. Sometimes I cried.

My grandchildren are only studying English at school. I am worried it won't be very useful. When I was young you needed money to learn English or German, and it's still the case today. I soon realized, even in elementary school, that those who got a place at the Lycée Masséna to learn English or German—"living" languages, as the teachers called them, and they are very welcome to that life of theirs—didn't learn their languages solely in school. Their parents had to be able to pay for language exchanges, study trips abroad. I was just a poor kid, and I still am in a way. Modern Greek wasn't offered by these teachers, nor was Italian, even though many of the children of foreign workers spoke that or Spanish at home. In 1891, the government attempted to bring in a reform to replace the teaching of Latin and Greek with that of living languages. Joseph Reinach wrote a thundering editorial: German and English might allow these young people to get to know other countries, but it would imprison them inside the particular, while studying the great texts of antiquity is an education in universalism. He wrote, and Theodore repeated it to me, "To understand Sophocles and Virgil, it is sufficient to be a man." Afterward, he went on, in a second phase, they can learn languages that could be useful for travel, business, industry. But first of all they had to learn how to think. Theodore claimed that if any more ancient music was discovered, we would one day be able to replicate its performance—if future scholars were still interested in such things.

"You have heard all those who say that the study of Greek is pointless, Achilles, that it serves no purpose. That in the world of today one must know how to drive an automobile, or build a bridge—I don't mean to be unkind to our friend Eiffel—everyone is supposed to be able to speak some vague and hazy English, which has only a distant relationship to the language of Shakespeare. (In my youth, you know, I translated *Hamlet*.) But it is precisely with what serves no purpose that one achieves great things."

31

"GET OUT!"

I see myself again insulting Monsieur Reinach. And him showing me the door, saying he never wanted to see me again in this house that, for several months already, without admitting it to myself, I had already begun to hate.

Directly above the statue of Athena, the staircase led to the Hermes gallery on the second floor. It was here, between Theodore's rooms and the servants' quarters, at the foot of the flight of stairs that went up to the roof, that Theodore chased me.

I almost snatched out of its niche the bronze copy of the statue discovered in the sea off the coast of Tunisia, to throw at his head. I was overcome by a fit of madness. He was stooped, leaning against the wall and talking to me. Basileus snoozed by his master's feet.

If the brazier had been lit, I would have tipped it over and set the house on fire. I wanted to. How pretty it would have been to watch from the beach as the Greek villa blazed. The curtains on the landing would have caught fire, the window frames turned into torches, the wind fanning the flames as the beams cracked and all the wooden furniture kindled into a single conflagration, papers and books feeding the inferno. The glow would have lit up the whole town.

I stopped to think for a moment. I knew that there was only one weapon capable of wounding him, a single word. I made my decision. I looked at him and said, "Thief." He stared at me. I think he understood very well what theft I was alluding to. I thought for a moment that he was about to salvage the situation, that he would give me back the gold crown, or tell me that I was the one who stole it from Dionysiou, and then he whispered, "Get out!"

I had been behaving very awkwardly around him for several weeks, without meaning him any ill. I knew what I owed him, but I resented that he was growing old and yet still held me in his thrall. The previous week, I had sold my first three paintings, received my first enthusiastic reviews in the newspapers, and it was intolerable to hear him talk to me like that. I didn't want to have to be modest any more. If I didn't dare show him my paintings, it was because I knew what he was going to say and that his condescension would be painful to hear. He was incapable of talking to me about them, or asking me any questions. For the previous year or two, I had much preferred the company of his brother Salomon, who was more open, more lighthearted—I even contemplated inviting Salomon to the dinner after my next exhibition opening. I would have asked him not to mention it to his brother.

The root of my ferocious disagreement with my "benefactor" had nothing to do with my new career as an artist. The quarrel was triggered by a difference of archaeological opinion that had been festering since the immediate aftermath of the Armistice. I had changed so much, and it seemed that he had remained exactly the same as he had been in 1914. At Eiffel's funeral at the cemetery in Levallois, after his death at the age of ninety-one, Theodore looked as though he had shrunk, and his gaze was blank as he watched his friend being lowered into a grave set slightly on a slant so as to be on the same axis as his tower. Theodore had no idea how his family mocked and mimicked him, albeit with affection. His children dared to find this man, the most brilliant of his generation, a little bit of a fool. I think he really didn't see any of that. He was publishing fewer articles, he was withdrawing a little, but he never admitted how much of his former glory he had lost. This didn't make me feel sad for him; he annoyed me. I could no longer stand listening to him going on about Greek history and numismatics when I had expected so much more from him. I remember how excited I was the day that Salomon, in his dingy office in the Museum of National Antiquities, said to me, "Look at these photographs, Achilles. Does this not look like the Phoenician alphabet, the inscriptions discovered on King Ahiram's sarcophagus at Byblos? Did you read the report by the French team in Lebanon? Can you guess when these date from and where they were found?" I shook my head.

"In a hamlet called Glozel."

"In Iran?"

"In France. Just outside a village of Ferrières-sur-Sichon, a few minutes' drive from Vichy. The finds include carved bone, arrowheads, terracotta urns painted with faces, definitely from the Neolithic era. Do you realize what this means?"

"That the alphabet—if it is an alphabet . . . "

"It certainly looks like one! And if it is, it means that the alphabet did not come into being 700 years before Christ on the shores of Lebanon, but 15,000 years ago in France!"

"Ferrières-sur-Sichon, cradle of civilization—that's going to come as something of a surprise!"

Salomon remained, nonetheless, skeptical. I helped him sort through the photographs and organize his papers, all densely covered in his untidy scrawl. Theodore's handwriting was fine and regular, with letters that sloped neatly upward. I was unsettled when I looked at the photographs Salomon handed to me. More so than I had been by the collection of pornographic images I had once come across: vases, sculptures, mosaics, statues . . . This time there were only geometric figures. I copied them into my sketchbook, comparing the various sequences of signs. I was sure it could be deciphered. I tried to match each sign with a syllable. Salomon was won over by my conviction, and from then on that was all we talked about. He borrowed me from his brother, as he put it, and we went down to see the trove—it was quite an adventure. That was what I loved about the three brothers: Joseph's passion when it came to defending Captain Dreyfus, Salomon's when he intuited a discovery—he became passionate about Glozel—the childish joy on Theodore's face when he played me the notes of the Delphic hymn to Apollo, which he had deciphered, like Champollion and the Rosetta Stone.

In 1926 Salomon and I spent two days talking to the country folk in Glozel, surveying the field, and weighing the clay tablets in our hands. On our return, with all the authority of an influential member of the Academy of Inscriptions, he announced that he believed the discovery to be genuine. He even published a short book of reproductions of the alphabetical signs.

Without suspecting a thing, I returned shortly afterward to Beaulieu. The success of my first exhibition had been a dream:

I began tracing signs in my paintings, images of the past layered over fragments of the future, which helped me make the transition from my early Cubist period. I was creating my own style, simpler, more elementary, somewhat primitive. On the train back I imagined new paintings, with rectangles, arrows, triangles, little watercolors, a whole new world that would be my home. I returned to the silent, gloomy villa, which no longer meant anything to me.

The moment he saw me Theodore flew into a rage. I had never seen him like that before. He swore at me. An alphabet! What next! Clearly someone had faked an entire archaeological site, perhaps there were a few authentic objects alongside these fragments of clay that were undoubtedly shoddy fakes. A whole alphabet invented for use in just one village? Only to be completely forgotten until it reappeared in Phoenicia, after a hiatus of over ten thousand years? Usually so calm, now he screamed and shouted. Because of me, his brother's career was going to end up a farce. Eventually he stopped shouting. His voice grew icy. I tried to defend myself:

"You made yourself ridiculous because of your own recklessness when the tiara was acquired, and now you are going to make yourself ridiculous again, but this time because of your excessive prudence."

I had never even alluded to the Saitapharnes affair before. He answered me in oily tones. He had heard such *wonderful* things about my paintings. His implication was that I might have set out intentionally to hoodwink them, I might have been the artist who . . . He was going to accuse me of being the author of the clay tablets discovered at Ferrières-sur-Sichon. That was the moment I realized I had to leave, at once. I walked away from him. My luck was that at last I was able to live on my own means. Glozel was just a pretext. I followed the advice that Ariadne's husband once gave me; he too had stopped coming to the house. But only a few weeks later I wept when I heard that Theodore had died. I joined the funeral procession to the Montmartre cemetery. His final resting place for all eternity—an eternity he perhaps did not believe in—was designed by Pontremoli. Greek in style, adorned with bronze palm trees, it was located near the graves of the Cahen d'Anvers, the Camondos, the Pereires, the Bischoffsheims, the Koenigswarters, and not far from the bust of his beloved Offenbach.

Theodore seemed to have come back to Kerylos with the sole purpose of going after me. He had long preferred the comforts of Paris, since he moved out of Rue Hamelin and into an apartment inherited from his wife on the corner of the Place des États-Unis, in the mansion that had once belonged to Jules Ephrussi. He went for slow walks with Basileus, also no longer very lively, on a leash. He lived down the street from a whole row of monuments, the mansions of the Deutsch de la Meurthe family, the Cahen d'Anvers family, the Bischoffsheims—theirs was the most sumptuous, and it became famous some time later for the legendary parties thrown by Charles and Marie-Laure de Noailles. The Glozel affair dragged on. People still occasionally talk about it even today. No forger was ever discovered.

I could never have imagined the oration at Theodore's funeral, even less that of his brothers. They were cultivated, brilliant—too brilliant, no doubt—too easy to hoodwink, ridicule, humiliate, yet they were still the best, they always had been, they couldn't help it, the best at chemistry, mathematics, geography, history, philosophy. And above all in the subject that was their greatest passion: Greece, its history, its language, its ruins, its statues, its tombs, its temples, and its houses. If Latin was the church and its priests, Greek was democracy and thus it signified France. They truly believed that. I often used to think about this when I was living with them, when I swam—that was when my brain functioned best, when my joints still supported me. They knew everything there was to know about Jewish history, were passionate about all religions, but their France was secular France, the kingdom that belonged to one and to all. With hindsight, I wonder if it was Theodore's fault I was so excited by Glozel: how could I resist the idea that the world's first alphabet had been born in France? Our only thought at the time was to serve our fatherland. Between the two wars, public opinion changed; nowadays, since the Liberation, the kinds of ideas that were born after 1870 are once more conceivable.

In 1898, in the middle of the Dreyfus affair, Theodore published the text of the speech he presented at the prize-giving ceremony for a Jewish charitable organization, which Adolphe gave me and I still have in my archives:

"Never confuse France with the agitation that sometimes disturbs its surface, temporarily, but with impunity. Continue to love this France, with all your strength, all your soul, as one loves a mother, even when she is unjust, or even wrong, because she is your mother and you are her children."

During the years after the victory, I became for him and for Salomon—I spent less time with Joseph, who died in 1921—I think I can say this with pride, a true friend, whom they could always count on. The moment of rupture, though it came as a relief, was also extremely painful. I had grown bored of seeing Theodore standing in the library, garbed in a white cloak that made him look like a prophet, where he would spend the entire morning writing. I could no longer bear to sit with him on a bench facing the blue rocks, listening to him recite his most recent articles or the ones that Salomon had sent him. He read out loud to me the whole of *Apollo,* his brother's short book, growling into his beard when, in the chapter on Greek art, Salomon cites Professor Furtwängler's theories about Phidias's sculptures. I'll never forget that. And yet, in the 1930s, I didn't want to remember. I went to all three funerals, I remained on good terms with the children, though I saw them less and less, and I never really wanted to renew the ties that had been broken in front of the statue of Hermes. I had my own house and my own family. For my wedding they sent a gift "from the whole family, with our best wishes." I had been expecting a gold Breguet watch, but I opened a box filled with straw and the full battery of copper pans from Kerylos, the ones that my mother had always admired. They must have changed over to aluminum.

They might have known everything, or almost everything, my beloved Reinach brothers, but in the end it was I who astonished them, when I discovered the greatest secret in the whole of Greek history. During our expedition to Dionysiou, I felt like Jason with his Argonauts, certain of finding the Golden Fleece in the kingdom of Colchis—one of the themes of the frescos on the walls of the peristyle. But it turned out that my golden fleece was not Alexander's crown, it was my art, created with my own hands after I escaped from the Labyrinth.

32

MADAME REINACH'S BEDCHAMBER AND HER SHOWER WITH ITS MULTIPLE JETS

For years I searched everywhere for Ariadne. It was my only purpose. I wondered if she ever came back to the coast, I went to visit all the ladies who offered drawing and watercolor classes, I wondered if she might have married the notary and taken on a different name—he had sent me an announcement of his rather late marriage—which would have been truly terrible. I explored all the brothels of Nice and Toulon during the war, I went to Mass at Matisse's chapel in Vence, the opening of which was the major event of 1951—I was sure that she would be there. I even used to peer at the faces of nuns who were about her age. When I bought my first car, when I developed my first color photograph, when I went for my first long vacation to Italy, when I bought my first 78 record—every time I thought of Ariadne, who wasn't there with me. I finally gave up looking for her several years ago. I realized that I wasn't mourning her anymore. Thinking about her made me happy, whether she was still alive or whether she had died. I had managed to banish the idea that she had a child who might have been mine, once I had my own two sons, like a proper father who asks no questions. It was when I used to swim that the images of Ariadne would return, taking me by surprise; later, drying off on the beach, I would forget her again, wholly occupied by my grandchildren.

Like many Corsicans of my generation, I never really liked the sea. It was Theodore who taught me to look at it, to call it *thalassa*, the sea of the Greeks, to see in it the "wine-dark" waves of Ulysses. Since then I have learned to enjoy boats, taken vacations to the real Greece, sailed around the islands with my family, I even thought about buying a bolthole in Thasos and ending my days there. Today I know the names of every seabird, I love the smell of kelp. I no longer swim.

Weep, gentle halcyons, sacred birds,
Birds beloved of Thetis, gentle halcyons, weep.

These lines by André Chénier—the author of *Odes to Fanny*—always make me think of the Reinachs. I lay down on the floor, fully dressed, with my sketchbook and pen, my white canvas trousers, my old American moccasins, a washed out blue polo shirt from before the war; if my children saw me they would tell me I looked like a tramp. Some days I make an effort, I shave and take out from my closet a white shirt and a pair of trousers the color of crushed strawberries; in Nice, once you're over fifty, you have nothing to lose by dressing like an old playboy, sitting on a bench on the promenade, eyes closed, soaking up the sun in silence. Today I have eschewed all elegance, lying on the ground on this Halcyon terrace making notes in silence, at the center of the wind diagram that has been half erased by the salt from the sea. I did my morning gymnastics here with Adolphe just a few weeks before his death. It was so unjust; I was a head taller than him, I could do fifty pushups where he could only manage fifteen, I built up muscle twice as fast as he—he blamed his scholarly heritage and inbreeding, congratulating me on my shepherd ancestors. I asked him what his great grandfather the cattle dealer had looked like, if he too was passionate about Latin, Greek, and Aramaic. He answered that being a cattle broker was already a step up from being a shepherd, and that he had ended up becoming the most successful dealer in Frankfurt, but that I needn't worry, things could go very fast, and no doubt my children would become professors of Sanskrit at the Collège de France, if I eased off the gymnastics a little to work on my language skills. Today I am the only person left who knows about this wind tower, this observation post, where you can forget the faded architecture of the house, a place where one feels free, happy. A place that makes you want to travel, do somersaults and stretches, drink champagne in evening dress, read, think.

Ornithes, birds, was the name of Fanny's bedroom, with its midnight blue paintings and its black and gold arabesques. I remember seeing Madame Reinach, with her bird-like profile against the clouds, standing by the open window in an evening dress and a turquoise silk cape, her cousins and sisters-in-law thronging around her in their bathing costumes. I didn't know quite how to relate to her, how to address her. It did not take long for me to begin calling Theodore by his first name, but I never dared call her "Fanny." I was never entirely sure to what extent I might tease them, about their obsessions, their taste, the way they had of only talking to each other about books, their conversations sprinkled with quotations as they unfolded their newspapers. But because I wasn't overly intimidated by them, I found a way to be natural. There were some things I didn't like: the first time I went to visit Salomon in Paris, I found everything hideous, which I told Theodore, thinking that he would send me packing, when in fact I think that it was one of the reasons he adopted me. Salomon very much liked his mansion on Avenue Van Dyck, the work of an architect called Alfred-Nicolas Normand. He had designed Prince Napoleon's Roman villa, which must have been one of the examples that they had considered, before Theodore decided on his own project. This palace, with its white and gilded wooden paneling, was palpably designed to dazzle.

The book chest in Fanny's bedroom was empty—what happened to all her Marivaux, Molières, the books by the two Corneille brothers and by Rostand, signed by the author? All her music scores have disappeared as well. Only a few photographs remain. The construction of this house was part of the rivalry between the three geniuses that had existed since their childhood. Had Madame Reinach been involved in the decoration of this bedroom, the most beautiful in the house, where the attributes of Hera, the wife of Zeus, alternate with floral motifs? Among the figures on the uppermost frieze her husband is visible—Adolphe once climbed a stepladder to give him a pipe and fix his beard, and the joke stayed. If he had been allowed, he would have liked to chisel on the walls some fake ancient graffiti, like the graffiti found at Pompeii . . . Lying on her bed reading, his adored aunt must have felt like a Trojan princess. I can't imagine how happy this must have made her.

Unkind gossips said that the beautiful Fanny, the first cousin of the first Madame Theodore Reinach, was the heir to the fortunes of her two uncles, Charles and Jules Ephrussi. Charles Ephrussi was a very important man, editor of the *Gazette des Beaux-Arts*, collector of Manet's asparagus paintings and the golden apples of Puvis de Chavannes, he loved ancient art and all that was modern, and knew everyone there was to know in Paris. Madame Reinach was not in the slightest bit worldly. She was entirely uninterested in any rivalry with the grandes dames of the region, among whose ranks figured her cousin Béatrice. She had no interest in receiving her neighbors. Egbert Abadie, who made his fortune in cigarette papers, had bought the Marquis de Rochechouart's boat and cultivated a friendship with the Prince of Monaco. She avoided him on principle. There were also the people who lived at the Chateau Marioni, descendants of a brigadier of the police who had explained to his children how to get rich, who were seen with the "Sun President" Félix Faure during his triumphal visit to the coast in 1896, even today a subject of conversation.

At Saint-Jean-Cap-Ferrat, there was a love nest: Paris Singer—of the sewing machine Singers, and Isadora Duncan's lover—had the villa "Mes Rochers" renovated, it was as beautiful as a Tuscan castle. All the talk there was of the Venetian palazzo owned by their great rivals, the fashionable American Curtis family, the owners of Villa Sylvia, whose garden Claude Monet once came to paint. They received the whole world at their residence on the Grand Canal. Madame Reinach saw them from afar at musical evenings and couldn't care less about them. She visited Èze a few times; the amiable nephew of the great poet Tennyson invited her to stay at his Chateau Aïguetta—a medieval fortress built for him—but I think she ceased to frequent him when she realized that he was ruining his family at the casino in Monte-Carlo.

At Èze, she liked to walk the path that Nietzsche used to take. She gave me *The Birth of Tragedy,* the essay where he splits beauty in two, inspired as much by Apollo as by Dionysius. She spoke to me of the sober architecture of Athens facing that of the great altar of the Pergamon, and I didn't dare admit to her she was telling me nothing I didn't already know. The philosopher stayed on the Riviera in the early 1880s, at a time when he was isolated and in despair, before he became a famous writer.

There was one couple who would have loved to be acquainted with the Reinachs and whom Fanny kept at a distance. Around the time that Kerylos was being built, the Villa Mirasol was also going up on the Cap d'Ail, where Gabrielle Réval reigned as a woman of letters. Suffice it to say that I was forbidden to read her books, whose very titles set me astir: *The Schoolgirl*, *The Trainer*, *The Fountain of Love*, *The Child with the Rose*. She had a husband who wrote historical novels with titles like *At the Time of True Love*, and *Checkmate*. After it was discovered that they had had the impudence to organize an evening in honor of the gods of Olympus, their names were no longer mentioned.

Theodore had two daughters from his first marriage. Inconsolable when he was widowed at the age of twenty-nine, he soon found consolation: Fanny said, "You're mad," and he replied, "Mad for you." I think Theodore truly loved her. He asked her to marry him straight away. They had four children together, Julien, Léon, Paul and Olivier. It was said that after all the children were born, they grew used to living separate lives, and that she found her own consolation, always with exceptional men. I don't really know what that means, nor if it was true. She was always charming with me, always ready with a word of encouragement and a smile. When she died in 1917, far too soon, Theodore was not even able to attend her funeral. The government had sent him to the United States to try and persuade politicians in Washington to join the war. Which is what happened, and the war was won. But he had lost the taste for happiness. He never remarried. He took refuge more and more in his reading, which I suppose must have taken him back to his adolescence. He used to stare at the clouds, as I am doing today.

During the days here when Ariadne and I loved one another, we slept several nights in Fanny's bedroom. It was the most beautiful of all the Kerylos bedrooms. I was looking after the house, and no one disturbed us. I told her how I wanted to paint, and she was the first to tell me not to put it off; if I wanted to be an artist I had to forget about everything else, devote every day to it. We could just make out the coast of Italy from the windows. The sun woke us. We ran naked to the shower that Theodore had designed for Fanny. It was shaped like a niche hollowed out for a statue. Standing on the slatted floor, raised like a pedestal, we posed like antique statues, Paris and Helen, Mars and Venus, Psyche receiving her first kiss from Cupid, now us. Very modern, worthy of a London hotel, the "cabin" possessed three jets, each with its own hot and cold faucet. Mosaic inscriptions in Greek explained everything. You turned the *Perikulas* and water gushed out in a circle, the faucet marked *Krounos* flowed with a fine mist, and then there was *Kataxysma*, a very unusual word which in Greek signifies only one thing: a sauce to pour on meat. Ariadne burst out laughing. It was just the kind of joke that Theodore would play on his wife, and which, at the time, made me so happy to be living at Kerylos.

33

ULYSSES'S QUARTERS

Next to the shower there was a bathroom called *Ampelos*, which is the name of a constellation, but more importantly that of a young satyr inspired by Dionysius. During those days when we were alone in the house, Ariadne would spend hours in the marble tub. On the walls was a stucco vine peopled by chaste-looking young girls staring at bunches of grapes, though not, apparently, tempted to pick them; it was very amusing. She talked to me, told me about how bored she was in her marriage, about miserable Grégoire's periods of depression, and then how intelligent he was when faced with a plan, his instinct for architecture, and I understood that she admired him and would never leave him. She also talked briefly about her desire for independence, for travel, parties, music; how she imagined herself opening a bookstore, a hotel, a boutique. I should have realized then that she was going to leave him.

The room next door, between Fanny's and Theodore's bedrooms, served as both a study for reading and the couple's private sitting room. In Greek it was called the Triptolemus, after the son of Gaia and Oceanus, born of the union between land and sea. Theodore didn't bother to go down to the dining room for every meal. Someone would bring him up a few plates of food that he would store in a specially made cupboard. Triptolemus once said, "Honor the gods by offering them fruits and not killing animals," but that was no reason to become a vegetarian. Theodore would eat his lunch in a hurry, on a pedestal table with a surface of polished silver, like the mirrors of the ancients. The walls were painted to suggest a garden, trees dancing among white columns.

Greek and Latin were the useless studies that have served me the most in my career. Without Greek and Latin I would have become an apprentice cook scouring caldrons in a restaurant kitchen; the children of my mother's peers all found jobs in luxury hotels catering to the whims of the nouveau riche. I cast all that aside. If I had followed the Reinach example, I would have become a literature professor. With my painting, I was able to establish myself on my own. I dined with the Duke and Duchess of Windsor, I was invited to the ballet rehearsals of the Marquis of Cuevas at Monte Carlo, I went yachting with Fulco di Verdura and the Viscount of Noailles, I own a nice house filled with antiques, two Picassos, and a Puvis de Chavannes, which I have hung alongside each other. I have a studio with a glass roof; it is not great riches, does not compare to the worldly success of captains of industry and bankers, I don't get talked about in the gossip columns, thank goodness, but it isn't too bad for a boy whose parents didn't finish school, whose grandfather was a shepherd and didn't read three books in his whole life. My whole life, I owe to Greek. If I hadn't known how to conjugate the aorist, where to put the stresses, how to recite mi-verbs, I would never have been able to escape my menial little existence. Declensions proved to be the instrument of my ascent. Charles de Noailles once showed me around his property, the Chateau Saint-Bernard, which was quite the opposite of a chateau in fact, a modern, functional house, "interesting to live in," according to this worldly gentleman who could not quite get over the fact that I knew Theocrites's *Idylls* as well as he. Theodore, back then, understood this too: living in a house is not a game. At the Villa Noailles there was a covered swimming pool and a gymnasium: at the age of seventeen I would have been much happier there than at Kerylos—if only I had been born twenty years later! But then again I might easily have never left the Eiffels' house, I would have never met anyone, and I would have remained poor. I don't think that would have been a terrible thing, but the life I have made for myself pleases me more. I know hundreds of ridiculous things. I have read hundreds of books that serve no useful purpose. I have learned rare languages that I will never speak with anyone. That is the debt I owe to the Reinach family. They did not teach me; they showed me.

"You see, Achilles, little tortoise"—I was barely sixteen, I was already a head taller than him—"Listen to me, I am quite fed up with telling people that the study of Greek will, in spite of everything, be useful: if they are politicians, it will enable them to think about democracy. If they are pharmacists, to understand the labels on their bottles. If they are tourists, to imbibe more from the monuments at Delphi and Olympia. It all sounds very nice, but it isn't true. Greek has nothing to prove. I like it precisely because it serves no purpose. Nothing is truly beautiful unless it cannot be used for anything, in the words of that old romantic Théophile Gautier. Have you read *The Romance of a Mummy*? I shall give it to you. Even Monsieur

Eiffel's tower serves no real purpose, which upsets him terribly; it is the measure of his future success. He is incapable of realizing it: he is not an architect; he is an engineer. Students ought to be encouraged toward the useless. Is music useful? Is running useful? Discus throwing, archery, are they useful? Are the rules of chess useful? Yet I shall always prefer those who play chess or the violin, if I have to choose whom to invite into my house."

"Because you like your guests to play the violin? You wouldn't stand it for five minutes. And you hate board games."

"You rascal. Those people would be able to talk to me about other things, they would understand allusions, be able to talk about things without naming them. I would be on the same level as those who had learned such things purely for pleasure. A long, difficult, tedious apprenticeship, but that is part of the fun."

"You mean the person who came first in the Beaulieu athletics? You would make him a cup of tea?"

"Insolent young man, you really are unique. Greek serves literally no purpose, but the fact of having learned it is what distinguishes us from the barbarians."

"And Madame Reinach, who is so distinguished, how much Greek does she know?"

"You are being most impertinent. She knows quite enough. And that is my business, not yours."

The master of the house's bathroom was baptized *Nikai*, the Victories, presumably because it was during his ablutions that Theodore came up with his most dazzling and implausible ideas. All at once the entire household would hear, from the "gallery" that led to these rooms—the elegant Grégoire banned the word corridor for being too prosaic; to annoy him I always said corridor—the master of the house talking to himself, ratiocinating in the hot water: "This braggart Barrès understands nothing about Greece! He should reread his own *Voyage from Sparta*! Ridiculous! Pontremoli met him once on a voyage, posing with his umbrella in the middle of the columns, the old fool!"

The stucco and the mosaics were particularly well done, rather more polished than those in Madame Reinach's bathroom, which tended dangerously toward the style of the Empress Josephine. The decor of the walls exalted swimming, to unintended comic effect. Pontremoli designed most of the mosaics himself, inspired by various antique vases that Theodore suggested. But I saw the stucco being applied by one of his old friends from the Villa Medici, called Jean-Baptiste Gascq. It involved a complicated process of mixing marble powder with plaster and then sculpting it as though it were a coin. Who else is here? Anatomical figures, copied from the famous vase known as the Euphronios krater, transposed into a subtle relief. Their muscles quiver as the light plays over their bodies. I used to wonder what chubby old Theodore must have thought as he climbed smiling out of his stone tank, when he caught sight of these naked men, with the broad shoulders and massive biceps of bodybuilders, being teased by their slaves. Perhaps he simply thought that with this morsel of bravura, he had surpassed the artists of antiquity—reflecting wryly that no one would ever know, for no one ever glimpsed inside his bathroom. For Pontremoli this taste for secrecy was not amusing: word was spreading that Kerylos was his masterpiece, the last word in modern-day architecture, the ultimate reconciliation of history and modernity, but, like Balzac's *Unknown Masterpiece*, it was impossible to see.

The master bedroom was called *Erotes*, which I translate not as Cupids, which sounds a little too romantic, but as Cherubim, for the throng of tiny winged figures painted on the walls against the red background bordered by a wide frieze. Theodore liked his children and his nephews and nieces to come and find him in his bedroom. He had Athena painted in there too, not the most loving of goddesses. He liked to read on his balcony, or daydream in front of the mosaic circle enclosing a boat with full sails surrounded by fish. As a gift for Adolphe's seventeenth birthday—a lot of people, but not me, called him Ado, as if he were an eternal adolescent—his uncle gave him a box camera with a shoulder strap, the latest craze. And, wonder of wonders, he bought one for me too. We were about to leave for Greece, and he thought we might take some interesting snapshots. Maybe he was having fun playing the prince and the pauper with Adolphe and me, paying me compliments in front of everyone to incite little Adolphe, the great hope of the family, and no fool, to work even harder. Theodore believed in using photography to serve archaeology. Salomon thought that only engravings, even etchings without any chiaroscuro, showing only the outlines, enabled one to see what inscriptions and sculptures really looked like. But since Salomon was not particularly inclined one way or the other, many of his books—particularly his works for the general public, rather than his scholarly articles—included a large number of photographs. When we got to Greece, I found I was not allowed to take photographs. The monks even threatened to confiscate my photographic plates. It is a great regret to me that I have no pictures to prove what we found in Athos.

The three brothers always got on well, in spite of the inevitable rivalry. It was as though they had divided up all human knowledge: one a scientist, one a historian, one an explorer. Theodore must have been the last man on the planet who knew everything. He did not do it to impress, but to put his knowledge at the service of those who, like me, understood nothing. They were people who had not been to elementary school, but believed that there should be elementary schools everywhere. They believed that after the fall of Napoleon III, France would become the new Athens. They believed that showing men the world would lead to their emancipation. In the Chamber of Deputies, Joseph continued to laud the Revolution. At a secondhand bookstall in Nice, I stumbled across a collection of articles by Salomon in three volumes called *Amalthea*, after the goat who nurtured the infant Zeus, with an amusing subtitle: *A Jumble of Archaeology and History*. It includes studies of Dutch goldwork, Renaissance painting, African fauna, medieval trials, the Serbian Neolithic period, Mycaenean Crete, Greek statues, late Latin literature.

I suspect that Theodore, in his heyday, had rather more lofty ambitions: he wanted to understand mankind, all the things that had remained unchanged in the human brain since ancient times, that were found from Brazil to India, that might have been found in the skulls of cave painters. He was a little surprised when he read one of Sigmund Freud's books in which Freud quotes Salomon on the history of religion. Theodore looked at me and said, "Do not ever read that man's books.

I have discussed it with my dear, respected brother, and he is mortified to find himself quoted in his book. These so-called Freudian doctors are like Cubist painters, or free-verse poets: they will soon be forgotten. Occasionally it can be interesting, but fundamentally it is improper. We must learn to order things according to our understanding. Do you really believe that the ego is not master of its own dwelling place? The doctors of this new school, led by this charlatan who believes himself the Copernicus of the mind, are going to do more harm than the Catholic confessors or the restorers of ancient paintings! Would you mind handing me my dressing gown? It will take a century or even two to repair the damage, while they make fortunes out of their new cult. When I consider that all this mumbo jumbo came about from our books, our studies, which required such effort from us . . . You see, paramount in the human brain is grammar, then architecture . . . "

EPILOGUE

DAEDALUS, ICARUS, AND ARIADNE

The dark wood staircase that leads up from the top floor bedrooms to the roof resembles nothing so much as a fitting from a yacht. Daedalus and Icarus, with their balconies, offer the best views. I always used to go upstairs feeling as if I were taking my place on the topmast of a ship. From the upper terrace, the human figures below blend with the landscape. Daedalus, the architect of Minos's Labyrinth, which we had visited in Crete, was Pontremoli. Did that mean that Icarus, with his loosely attached wings, was Theodore? Icarus's dream was to fly without burning his wings. Theodore got burned rather frequently. These two rooms, where Fanny used to put up her friends, were empty when there were no visitors. I liked to lean out and look at the blue rocks, like a cartographer locating reefs—I would look for them later when I went swimming.

Today I went up to the terrace to see the sun, low in the sky. I couldn't take the risk of staying until nightfall, for fear that the caretaker might find me there while doing his evening rounds of the house, or that he might decide on an impulse to go up to the terrace to watch the fireworks over in Monaco. It took me ten years to be able to watch fireworks again after the Great War. The noise was intolerable. It no longer bothers me now. I am cured.

I came back down and found my way out through the alleyway.

I had hoped to leave with Alexander's crown. It was almost dusk. I hadn't found the finely wrought olive leaves, so light and delicate, the masterpiece of the Macedonian goldsmiths, which I had once held in my hands and not dared to place on my head. I might go on another voyage to the monastery of Dionysiou. Perhaps I should stay there and end my days in that landscape of ordinary peace, a holy man walking in sandals on his way to night Mass, over the pebbled terrace that perhaps conceals the mortal remains of the great hero. In Dionysiou, when a man dies he is buried without a coffin, facing the sea. The gardener monk waters him every day for two years. Then the bones are exhumed, scrubbed cleaned, and piled up in the chapel. The name of the deceased brother is marked in red upon his skull. I am not sure that this is what I want, or if I would really have the courage to leave everything behind. The crown must still be somewhere. One thing is certain: Theodore did not give it to a museum, for fear that some so-called expert would insist that it dated from the Renaissance, or prove without doubt that it had been fabricated in a Byzantine monastery, and then it would be locked up with the tiara in the museum reserves, or in a cupboard in Saint-Germain-en-Laye alongside Salomon's research on the clay tablets from Glozel. I suppose that the Germans took the crown, but how did they know it was here? I never told anyone about it—except once, one person, in the room named for the Naiads. Ariadne was incapable of betrayal, of betraying me. Or was I too naive? I have no idea what she did during the last war, if she was even still alive. This evening I left, without the crown, without being sure I will return to Kerylos before I die, without having filmed everything I wanted to or have room for on the film reel. I went back to the café, exhausted, the crumpled copy of *Paris Match* in my camera bag, and this strange postcard of the Labyrinth. I note—because I must recount every detail of how this day ended—the attention with which I flicked through the magazine in the heat, to keep myself from thinking, as if in a trance. I looked at every photograph of the future princess in her enormous hat arriving in Monaco on the *SS Constitution*. A few pages on I read an article about a world I knew barely anything about, a club called the Minotaur, half-cabaret half-jazz cellar, a photo of a woman dancing barefoot who welcomed "young men with long hair, spirited young women, and cinema producers in white dinner jackets. Some evenings you might even see Jean Cocteau, who is currently decorating a sailors' chapel in Villefranche-sur-Mer." I haven't yet seen the Villefranche chapel, though I would like to go and see him at work. Apparently he has assistants and doesn't spend every day up on the scaffolding. Nothing scandalous, but the fine upstanding people who spread this news concluded that Cocteau was an imposter, no more than a beachgoing Michelangelo.

I spent an hour or so flicking through the whole magazine, skimming articles about this new Côte d'Azur that was like a foreign land to me. I am only seventy, younger than Clemenceau was in 1914, and who knows, maybe the greatest role of my life lies ahead of me. This is what I tell myself, to furnish the echoing rooms of my soul. I read a gossipy report from Grace Kelly's home in Philadelphia by a "special correspondent" to the principality. The old café I used to know is now a restaurant. I ordered sea bream, which I enjoyed.

According to one article, which was accompanied by photos of the Hotel du Cap-Eden-Roc and La Croisette, the Côte d'Azur is the stuff of dreams because it is "so international." The Reinachs were patriots; they loved Gambetta and the Republic and Clemenceau as much as they loved Monet; they would have been surprised to hear the priest, the pastry cook, the blacksmith, and the waiters from the various hotels, the dairywoman who knew everything there was to know about anything, and nothing at all—they too were France of course—discussing in detail all their comings and goings, pointing at them and calling them "foreigners." The Reinachs were wealthy and generous, which led to the other despicable thing that was said about them: they left excellent tips. The people who pocketed them felt humiliated. I am not sure that the producers in their white dinner jackets give anything to the doorman when they leave the Minotaur.

The little port of Beaulieu had never understood this family. They would have preferred them to talk about the latest ballets in Monaco, about the dancers they kept, they would have liked to mock them for buying Renoir and Degas paintings, but from what planet could these bespectacled men have fallen, with their pleasant, reserved wives, who spent the afternoon walking along the jetty and debating aloud how the walls of the city of Metaponto had been built, if they had arrow slits, and how the defensive system was designed. The cheese monger overheard a conversation on the different forms that the cult of a certain Isis in Alexandria took, and he initially thought this Isis must be an opera singer, until he heard the unfamiliar words "inscriptions," "epigraphy," "minting," from which he concluded that they must be a couple of engineers discussing the telegraph, though he instinctively realized that he had failed to grasp the logic behind it all. Choreography yes, epigraphy, no. The young lady at the post office, when she was quizzed about whom these people corresponded with, defended them; it was quite clear that they were doctors, important medical doctors, who had made major discoveries, and she once asked Monsieur Theodore if he would mind vaccinating her little boy. He had laughed and sent one of his colleagues from Nice, who did the vaccination for free: these Reinachs were benefactors of all mankind.

No one had understood a thing. Kerylos itself was a misunderstanding. The Reinachs believed they were becoming part of the very lifeblood of France, its culture. Among the better-educated people of Beaulieu—the doctor, the horrible notary, and a retired clerk of the court—they were called snobs, spoken about with contempt; the local lords and ladies who held court between Antibes and Menton did not even bother to invite them, since as it happened they held the same opinion as the dairywoman. Once they learned that the Reinachs came from Saint-Germain-en-Laye, they concluded that they had been rattled for no good reason—it was not as if they came from the *real* Saint-Germain, in the heart of Paris!

The Reinachs could have sufficed with the Minotaur club and a jazz soundtrack. Had Fanny and Theodore been born thirty years later, they would have been photographed with Giulietta Masina and Marcel Pagnol sitting in front of a platter of fried calamari, then left in peace. Theodore had loved the Saitapharnes tiara with a solid gold passion, he had loved his villa, and he had loved his books. His wife should have acted jealous and stopped him before it was too late. At the end of the ravine down which he was rushing headlong was the fall—and as in every Greek poem, he foresaw nothing. Daedalus loses, Icarus falls.

This evening, because I didn't know what else to do, and because I had read this article on the fashionable places on the "new Riviera," I decided I wanted to get drunk. I got in the car and drove here, to the Minotaur club, parking my Peugeot by the sign that had caught my attention, just behind a Rolls-Royce. A young American, slightly tipsy, came out of the club and began bending my ear. He was perfectly pleasant, like a golfer on vacation, the scion of a well-to-do East Coast family in a cotton polo shirt and deck shoes. He spoke French.

"Will you look at that masterpiece, the Rolls-Royce radiator, the very quintessence of British style? It took centuries to achieve such balance. Face on, with those columns, it looks just like a Greek temple, from the side, with the radiator plug, the energy of the woman with her outspread wings, it's like an antique statue, Dionysius poised above Apollo, utter perfection, I could look at her for hours."

"Yes," I said, "You're quite right. The harmonious rigor of Athens combined with the controlled energy of the Pergamon sculptors gives you this cross between Westminster and Miss Liberty." He opened his eyes wide, then enfolded me in an embrace: "Let me buy you a drink." And together we went into the club.

At the entrance to the long room, a pair of revolving postcard stands, like geometric steles, were filled with postcards of a single image, the same one as on the sign outside: the Labyrinth of Kerylos. The same card I had bought at the tobacconist in Beaulieu, the same one I had been mysteriously sent. A hundred of them for customers to help themselves to. "Who hasn't got their Minotaur?" said my American, laughing a little too loudly. This talkative dandy was the same age as my eldest grandson, and I would have liked them to meet. The American was finishing his PhD, on Pindar's poems, at Yale, in Connecticut. I have never been there. I told him I thought that of all the Greek poets, Pindar was the most difficult to understand. He said that Pindar's odes are first and foremost melody; he always reads them out loud. Archaic Greek, he told me, was all the rage in the United States. We ordered two gin and tonics and he asked me if I preferred the Olympic or the Pythic Odes, we drank and I answered that I couldn't remember very well, and then I ordered two more gins.

The sound of the music swelled like a wave, drowning out our conversation, then ebbed away. The bar was in a former boathouse, and the designer had seen fit to leave the ropes and sails as decorations. I was not the oldest person there. Wrinkled yachtsmen sat drinking champagne. All the tables were occupied. Young people were sitting around the tiny dance floor, others on the stairs that led to a little stage where a pianist and saxophonist, whom I could hardly make out at first in the fog of cigarette smoke, were playing some improvised jazz. Next to them, right at the back—I took a little while to notice, because the loquacious American was now lecturing me about ceremonies of initiation into the mysteries of Eleusis and the ruins of Phidias's workshop that had been discovered near the site of

Olympus—I saw the elegant figure of the proprietress whom the article had mentioned. The musicians stopped playing, and a few people at the tables applauded. She leaned down to the pianist, and then he began playing a melody that I didn't immediately recognize. After a few minutes, I picked out a little phrase that anchored itself in my head, then was swallowed up in a variation, then repeated. I parted my lips to sing. I couldn't believe what I was hearing, it was like a dream: the Delphic hymn to Apollo.

"Call me Erwin, by the way. Gee, will you look at that crazy little temple, looks like a kennel. It's even got an inscription: 'Basileus'! It's for us! Do you think it means the kennel belongs to the king? I'd like one like that, if you please!"

I had not set eyes on this object for over thirty years. I had not even noticed its absence at Kerylos. Nor had I ever interpreted "belongs to the king" so simply. *What this box contains belongs to the king*. It was as simple as that. I stood up and walked over toward her. She didn't dye her white hair; according to the journalist, that was part of her legend. In the picture in the magazine, it was hard to make out her features. Now, among the sculpted neon lights, standing in front of a wall of mirrors, I saw her beautiful braids and her blue eyes. I could hardly bring myself to believe that it was she who had sent me the postcard.

She took my hand and rolled up my sleeve to reveal the little goggle-eyed octopus done for me long ago by an old tattoo artist in the port of Thessaloniki. From the top of the staircase, Ariadne had come down to greet me, smiling, her arms wide, dressed in a blue linen tunic that fell to her feet, a gold crown upon her head, my Victory.

A FEW HISTORICAL CLARIFICATIONS AND ACKNOWLEDGMENTS

I am grateful to the president of the Fondation Théodore Reinach, Michel Zink, professor at the Collège de France, permanent secretary of the Académie des inscriptions et belles-lettres, and novelist, who first invited me inside Villa Kérylos, which is owned today by the Institut de France. During several wonderful conferences in which I was invited to take part, Odile and Michel Zink showed me that the freedom of spirit and the wonderful imagination of the Reinach family was still alive on the Pointe des Fourmis. Every year, the Académie, of which Salomon was a member and Théodore was what is called an independent member, organizes scholarly celebrations in their memory.

When I first began writing this novel—several chapters of which were written at the villa itself, looking out to sea—I was indebted to the always affable and marvelously well-read Bruno Henri-Rousseau, for his unwavering courtesy and efficiency. He showcases the site to its best advantage and with great respect for its spirit. I had the great fortune to live at Kérylos for several days. Today, the Center for National Monuments, with the support of its president Philippe Bélaval, maintains and is restoring the villa, which is open to the public all year round. Bernard Le Magoarou, the administrator, takes magnificent care of Kérylos.

I would like to thank the participants of the annual conference at Kérylos, who have all offered me ideas: Antoine Compagnon, Philippe Contamine, Xavier Darcos, Jacques Jouanna (to whom I owe the story of the supposed statue of "Sophocles," with which I took a few liberties, by siting it during the lifetime of Madame Reinach), Béatrice Robert-Boissier, Arlette and Jean-Yves Tadié, Monique Trédé, Benoît Duteurtre, and Henri Lavagne, who filled me in on many details regarding the villa's decoration and furniture, and will forgive, I hope, my occasional novelistic license.

For the reader who wishes to find out more about Villa Kérylos, several books are available:

Joseph Chamonard and Emmanuel Pontremoli, *Kérylos, la villa grecque*, Editions des bibliothèques nationales de France, 1934. Republished (with a preface by Jacqueline de Romilly), Marseille, Éditions Jeanne Laffitte, 1996.

André Laronde and Jean Leclant (editors), *Un siècle d'architecture et d'humanisme sur les bords de la Mediterranée. La villa Kérylos, joyau d'inspiration grecque et lieu de mémoire de la culture antique*, Actes du XIXe colloque de la Villa Kérylos, 10–11 octobre 2008, *Cahiers de la villa Kérylos*, n° 20, Académie des inscriptions et belles-lettres, De Boccard, 2009.

Georges Vigne, *La Villa Kérylos*, Éditions du patrimoine, collection "Itinéraires," 2016.

Regis Vian des Rives (dir.), *La Villa Kérylos*, preface by Karl Lagerfeld, photographs by Martin D. Scott, Éditions de l'Amateur, 2001.

Jerôme Coignard, *La Villa Kérylos, Connaissance des arts*, hors-série, 2012.

Françoise Reynier, "Archéologie, architecture et ébénisterie: les meubles de la villa Kérylos à Beaulieu-sur-Mer," *In Situ* [online], n° 6, 2005.

Anne Sarosy wrote a remarkable dissertation in 2015 as a student at the Sorbonne on the sources of Villa Kérylos, which I hope will soon find a publisher.

Théodore Reinach is still awaiting his biographer. The most recent study of this complex figure, by Michel Steve, *Théodore Reinach*, Nice, Serre éditeur, 2014, combines excellent architectural analyses with dialogues imagining conversations between Reinach and Pontremoli.

Other interesting works include Gustave Glotz, "Éloge funèbre de M. Théodore Reinach, membre de l'Académie," in *Comptes rendus des séances de l'Académie des inscriptions et belles-lettres*, 72e année, n° 4, 1928, pp. 321–326; and Rene Cagnat, "Notice sur la vie et les travaux de M. Théodore Reinach," in *Comptes rendus des séances de l'Académie des inscriptions et belles-lettres*, 75e année, n° 4, 1931, pp. 374–393.

For those who would like to know more about Théodore Reinach, it is still possible, even today, to read his work. Among his copious publications, the book that undoubtedly gives the best idea of the subtlety of his analysis and his style is his *Mithridate Eupator, roi de Pont* (Firmin-Didot, Bibliothèque d'archéologie, d'art et d'histoire ancienne, 1890). His erudition here is put to the service of a deep understanding of the ancient world, with a true geopolitical vision: the archaeologist and numismatist make way for the great historian, unjustly forgotten and misjudged today. This book—inaccessible today except online, on gallica.bnf.fr—also testifies to the appeal the banks of the Black Sea held for him, from where the tiara of Saitapharnes was supposed to have come.

The best book available about the Reinach family is the collection of conference papers entitled *Les Frères Reinach*, edited by Sophie Basch, Michel Espagne, and Jean Leclant, Académie des inscriptions et belles-lettres, De Boccard, 2008. The volume teems with fascinating articles, and the foreword by the much-missed Jean Leclant, as well as the contributions by Alexandre Farnoux, Dominique Mulliez, Jacques Jouanna, Annie Bélis, Agnès Rouveret, Élisabeth Décultot, Roland Recht and Antoine Compagnon, I found particularly helpful.

To understand the milieu of the Reinach family, there are two immensely useful books, one by Pierre Birnbaum, *Les Fous de la République*, Fayard, 1992, which devotes a chapter to the family entitled, *Au coeur de la République républicaine, les Reinachs* (pp. 13–28), (available in English as *The Jews of the Republic: A Political History of State Jews in France from Gambetta to Vichy*, Stanford Studies in Jewish History and Culture, Stanford University Press, October 1996), and one by Cyril Grange, *Une* élite parisienne: les *familles de la grande bourgeoisie juive (1870-1939)*, CNRS Editions, 2016.

Two other books bring this social milieu to life: Pierre Assouline's *Le Dernier des Camondo*, Gallimard, 1997, and Edmund de Waal's *The Hare with Amber Eyes: A Hidden Inheritance*, London / New York: Chatto & Windus / Farrar, Straus & Giroux, 2010.

In order to describe the construction of the villas in Beaulieu-sur-Mer and its environs I used the book by Didier Gayraud,

Belles démeures en Riviera (1835–1930), preface by Georges Lautner, Éditions Giletta-Nice-Matin, 2010.

To describe Villa Eiffel, I turned to the catalogue of the exhibition *Les Riviera de Charles Garnier et Gustave Eiffel*, edited by Jean-Lucien Bonillo, with contributions from Béatrice Bouvier, Andrea Folli, Jean-Louis Heudier, Françoise Le Guet Tully, Jean-Michel Leniaud, and Gisella Merello, Imbernon, 2004.

Readers curious to know more about Edmond Rostand's villa in Cambo-les-Bains can turn to the book by Jean-Claude Lasserre, *Arnaga*, Le Festin, 1998.

Those interested in finding out more about Villa Ephrussi may turn to *La Villa Ephrussi de Rothschild*, edited by Regis Vian des Rives, with contributions by Jean-Pierre Demoly, Alain Renner, Michel Steve, Pierre-François Dayot, Christina Ulrike Goetz and Guillaume Seret, and photographs by Georges Veran, Éditions de l'Amateur, 2002.

For more about Villa Primavera, which, although it is mentioned only in passing in the novel, and was built a little later than Kérylos, offers an interesting example of construction in the Greek style, there is a remarkable study by Henri Lavagne, "La villa Primavera à Cap-d'Ail (1911–1914): témoignage d'une culture ou déclaration de grécité," in *Monuments et mémoires de la fondation Eugène Piot*, Académie des inscriptions et belles-lettres, De Boccard, 2013, t. 92, pp. 177–247.

The life of Léon Reinach, musician, composer, and husband of Béatrice de Camondo, is told by the Italian novelist Filippo Tuena in *Le variazioni Reinach*, Rizzoli, 2005.

The most valuable source on Adolphe Reinach for me was the excellent edition introduced and annotated by

Agnès Rouveret, of his posthumous work, first published by Klincksieck Editions in 1921, *Textes grecs et latins relatifs* à *l'histoire de la peinture ancienne (Recueil Milliet)*, and republished with a commentary, under the patronage of the Association des études grecques, with a foreword by Salomon Reinach, Éditions Macula, 1985.

The account of the 1908 cruise comes from a letter by Hervé Duchêne, "En Mediterranée orientale avec les frères Reinach : Joseph, Salomon, Théodore," reproduced in the papers from the conference *La Grèce antique dans la littérature et les arts, de la Belle* Époque *aux années trente*, under the direction of Michel Zink, Jacques Jouanna and Henri Lavagne, *Cahiers de la villa Kérylos*, n° 24, Académie des inscriptions et belles-lettres, De Boccard, 2013, pp. 19–36.

The descriptions of the restoration of archaeological sites in Crete were inspired by the excellent catalogue that accompanied the exhibition *La Grèce des origines, entre rêve et archéologie,* published under the direction of Anaïs Boucher, National Museum of Archaeology, Saint-Germain-en-Laye, RMN, 2014. The Phaistos disc was in reality discovered a few months after the sea voyage that the Reinachs undertook in August 1908, but it is highly revealing of the era's taste for spectacular discoveries that were almost immediately controversial.

At the French School at Athens, Alexandre Farnoux, the director, spoke to me at length about the Reinach family, about whom he is a specialist. He showed me the documents kept in the library, including the lengthy rough draft of the letter from Théodore concerning the affair of the tiara of Saitapharnes, which Dominique Mulliez refers to in his article "Les Reinach et l'École française d'Athènes," in the collection of papers from the conference *Les Frères Reinach*, *op. cit.*, p. 56.

The voyage made by Théodore and his nephew Adolphe to Mount Athos is entirely imaginary, as is the search for the grave of Alexander the Great. I owe a great deal to Olivier Descotes, director of the Benaki Museum, and David Levi, who is passionate about the holy mountain, who took me along with them for a memorable Holy Week.

I searched in vain for the description of the fresco representing Saint Sisoes discovering the tomb of Alexander the Great and the inscription that accompanies it in the learned work of reference by G. Millet, J. Pargoire and L. Petit, *Recueil des inscriptions chretiennes de l'Athos,* 1re partie, Paris, Albert Fontemoing, 1904, republished in Thessaloniki in 2004. Yet the painting certainly exists (a panel conserved at the Byzantine and Christian Museum in Athens also shows this rare iconographic theme); the fresco is located where I describe it, and I have a photograph I took of it there. The chapter about the Dionysiou monastery (pp. 456–495), however, is somewhat sketchy. The treasures of the Athos monasteries remain highly mysterious and largely inaccessible. The best of the recent books on the subject is without doubt Ferrante Ferranti's *Athos: La sainte montagne*, Desclée de Brouwer, 2015.

To gain a sense of what Mount Athos might have been like at the beginning of the twentieth century, before it was discovered by the travelers who made it popular, alongside works by Jacques Lacarrière (*Mont Athos, montagne sainte*, Seghers, 1954) and François Augiéras (*Un voyage au mont Athos*, Flammarion, 1970, and Grasset, "Les Cahiers rouges," 2005), I also drew on an older account, a magnificent book that would be worth republishing, by Francesco Perilla, *Mount Athos* (Thessaloniki, published by the author, 1927), that the intrepid author illustrated with his own drawings and watercolors, much as Achilles, the hero of my novel, does.

The Greek-Corsican village of Cargèse is well known, and its story is told in the classic book by Count Colonna de Cesari-Rocca and Louis Villat, *Histoire de Corse*, Furne, Boivin et Cie, 1916, and by Patrice Stephanopoli, in *Histoire des Grecs de Corse*, Ducolet brothers, 1900. The story of this episode was told to me by Monsignor Florent Marchiano, Archimandrite of the Greek parish of Cargèse and priest of the Latin parish, prelate of His Holiness, whom I was fortunate to meet before his death in 2015.

The story of the Saitapharnes tiara is known thanks to the work of Alain Pasquier, who published an early article on the subject in the catalogue of the exhibition at the Musée d'Orsay, *Jeunesse des musées*, under the direction of Chantal Georgel and Catherine Chevillot, Musée d'Orsay, RMN, 1994: "La tiare de Saïtapharnès: histoire d'un achat malheureux" (pp. 300–311) with an additional essay, "La tiare de Saïtapharnès, description et analyse" by Catherine Metzger and Veronique Schiltz (pp. 312–313). Other valuable information can be found in the article by Dominique Mulliez, "Les Reinach et l'École française d'Athènes," in the collected papers from the conference *Les Frères Reinach*, *op. cit.*, pp. 21–40. Veronique Schiltz continues her research to this day. She has published "Du bonnet d'Ulysse à la tiare de Saïtapharnès," in Kazim Abdullaev (ed.), *The Traditions of East and West in the Antique Cultures of Central Asia*, *Papers in Honor of Paul Bernard*, Tashkent, "Noshirlik yog'dusi," 2010, pp. 217–234, as well as "Le savant et l'orfèvre," in *Comptes rendus des séances de l'Académie des inscriptions et belles-lettres*, 2012, I (January–March), pp. 585–618. Thanks are due to Christine Flon-Granveaud, who introduced us; I was able to interview Veronique Schiltz on the lesser known aspects of the history of the era's predilection for a Greek world far from that of Pericles.

Some of Israel Rouchomovsky's pieces still exist. He was a great artist whom posterity continues to call a forger: thanks to Nicolas and Alexis Kugel I had the opportunity to hold in my hands one of the pieces he made in Paris after the affair of the tiara and it is impossible not to think of Fabergé when you see it.

The president-director of the Louvre, Jean-Luc Martinez, has long loved Kérylos and Beaulieu-sur-Mer—it was he who conceived, with Alain Pasquier, the gallery of plaster casts of antique sculptures found in the interior walkway that surrounds the villa. Françoise Gaultier and Cécile Giroire showed me the famous gold tiara, which is kept in the museum's vault, certainly the most famous and valuable fake in France's national collections.

I owe an enormous debt of gratitude to the people who first took me to Kérylos, Marike Gauthier, Bruno Foucart, and Roselyne Granet—who told me the story of the Eiffel and the Salles families—as well as those who later on, during various conferences at Villa Kérylos, encouraged me and gave me ideas; Madame Jean Leclant first and foremost, Lory Reinach, who shared with me memories of her husband Fabrice Reinach, Théodore's grandson, Thomas Hirsch-Reinach, Théodore's great-grandson, and his family, whom I met by chance, quite as if it was fated, while I was in the middle of writing this book. I must also thank Hervé Danesi, secretary general of the Académie des inscriptions et belles-lettres, who is also a champion of the house.

I was welcomed to Kérylos by Vassiliki Mavroidakou-Castellana, head of development, who told me about the photographs of ancient Greece at the time of Théodore Reinach. I enjoyed long conversations with Paulo Chavez, who has known the villa for a long time and is responsible for its maintenance. I am deeply grateful to them both for having shared their love for this unique place.

For the final scene, I had in my head the lecture given by Erwin Panofsky entitled "The ideological antecedents of the Rolls Royce radiator," a sixteen-page pamphlet published by the American Philosophical Society in 1963. For the idea that Achilles became an abstract painter after 1945, I was inspired by the thrilling exhibition at the Musée des Beaux-Arts in Lyon: *1945–1949. Repartir* à *zero. Comme si la peinture n'avait jamais existé*, with a catalogue under the direction of Eric de Chassey and Sylvie Ramond, Hazan, 2004.

I also owe thanks to those with whom I have had so many conversations in France and in Greece: Lucile Arnoux-Farnoux, Sophie Basch, my dearly missed friend Laure Beaumont-Maillet, Christophe Beaux, Violaine and Vincent Bouvet, Marine de Carne, Laurence and Cécile Castany, Adelaïde de Clermont-Tonnerre, Valérie Coudin, Mathieu Deldicque, Bertrand Dubois, Béatrice de Durfort, Côme Fabre, Olivier Gabet, Annick Goetz, Elisabeth and Cyrille Goetz, Mickaël Grossmann, Constance Guisset, Aline Gurdiel, Matthieu Humery, Barthélémy Jobert,

Jacques Lamas, Laurent Le Bon, Isabelle le Masne de Chermont, Jean-Christophe Mikhaïloff, Christophe Parant, Paul Perrin, Polissena and Carlo Perrone, Alain Planès, Nicolas Provoyeur, Jules Régis, Bruno Roger-Vasselin, Brigitte and Gérald de Roquemaurel—thanks to whom I first encountered Cargèse and its Orthodox church—and Béatrice Rosenberg.

I must of course thank my editor at Éditions Grasset, Charles Dantzig, himself a writer with deep knowledge of the history, art, and literature of antiquity.

My thoughts turn to my uncle, Jean Goetz, a classics teacher, who gave me my first Greek lessons—I was not a good student—and played for me when I was in middle school the Delphic hymn to Apollo. How I wish he could have read this novel, which is dedicated to his memory, on one of the Cretan beaches he loved.

And finally my thanks go to Marie, Julie, and Lucile, for whom every pleasurable holiday must include a swim in the sea at Beaulieu-sur-Mer, the most beautiful of all the resorts on the Côte d'Azur.

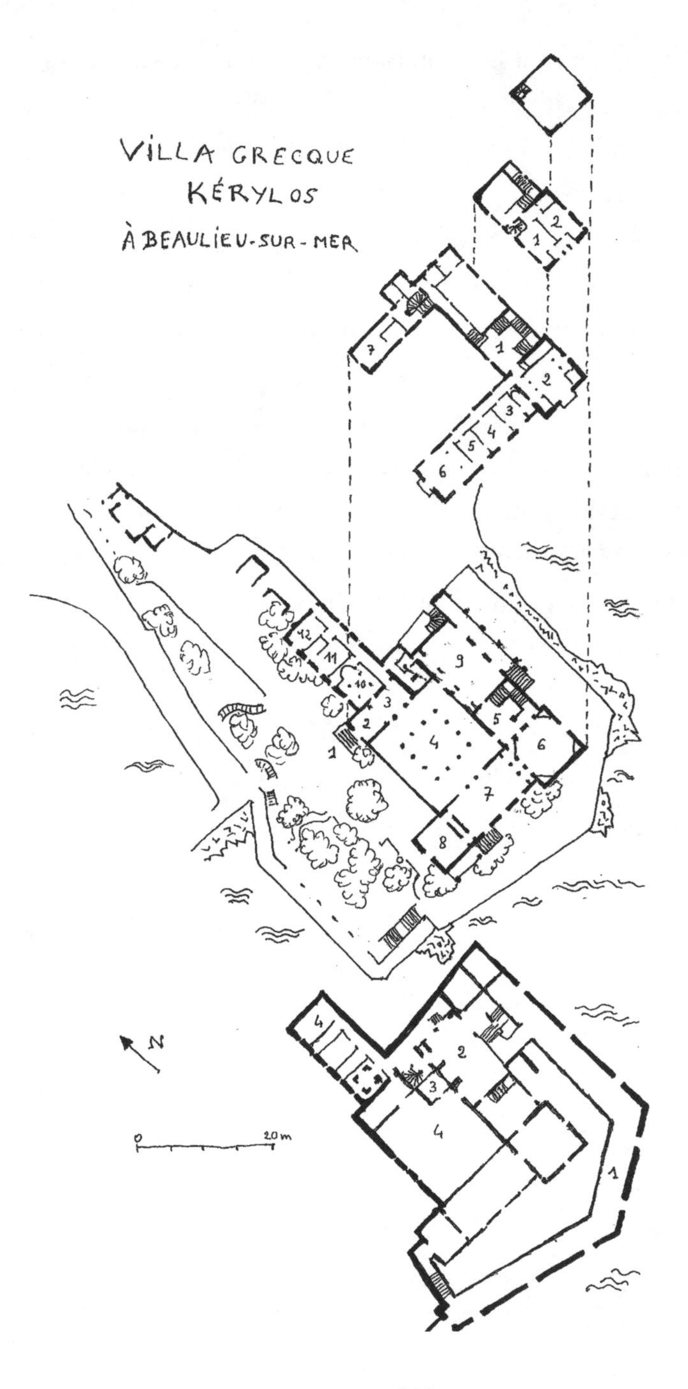
VILLA GRECQUE
KÉRYLOS
À BEAULIEU-SUR-MER
N
0
20 m

Terrace

Third Floor

1 Daedalus
2 Icarus

Second Floor

1 Hermes gallery
2 Ornithes (birds, the name of Fanny Reinach's bedroom)
3 Ampelos (grapevine, a bathroom)
4 Triptolemus (sitting room)
5 Nikai (The Victories, bathroom)
6 Erotes (Cherubim, Theodore Reinach's bedroom)
7 Euormos (guest quarters)

First Floor

1 Main entry
2 Thyroreion (vestibule)
3 Proauleion (entrance hall)
4 Peristyle
5 Amphithyros (stairwell)
6 Triklinos (dining room)
7 Andron (reception room)
8 Oikos (music room)
9 Library
10 Naiads (thermal baths)
11 and 12 Philemon and Baucis (guest rooms)

Basement

1 Lower gallery
2 Kitchen
3 Hot water heater
4 Service rooms

ADRIEN GOETZ is a novelist who teaches art history at the Sorbonne in Paris. He is the editor of *Grande Galerie,* the quarterly magazine of the Louvre Museum.

NATASHA LEHRER has translated books by Georges Bataille, Robert Desnos, Victor Segalen, Chantal Thomas, and the Dalai Lama.